I0585502

The Secrets We Keep

A Love Story

D. R. Coghlan

Web site and Newsletter: www.drcoghlan.com
Facebook: www.facebook.com/drcoghlan.author
Amazon: www.amazon.com/author/drcoghlan
Goodreads:www.goodreads.com/author/show/18517543.D_R_Cog
hlan
BookBub Follow: www.bookbub.com/authors/d-r-coghlan

Dedication

To JM for all that you were and all that you could have been

And to MJ for allowing me the space to be all that I can be

The secrets we keep:

They bind us, they blind us, they break us apart.

Let there be secrets no more.

***

I write this in your honour my sweetheart,

That the world may know you, and the love we share.

Oh, how I hunger for you;

Your kiss, your scent, the sound of your voice.

I close my eyes and am soothed by the touch of your hand.

Your love surrounds me in a whisper.

Yet still my heart aches, my spirit cries out

As your beautiful eyes smile back at me from the face of
our child.

Come back to me, come back to me, come back to me,
please ...

The Secrets We Keep

One

It was Friday night late in the Summer of 1989 and I was a woman on a mission. I had driven the two hours from Melbourne to the family farm at Kangaroo Springs to see my folks. My twin brother, Jack, was fresh home from the northern shearing season and we were all having a beer at the kitchen table as dinner cooked. I laughed and chatted along, all the time looking for the ideal moment to spill my guts. It was like skipping rope, waiting, watching as the conversation flowed, sensing the rhythm, looking for the right point to jump in, hoping not to screw up.

My father, sitting at the head of the table, in his standard dress of khaki work shirt with the sleeves cut out, recounted the story of how he had narrowly escaped being bitten by a snake up in the back paddock. He told the story in his usual country drawl and we all sat, listening with great interest, all aware that he was likely exaggerating.

"If I hadn't put the shovel down just when I did, he woulda had me." He shook his head. "I hadn't even seen it. First thing I knew was the thump as it hit the bloody shovel blade. Nearly shit meself!"

We all laughed.

"What sort was it?" Jack asked.

"Brown, not that big, around four foot I reckon. I was too shit scared to even have a crack at it for a start. I stood there, holding the shovel in front of me, shaking in me boots watching it, hoping the bloody dogs wouldn't come sniffing around. You shoulda seen the damn thing." Dad rested his weather-beaten elbow on the table, forearm vertical, hand curled over, darting about, imitating the snake's movement. "It sat up and looked at me for about ten seconds, seemed like half a friggin' hour, then it turns and heads off through the grass."

"So, did you get it?" I asked.

"Yep, the minute the bastard turned its back on me I let it have it. It won't be bothering anyone again that's for sure. I chucked it on the back fence, away from the dogs."

I waited for a moment. I needed to be sure he had finished. I took a swig of beer then jumped in.

"I've got some news." My gut churned as all eyes turned in my direction.

"What's happening with you?" My father turned his full attention to me as he asked.

"I'm going to Europe."

"You're what?"

"What?"

"When?"

"In about five weeks. I've booked and paid for my airfare. I'm giving four weeks' notice at work on Monday, I've sold the car to a guy at work, I'm all organised." There, it was on the table.

"Just like that? Don't you think you shoulda come home and talked about it before racing in and organising it all like that?" That was Dad of course.

I shrugged. "This's been my goal for years. I've always wanted to go. I've been researching, reading guidebooks, talking to people who have done it. I've bought myself a Eurail train pass and everything."

"How long are you going for?" Mum's face had fallen.

"I'm not sure, maybe a year."

"A year, a friggin' year?" Dad again. "Bloody hell Laura. What the hell are you gonna do for a year? Where are you gonna live, what are you gonna do, swanning around Europe for a year? Shit, girl." He ran his hand over his bald scabby head, becoming agitated. "Sounds like a bloody waste of time and money. What about your job? It's a good job. How can you chuck your job like that and go on holiday for a year?" He was relentless. "Don't you think the rest of us would like to chuck our jobs in and piss off like that? What gives you the right?"

The room fell silent, the laughter had disappeared.

I shrugged again, struggling to contain my fear, my anxiety. I expected as much from them, particularly from him. That's why I had done it like I had. I made sure everything was organised, booked and paid for before telling them. That was essential because, despite being 24 years old and having lived in Melbourne, Australia's second largest city, for over six years, they still possessed the ability, and also thought they had the right, to pull my decisions to pieces. They were very good at undermining my self-confidence and crushing my dreams into little bits.

"Laura, couldn't you go to New Zealand, on a Contiki tour, like your brother did?" Mum was trying for the compromise as usual.

I smiled at her. "No Mum, that was Jack's plan, not mine."

"I'm sure he'd like to squander his friggin' savings on a year-long holiday too but he's got more sense of responsibility than that." There was no point taking my father on. I needed to tread the careful line between respecting and acknowledging him but not engaging with his argument. I knew where that would go.

I looked across at Jack. He played his typical game, holding back, letting "the olds" get it off their chest. We locked eyes, and he gave me a faint smile before speaking up.

"It's not that big a deal. There's lots of people doing it. You can pick up work in London. Get a working holiday visa, can't ya? Travel in your time off." He nodded. "Sounds good Lozzie."

"Yeah, thanks Grub." I agreed, smiling my appreciation across to him. "It's easy to get a job over there."

"What about your flat, have you told Jess?" Mum spoke as she rose to take the casserole out of the oven. I stood up to clear the chips and empty stubbies from the table.

"Yeah, she knows. She's already got someone else lined up to move in, another one of the crew from the theatre company."

"So, who's moving in?" Jack had met most of the gang from the amateur theatre group I was part of.

"Ray."

He nodded. "Gay Ray?"

"Yeah, gay Ray." The truth was, Ray was possibly the only person yet to realise that Ray was gay. He had even asked me out at one stage. I loved him to bits, but he must have been so deep in denial, so unhappy. "And as for my stuff, I'll give some of it away and I'm hoping to put a few things in the shed."

"Well, that shouldn't be a problem." Mum was trying her best to digest it all. "What about Kelvin? What is happening with you guys? Is he going with you?"

"Ha!" I shook my head. "Nah, that's history. He has been trying to persuade me to take him with me. In fact, his Mum has even been working to get me to take him but, nah, not gonna happen. I'm doing this on my own so I can do what I want. I don't want to be fitting in with what anybody else wants to do."

"Oh dear, will you be safe?" Mum's eyes were full of concern as we took our places back at the table in front of steaming plates of lamb casserole and mash.

"Yeah, of course. I'll be very careful. I may be going on my own but I'll be staying in youth hostels, meeting heaps of young travellers doing the same thing. There'll always be someone travelling in the same direction as me ... I won't be out at night by myself etcetera etcetera."

"Well, there's no point discussing it then is there? It's all done and paid for." Dad was a bit out of sorts but settling down. "You should have come home first to talk it through. You shouldn't be making decisions like that on your own, just a young girl and all."

I bit my lip. I'm sure if I had a penis, he would have given me more credit, but I kept that opinion to myself for the sake of peace. None of it counted, anyway. I had carefully stacked the deck this time. I would not give them the chance to defeat me. I was going to Europe in five weeks. Nothing else mattered.

Two

I had been longing to go to Europe most of my life but it wasn't until I started work in Melbourne as a young junior accountant, I met people who had been there and done it. Previously, the only person I had known to travel to Europe was my Grade six teacher. He had sent me a postcard from Paris. The whole idea was just so exotic and exciting, especially to a young girl growing up in a farming family in country Australia. When some of my co-workers shared their stories, I was captivated. I wanted to ask a million questions as I realised it really was possible for the average nobody, like me. It had been my main life goal ever since.

The next five weeks whizzed by in a blur of preparation, packing, and parties. Kelvin made a last-ditch effort at trying to get me to take him with me.

"But we've been so good together. Why are you doing this?"

"I'm sorry Kelvin, but no, we haven't." I had rehearsed this speech, determined not to give in, though I hated hurting him. "You are a great guy and we've had fun, but it's time to move on. We both need to move on. You know that. As soon as I'm out of the way, you'll see —"

"But I love you ..."

"I realise it's hard now but give yourself a chance. You'll find the right woman. You know it's not me."

Then Ray got drunk and turned up on my doorstep professing his love for me.

"I love you Lolo. There's just something different about you, you're not like other girls." He cried and hugged me, pressing me into his chest and I sagged under the weight of his drunken unsteadiness.

"Ray, Ray, get off." I reclaimed my space and let him in, taking him through to my room so we could play out this little heart to heart in private.

"Yeah, Ray, you're not like other guys either. I love you lots but I'm not the one for you, I'm really not, sweetheart." I handed him some tissues and stroked his beautiful dark curls as he tried to clean himself up.

He ran his fingers through my short hair. "What colour do you call this?"

"It's brown, just brown, Ray."

"No, it's not. It's like golden honey or ... or ..."

"Baby poo."

"Oh Laura. Don't say that, I love your hair."

"You must be drunk. Nobody loves my hair, I think it fell off a scarecrow. It's straight, it sticks out and never does what it's told."

"But it's a lovely mess. Can I stay the night, here with you, please?" He patted the bed beside him as he spoke.

"Ray? Are you asking to have sex with me?"

"Oh no, no Lolo, no, I'm not, really I'm not." He threw his large hands in the air in all of his theatrical gayness. "Not that." He looked at me. "You're gonna be gone next week and this ... this is gonna be my room." He stopped and looked about him. "I wanna, just wanna ... I just wanna cuddle ... then ... when I am here, I can remember you." His voice cracked, and he cried again, like a little lost boy.

"Oh Ray. Alright. You're too drunk to drive home, anyway. I'll find you a toothbrush. You can sleep in your t-shirt and jocks but no poking me in the back with Mr Happy alright? And if you keep me awake with your drunken snoring, you'll be on the couch."

"Oh, Laura!" He chuckled, a bit embarrassed. "Yes, thank you, I don't snore, I ... indeed, I'll ... I'll be quiet as a mouse, I will." I knew he would be more embarrassed in the morning. He was a bit pathetic in that moment, but I really liked him, he was such a sweetie.

The guys from the theatre group helped me pack my stuff into the trailer to take back to the farm. I handed my keys over to my housemate Jess. We had lived harmoniously but independently. We hadn't ever been mates. She was younger than me and apart from a joint passion for the theatre we were totally different. She was short and round and loved bluegrass music, boot scooting, TV soaps and mac 'n' cheese. I was tall and slim and more of an uptight tree-hugging, new age, quasi-vego.

I finished the last round of hugs, extricated myself from Ray's arms, smiled and nodded at Kelvin and jumped in the car. I waved and tooted as I pulled out in Jack's old wagon I had borrowed for the trip. It was a slow drive home with everything rattling and banging about in the trailer behind me.

Departure day arrived soon enough, and I carted my bags out to Jack's wagon, ready to drive down to catch my 3pm flight. We had agreed after some discussion that Jack would take me to the airport. I was relieved, happy to get the farewell to my folks over with. I looked about me, at the old farmhouse, the dairy, the hay shed, the cows grazing off in the distance; the calves frolicking closer to. I closed my eyes and breathed deep, imprinting the sounds and scents on my memory. I felt a heavy sense of the way time would continue to grind forever onwards in my absence, and I knew I would miss the natural simplicity of the farm.

I wandered out onto the large side lawn, "the park" as we called it. Chester, my gorgeous rescue sheep stood up on his fat little legs and baaed a happy greeting as I walked towards him. He was tethered to an old car wheel near the willow tree. Jack reckoned he was the fattest sheep in Australia. He was certainly one of the cuddliest. I sat on the grass beside him and he buried his soft fluffy head in my lap as I scratched his ears. Jack had brought Chester home for me to care for after he had found him in pretty bad shape somewhere up the track. He knew the poor lamb would die if he didn't step in and was confident, I would be the person for the job; I had always been a rescuer.

"I love you Chester. I'm gonna miss you, you woolly old thing. You be good and don't get too fat, you hear." Chester looked up at me with his lovely light brown eyes, understanding nothing except the right here, right now of his existence.

Our two dogs, Dick, the old German Shorthaired Pointer and Johnson, the young ball-obsessed Kelpie joined in. They scrambled in the mix for attention while the cats, Betty, and Ginger, rubbed and purred around us all.

My mind travelled back to a scene over six years beforehand. I had been sitting in that same spot playing with Chester as a young lamb, still limping from the leg wound he had arrived with. On that day, I had been waiting for my year 12 results to arrive in the mail. After the mailman left, I ran the hundred metres up the driveway, across the bridge over the channel, to the mailbox on the roadside. Behind me came a procession of animals with Dick in the lead. He was closely followed by Chester, Copper, the old farm dog, and three domesticated feral cats. I looked like the Pied Piper. It was one of my favourite memories ever.

In my backpack, ready to go with me to Europe, I included a little family photo album, complete with pictures of Mum, Dad, Jack, Dick, Johnson, Chester, Betty, and Ginger — my family.

I lay back on the grass and let them crawl all over me. Johnson licked my ears clean, Dick had his front paws and head on my chest, the cats nuzzled my neck and body and Chester was rubbing the top of his head into my side. I loved it and rolled around laughing and playing with them, realising I would probably never get to do that again.

Mum called out from the side door. "Laura, it's ten-thirty. Do you want a cuppa before you get ready?"

I sat up. "Oh, yeah, thanks Mum, I'm coming now." I swung back to my furry friends as they stood watching me, waiting for our game to resume. "Sorry, I gotta go, guys. I love you all, miss you already." I kissed and scruffed the heads of each of them in turn, a lump rising in my throat and tears prickling my eyes. "Be good. Be well ... and thank you." I started walking towards the back door, dogs, and cats bounding around me. Chester bleated his objection at being left behind. I turned, ran back, gave him another quick bear hug around his fat woolly frame, whispered sweet nothings in his ear, scratched his head, then ran inside. I smelt like the whole farm which I loved, but I didn't think my neighbours on the plane would enjoy soaking in the aroma for hours on end.

It was time for a cup of tea, a hot shower, an awkward goodbye then off to the airport, and life's big adventure.

The worst part was the goodbyes. Mum was a bit teary, Dad was hiding his concern by being cheerful.

"Are you sure you've got everything?"

"Yes Mum." I gave her a big hug.

"You be careful." She patted my cheek. "I'll miss you."

"I'll miss you too." I kissed her on the cheek. "Thanks."

"I love you Laura."

"Love you too Mum."

I turned to my father. "Bye Dad."

"Yep, bye now." He pulled me in close. "You take care of yourself, don't do anything stupid."

"I won't. You take care of yourself too."

"Come on," called Jack, standing at the car, "Time to move."

"Okay, bye." I grabbed my day pack and jumped into the passenger seat.

"Bye, have fun. Make sure you write."

"Yes Mum, I will. See ya."

As the car drove out the driveway, I turned to see them still standing, waving. I waved out the window then reached over and beeped the horn. Sitting back in my seat, I breathed a sigh of relief and at the same time felt the excitement growing inside. This was actually happening.

Jack pulled up in the one minute drop off at the airport and jumped out to help me with my bags.

"You got everything?"

"Yep, reckon so."

He gave me a big hug. "See ya Lozzie. Have fun, stay safe. I look forward to hearing your news."

"Thanks Grub, thanks for all your support. I'll miss ya."

"Ah, piss off will ya, you're gonna get me all emotional."

I smiled at him. "I love you."

"Yeah, whatever." He grinned. "Love you too." He waved his hand and jumped back in the car.

I watched him drive off then dragged my stuff over to a trolley. Time to get checked in, have a wander around duty free then settle down with my book in the waiting lounge, as I counted down to take off.

As the plane sped on through the heavens, the increasing distance between myself and everything I had ever known excited me. I hoped I had left my former life and my old secrets behind. My life had been complicated, messy, unhealthy. No one was aware I was recovering from a broken heart, broken by a man I had no right to love. I also carried guilt over Kelvin and knew I had not given him my best. I hadn't allowed him sufficient space in my life, but had used him as a salve for my woundedness. I needed to shed some emotional baggage, to move on and make better choices with my life and relationships.

Two days after flying out of Melbourne, and a brief stop-over in Kuala Lumpur, I arrived in London at Heathrow Airport. I had no bookings past the next two nights in a cheap London hotel. I didn't care. I was an adventurer, exploring the world. I didn't need schedules and rigid plans. The young Singaporean guy who sat next to me on the plane could not understand why I would "choose to be a bum". This guy would get along really well with my father, I thought. I was not a bum. I held a degree and professional experience that would get me a job when it mattered. I brought sufficient money in travellers' cheques to last at least 6 months, a Eurail pass, a new bulging backpack and an overstuffed suitcase.

There was a tube strike and a heat wave to greet me in London. These threw me for a start. Neither possibility was mentioned in any guidebook I had studied. I was supposed to take the underground, the Piccadilly line, to the middle of London. I pushed the luggage trolley through the crowded airport distracted by the colours, cultures, shapes, and sizes of the surrounding people. Each person was the centre of their own universe. Each individual was living out his or her destiny in a way that was separate and distinct, yet so intricately related to everyone else around them.

I brought my thoughts back on task. It took persistence, but eventually I asked the right questions, found the right bus and got off close to my hotel. I took a moment to review my London A-Z to get my bearings. The short distance was a serious struggle as, weighed down by the oversized pack on my back, I also tried to lug my heavy suitcase along. They were the days before suitcases were made with wheels, well, at least the cheap ones like mine. I swore and sweated and felt nothing at all like a light-hearted adventurer as I inched along the footpath becoming hot and bothered. I passed my first traditional English pub, decorated in black and gold. It was crowded, overflowing onto the street with festive cheer as the young white-collar crowd cooled their throats and quenched their thirsts at the end of a long hot day. I trudged past unnoticed as if in a parallel universe.

I will always remember waking early the next morning. I watched the eerie redness of the sun spreading across the hazy morning sky over the row of roof-top chimney pots across the street. I jumped out of bed and leaned on my fifth-floor window taking it all in through bleary eyes. Opposite my hotel I could see an immaculate row of white terrace houses. The pavement below was still quiet in the early dawn. "Welcome to London," I said to myself with a grin.

Three

After my two nights were up, I power lifted my gear down to a quad room in the Walkabout Club. It was in Craven Terrace, Lancaster Gate. What a great place. It was alive with backpacks, hippy scarves and travel stories from all over the globe. Lots of Australians, Kiwis, Canadians, and Americans with the occasional German, Italian or Scandinavian. I loved the whole, "Hi, I'm Laura, I'm from Melbourne Australia, and you?", "Hi, I'm Jane (or Tommy or Simon or Katherine or Paolo) and I'm from ..." I was full of questions and keen to hear their tales of adventure, mishap, friendship, and chance. Where had they been? What was it like? Where were they going next? What work were they doing?

I was like a sponge, so hungry for their knowledge and experiences. I wanted to roll in their energy, like a dog in a bad smell, incorporating them into my identity. Inside me, barely consciously, I thought if I travelled to the places they went and had the experiences they had I would become one of them. I wanted to be surrounded by happy, laughing, cool looking people who searched me out in a crowd. I wanted to laugh and joke and smile and love myself, but I didn't. I was pretty insecure and full of self-doubt just as I had been at home.

There was my first glimpse of my tragic reality. I had paid my money, farewelled my loved ones at home, journeyed to this place on the other side of the world — the traveller's Mecca, but nothing inside me had changed. I was the same person as when I left. I hadn't shed or attained anything as I stitched the Australian flag onto my backpack, or as they stamped my new passport with visas allowing me to go to interesting places. I hadn't changed when I arrived in London when I took up residence among the seasoned travellers in the Walkabout Club. I hadn't become "somebody" because I had travelled. I didn't suddenly believe in myself.

But hey, I had just arrived. I was on an adventure — the adventure of a lifetime. I wanted to leave my tendency towards "analysis paralysis" behind. I just had to find where I belonged in that crazy world.

I put my day pack on and went exploring. My path led me through the beautiful gardens in Hyde Park where I laughed with delight to see the squirrels scampering to-and-fro. I breathed in the garden air, laden with the sun-warmed fragrances of late Spring. There I found peace and wholeness. There I felt embraced. I reached out to connect with the oak trees — the smooth green leaves, the arching branches, the rough, crumbly bark. I sank to the ground, resting against a large old trunk, closed my eyes and relaxed.

Nature had always been my refuge. In the darkest moments in my life, when angry voices were shouting, glass was breaking I ran to nature. I had been all but paralysed with fear as I inched away, escaping to the forest, merging with the trees, the leaves, the grass, often with Copper, the cattle dog, for company. Dogs are such good listeners. Burying myself in the rocks, the moss, the bracken fern I would sit and cuddle Copper and sob.

I spent the next few days wandering around London and ticking off a few "must see" items. I loved the British Museum, window shopping in Carnaby Street and the market stalls of Piccadilly Circus. It was in a little market stall that I bought my first hippy travellers' scarf, but I soon grew restless with the sites of London and booked a ticket to Ireland. I repacked my backpack, leaving most of my gear at the Walkabout Club. I said a few quick goodbyes and set off in the crowded bus on my way to Holyhead in Wales to catch the ferry across to Dublin.

The bus to Holyhead was full of Irish folk heading home. They were cheery, chatty people and spoke their truth in no uncertain terms. The dangers and discomfort of passive smoking were just coming to the fore and the bus company had complied with the emerging legislation by declaring the front half of the bus to be a

"No Smoking" zone. To the happy-go-lucky Irish, who comprised about ninety percent smokers, this was not more than a slight inconvenience. Those smokers in the front half of the bus simply had to walk over the halfway line in the aisle and light up while they chatted to their fellow travellers. I had an aisle seat in the last non-smoking row, in the middle of the bus which meant my whole trip I had to contend with bumping hips, bums and even groins in my face, along with choking clouds of smoke. Cigarette smoke in enclosed spaces has always made me nauseous. I sort of hoped for the opportunity to puke on someone's shoes but had to be content with getting off the bus smelling like an ashtray and with a splitting headache.

Once out of the bus we made our way down to the ferry terminal and boarded the ferry. The Irish sea tossed and gurgled beneath us but the ferry stayed steady. I spent the first while out on the deck, enjoying the sea spray as I breathed a deep belly-full of cold fresh salty air and allowed the wind to blow away the stench of cigarette smoke.

When we reached shore, I made my way down and off the ferry and scrambled onto another bus for the trip into Dublin. I sat beside a young bleached blonde traveller also nursing a backpack.

"Hi, I'm Laura."

She smiled. "Hi, I'm Roxy, where are you from?"

"I'm from Australia, and you?"

"Australia? The land down under? I'm from the States."

I smiled and nodded. "Where are you headed?"

"I'm looking for a youth hostel in Dublin, how about you?"

"Me too." We looked at each other, smiled and nodded in silent agreement.

I liked Roxy straight off. She was about two years younger than me, more attitude, wearing a Sinead O'Conner t-shirt.

"Travelling on your own?"

She nodded. "Yeah, I left my boyfriend behind in New York. You too?"

"Yep. Left mine behind too. A good decision."

She laughed. "I'm going back to mine, we're still together."

"Good on you. He must be worthwhile. Where are you going after Ireland?"

"Yeah, he's alright." Her face became reflective for a moment. "I'm getting the ferry across to Europe, then Germany to my Aunt's place in Dresden. She's about to have a baby. I'm hoping to arrive in time. What about you?"

"Sounds great. My plans are pretty loose, I'll be going back to London ... I'm not sure after that."

We found our way to the newly opened International Youth Hostel in the old school building in Mountjoy Street. Five and a half Irish pounds bought us each a comfortable bunk bed in a dorm room and a free breakfast. In fact, the hostel was so new we were the first to sleep in our assigned bunks. As we entered the dorm room, they were still putting the bright red powder coated frames together. Others marched in with mattresses, pillows, sheets and covers. What a treat! Roxy and I pitched in and in no time, we had the brand-new dorm room sorted. What a lovely old building and our room at the front had a bay window facing out onto the street.

"You ready to go exploring?" Roxy had unpacked and was full of enthusiasm.

"Yeah, sure, let's go."

In the days to come Roxy and I became a real team, we made decisions together easily and talked and laughed our way through a broad range of topics. Roxy could be brash and effusive and she brought me out of myself. A relationship like that didn't come naturally to me. I found it a little awkward, but I liked it. I had had few close girlfriends before.

Dublin was great. The markets, the pubs, the people. I was, however, shocked to see so much poverty. I will never forget the face of a skinny little straw-haired girl, dressed in rags, begging on the street. She was small, the size of an average five or six-year-old but I would guess she was closer to twice that. Her skin was pasty and flaky with red inflamed patches and she had dark circles under her vacant world-weary eyes. I noticed her mother nearby also looking bedraggled, undernourished and exhausted, sitting on the pavement on the approach to one of the central bridges over the river Liffey, with a young baby clutched to her flat old breast. I had never seen such absolute poverty, and I struggled to reconcile that with the beautiful old buildings, the richly painted pubs and the general cheerfulness of the Irish people.

We finished the afternoon in a pub in the centre of town with a pint of Guinness.

"I can't get over that little beggar girl." My heart was heavy, and I shook my head. "I wanted to rescue her ... I so wanted to get involved, but where the fuck do you start?"

"Yeah, same." Roxy put down her beer and looked at me, eyes full of concern. "I wanted to buy her a sandwich, but then I see Mum sitting there with a baby ... you realise you can't even scratch the surface, what's a fucking sandwich going to do for her? We have no bloody idea what she goes home to, and who knows how many more kids Mum has begging 'round town."

"It's just wrong. I hate how we can laugh and dance around and swill beer like overstuffed friggin' tourists when there are people right outside the door, outside that bloody door, seriously starving to death." I swallowed another mouthful of Guinness, not enjoying it anymore. "Do you see that in the States, that level of poverty? We don't in Australia. Well, let's be honest, among the Aborigines, yeah, I haven't seen it for myself but I've read articles saying there's real poverty, sickness, etc."

"Yeah, we have it in the States. To be honest, I haven't really seen it though. It's mostly in ghettos, you know, specific areas. Not sure it's that bad though." She shrugged. "I guess it's confronting here coz they're not a minority, or anything, they are not black or Hispanic or native or anything like that. It's easy to blame minorities for being poor, fucking wrong, but easy. These guys though could be us, they're not some immigrant minority or mistreated native, they're just fucking poor."

"Yeah. And it's right there on the bloody street, not hidden away in some slum somewhere." I fiddled with a coaster on the table as I tried to get my thoughts straight. "I'd like to care, I mean I do care, I'd like to ..." I ran out of words. "I don't like it, and I don't know what to do about it. I guess that's why I haven't found out more about the ... the Aborigines at home, it overwhelms me, I'm useless, what can I do?"

"I know what you mean. I agree. The world's fucked, it's just fucked."

Two days later, having had our fill of the wonderful and tragic sites of Dublin we set off to explore the country. Before leaving though, at Roxy's urging, I pulled over six kilos of clothes and crap out of my bulging backpack and mailed it back to the Walkabout Club. Best decision ever.

On the advice of the various bar tenders we had encountered across Dublin we passed by the option of public transport, choosing to hitch our way around southern Ireland. Neither of us had ever hitch-hiked before but we were keen for the challenge. A local bus took us to the western outskirts of town where we self-consciously raised our thumbs, aiming for Galway on the west coast.

Four

We hadn't been walking long before a combi van pulled up. We approached with caution to find a friendly-faced Englishman, travelling solo. Roxy and I locked eyes as we silently weighed this opportunity and agreed to join him.

I hopped in the front and Roxy jumped in the back with our packs through the sliding door. The man, James, was returning to his family at Fanore in the Burren, just south of Galway after a business and shopping trip to Dublin. He and his wife had three small children and ran a little hostel. He offered to stop on the way for us to buy dinner supplies if we would like to end our journey that day at their digs. Roxy and I considered this, again, more through silent eye contact than words. Sure, we agreed, let's do it.

James was a passionate historian. His speciality was religious history. This meant for four and a half hours as we crossed Ireland, stopping from time to time for James to run errands, I received a very detailed run down on English and Irish religious history. He wore my ears out. Meanwhile Roxy curled up in the back reading her book, snoozing and just chilling. Occasionally I eyeballed her, "how did you get the back seat?" She smiled back with smug sweetness.

The next day, we took off from the hostel at about nine and walked down to the beach then south along the sand and rocks towards Doolin. A beautiful sunny summer morning put us in high spirits as we sang and laughed our way south. I tried the water, but it was freezing cold.

After we had exhausted our repertoire of songs and jokes, we fell silent for a while. I was lost in my own thoughts when Roxy spoke.

"I love your hair."

"You what?"

"Your hair. It's so, I don't know, different. Makes me want to pat your head."

"Ha, yeah well I wish it was on a different head, we don't really get along. I don't know why people seem to like it."

"It's the colour, a really nice goldy colour and just the way it does its own thing. Is it like your Mum's or your Dad's?"

"No, it's not like anybody. I don't know what I did to deserve it."

She was quiet for a few paces then asked, "Are your parents still together?"

"Yeah, but it's not something I celebrate. What about yours?"

"Nah, they split when I was little. I don't have much of a relationship with my Dad. He remarried, moved away. Haven't seen him in years."

"What about your Mum, did she remarry?"

"Well, she's had a couple of long-term partners but she's on her own now, that's probably a good thing."

"Why?"

"It's just that, you see, her relationships always seem to be complicated, dramatic. I think she's happier on her own."

I nodded. "I reckon my Mum would be happier on her own."

"Why?"

"Coz my father is a difficult person to live with. I mean, he's not ..., he's ... well, it's hard to talk about, he's sort of schizophrenic."

"How can someone be sorta schizophrenic?"

"Well, when I was growing up, he would get really angry, really scary, froth at the mouth angry." I had a hard time trying to talk about it because it was such a deeply held secret in the family. "They just told us that Dad had nerves."

"Did he ever get diagnosed?"

"I suppose so, he must have. No one ever talked about it. We all just did whatever we could to not upset Dad. If he got upset, it was always our fault, we copped it."

"Did he hit you?"

"No, that's the funny thing, he never laid a hand on us ... we were so shit scared, he was psychotic at times, really bat shit crazy angry and really intimidating ... he didn't need to hit us."

"So, how do you know he had schizophrenia?"

"Well, he's had these pills for years but he almost never takes them. I wrote down the name of the pills and asked a retired psych nurse I had counselling with. She told me the pills were for schizophrenia, that the dose he was taking meant he was mildly schizophrenic, whatever the hell that means."

"Fuck. So, does your Mum know?"

"Yeah, I told her what the psych nurse said, and she just nodded. She knew." I stopped, sat down on a rock, my insides churning with a whole range of emotions. "All our lives they told us it was our fault if he lost his shit, the bastard. I don't love him, I ... I don't give a shit about him ... don't care if I never see him again. Prick."

Roxy dropped onto the rock beside me, put her arm over my shoulders and together we stared in silence out at the waves for a while.

"Come on," I said, standing and pulling Roxy to her feet. "Enough shittiness. Time to come back to the present. We are in Ireland, diddly dee potatoes, to be sure to be sure."

"Your Irish accent is so bad."

We both laughed and continued on our way down the beach.

After two hours of walking, we headed up to the main road in search of a drink. We found a tiny village, just a few houses and a pub and charged straight into the bar at the pub.

A cheery barmaid greeted us through the smoky, stale atmosphere. The only other patron was a wizened old Irishman with nicotine-stained whiskers and a half-smoked rollie between his fingers. We ordered water then cola and drank it down thirstily. As we chatted with the barmaid, the old Irishman came over. He said something up close then put out his hand. I thought he wanted money.

"What did he say?"

The barmaid laughed. "He wants to look at your hand?" She had a broad Irish accent.

"My what? My hand?" I extended my hand to him, thinking he wanted to shake it. He took it in both of his and turned it over, running his yellow stained fingers over the lines in my palm.

His old rheumy eyes met mine, and he said something in Irish.

"What did he say?"

The barmaid conferred with him. "He says to find love, you must first find yourself, that you won't find it where you think it is."

"Okay," I was a bit uncomfortable, but I smiled at the old fella, puzzling over the message and eager to have my hand back.

He spoke again and smiled a yellow gappy smile through his whiskers. The barmaid snorted with laughter.

"Now what?" He still held my hand.

"He says he wants a kiss."

"Oh," I smiled in awkward surprise, retrieving my hand with a jerk. "Is that the time? Must be off now. Let's go Roxy. Thank you, thank you." We downed the last of our drinks and headed for the door.

Back on the road we pissed ourselves laughing, taking off the old fella. It had been a curious little scene. He hadn't appeared to even glance at Roxy; he was only interested in me. Maybe I should have kissed the old bugger.

We continued on down the road for another hour or so till we came to Doolin where we checked into the Rainbow Hostel. Our host showed us to our dorm room, pointing out which of the seven beds were free. The room was empty so Roxy undid her heavy black jeans and pulled her top over her head, revealing her ample bosom as it strained to break free from her black lacy bra. As she opened her pack, half undressed, the door opened, and a man walked in. He was wearing neat hiking gear and the essential hippy scarf knotted at his neck.

The first thing he did was wave his hand towards a bunk to his left. "Hi, that's my bed," indicating a bottom bunk by the door. We hadn't been told it was a mixed dorm but after the initial shock and mental readjustment it didn't really matter. The two of us started the "Hi, what's your name, where are you from?" routine, playing it cool as Roxy scrambled to find a clean t-shirt to cover her modesty. He was tall and lean with broad shoulders, smooth olive skin and short sandy coloured hair that promised to be gorgeously curly if left to grow wild.

"Hi, I'm Laura and this is Roxy."

"Hi, I'm Jordi, I'm from Barcelona." He had gold-rimmed glasses that framed his bright but intense blue eyes, and his face lit up when he smiled.

"Ah, you're Spanish?"

He frowned and shook his head. "No, I am Catalan, not Spanish."

"Catalan? What is that? Isn't Barcelona in Spain?"

"Well, technically yes, but it is actually the capital of Catalonia which is an independent country that the Spanish are occupying."

"Really? I didn't know that. Your English is very good."

He shrugged. "I studied classical languages at Cambridge."

"I see, that explains that."

There was an immediate chemistry between Jordi and me. I loved the sound of his voice. It was deep and earnest. He had a beautiful posh and slightly sing song sort of accent and I've always been a sucker for accents. It was Jordi's third time in Ireland. He had arrived in Doolin just the day before, wanting to catch some traditional music in the pubs before heading north and out to the Aran Islands.

The three of us hired bikes and pedalled out to the Cliffs of Moher together the next day. This proved to be a challenge. Roxy was quite unfit and fell behind, puffing and spluttering as she pushed her bike up the hills against a strong head wind. Jordi and I waited for her the first couple of times, chatting and getting to know each other but Roxy, picking up on the chemistry, told us to fuck off, she would make her own way out there. Then my chain started slipping when I dug deep to get up a hill, I struggled and swore and fell further and further behind Jordi. He did not prove to be the gallant gentleman and swap bikes with me. "Treat 'em mean, keep 'em keen" entered my mind more than once, along with many "fuck you, buddy!"s as I watched him cycle ahead, handicap free.

"Well, thanks very much." I exclaimed on finally arriving at the cliffs.

"What?" Jordi's face was blank.

"My bike chain was slipping, you could have waited, helped me ..."

"My bike was fine." His smile seemed a little condescending.

"So I noticed."

Roxy had rallied and arrived not far behind me.

I turned to her. "You okay?"

"Yeah," she was panting heavily but grinned. "So unfit."

The cliffs were spectacular. Well worth the effort to get there. They towered 240 metres above sea level. As we looked along the coast, we could see the white frothy wave tops, highlighted in the dark coldness of the North Atlantic Ocean crashing against the cliff face way below. Standing on the cliffs, looking out across the water I was in awe wondering, if I could take off and fly due west, what land mass would I encounter next? I have had a similar sensation just once since, standing on the cliffs in the Great Australian Bite, staring south, with nothing but water between me and the continent of Antarctica.

We went to the pub after dinner with a group from the hostel and had a few beers. Roxy had found two other girls from her home state and was having a rave with them, meanwhile the sexual tension between Jordi and I was ramping up. We couldn't keep our hands off each other. The shout for last drinks went out and while the others were scrambling to have their orders filled, Jordi looked at me seductively.

"Do you feel like a walk?"

I smiled back at him. "Yes, let's go."

We slipped out into the street and down between two buildings towards the sea. We stopped out of sight in the shadows and hungrily devoured our first kiss. Oh, my God. So much passion, so much sexual energy. My insides were exploding with sensual overload. The taste of him, the scent of his hair, his body. I pulled his shirt out of his pants and allowed my hand to wander up over his back, shoulders, chest, stomach. A small gasp escaped me as I explored his firm well-muscled torso.

Five

We kept our clothes on that night, just kissing, touching, caressing, whispering with no physical relief. The hostel was quiet and dark when we arrived back. It was weird then, undressing in the dark together in a room full of sleeping bodies. I was in bed when I saw him coming over in the darkness. I could see his body outlined in his jocks and t-shirt. Oh God, I thought. Is he planning to get into bed with me? I had no will to resist. But he didn't. He knelt down, placed one hand behind my head so he could caress my hair and kissed me with warm soft lips.

"Goodnight Laura," he whispered, pronouncing my name in the Catalan way, which made it almost sound like "louda" but with a rolled "r". "And thank you. I've had a great day. Now, sleep well."

I was so churned up inside I didn't know how the fuck I would go to sleep at all, let alone sleep well but the exercise of the day and the sea air led to a gentle heaviness in my body, my thoughts slipped out of my head and I was soon fast asleep.

The next day Jordi continued north and we south. Our parting was both passionate and romantic.

He picked a flower and gave it to me.

"Keep this," he instructed me. "Give it back when I see you next." We had agreed to meet up in London in about ten days' time at a youth hostel in Earl's Court.

Roxy and I packed and left after breakfast, heading south along the road out of town. We struggled to get a decent lift, ending our day half way to Cork somewhere in a caravan in someone's backyard. "There's only one bed, if that's okay," explained our host, a rosy-cheeked Irish woman in her late 30s, as she showed us the van. We exchanged looks that said "If it's okay with you, it's okay with me," and I let the woman know one bed would be fine.

"There's a shower and toilet in the shed there for you to use and if you tell me what time you want to go in the morning, I'll bring you down some breakfast."

Breakfast, wow, we were so happy to hear that. We made a meal of some stale bread and cheese, fruit and biscuits and thought of the cooked Irish breakfast that would greet us in the morning.

It surprised me how comfortable I felt getting undressed and sharing a bed with Roxy. I hadn't shared a bed with another girl since I was about nine years old. With no sisters or female cousins my age I had little experience of warm intimate relationships with women. I was awkward and often left out by my female friends at school.

We talked about our plans for the next day, read a little then switched the light off when it was still early. We were both tired.

I still remember the soft warmth of Roxy's body and the rhythm of her breathing as she slept beside me. I inched closer till I could just connect with the rise and fall of her breasts against my back. As I drifted off to sleep sexual thoughts and images played in my mind. What would it be like, being able to caress Roxy's beautiful body with its soft voluptuous curves, to run my hand through her short blond hair as I looked into those brilliant deep-set eyes? In my dreams I kissed her. I kissed her beautiful expressive mouth as my hand explored her generous warm breasts; her erect nipples. The scene played over and over in my mind. I felt myself moisten and the warmth flood through my whole body. My hand moved lower down over the roundness of her stomach and through her soft, silky pubic hair. She writhed in pleasure and a small moan escaped my lips, bringing me back to wakefulness with a jolt. I froze with my eyes and ears wide open. What was I doing? Had I been discovered? Had she heard me? No, her rhythmic breathing told me she was still asleep. I moved my body and my thoughts away, emptying my mind and drifting off to sleep again.

The next morning was business as usual as we munched our way through baked beans, toast and jam and a pot of black tea before we headed back out onto the road. My vivid dreams and my conflicting emotions and desires somewhat distracted me. I shook my head as I reflected on the day before, beginning with the passionate farewell with Jordi and ending with my fantasy about Roxy. Really? The inner judge was not impressed. In the same day? What did that say about me and about my relationship with Roxy, with Jordi, with myself? I wasn't sure what was real and what was delusional? Was it purely the convention that led me to explore a relationship with Jordi and not Roxy? A friend of Jess's in Melbourne, Carol, had come out of a torrid relationship with another woman. She started dating a man. She said she was attracted to a person, a soul, a spirit, not a set of genitals. I could relate to this more clearly now. I wondered whether it was more social convention than anything else that led me to fan the flames of my feelings for Jordi while turning my back on anything I may have experienced with Roxy.

We were not long in getting a lift from two young wild-haired fellas and a girl in a beat up, rusty old car. The boys were from the Aran Islands and only spoke a few words of English, well only a few words we could understand. The girl, their cousin from Galway translated for them from where she was squashed into the corner beside us in the back seat. The boys grinned at each other in the front. It was clear the experience of picking up a pair of foreign girls in their old car delighted them. They snuck cheeky glances at us and at each other, and I am sure they were imagining possible outcomes from this chance encounter, but we were never unsafe, they were good, respectable lads. In fact, I think they would have been shit scared if Roxy or I had tried to make a move. I'm sure they had fun later sharing an embellished version of the story with their friends. It was a fun trip, and they dropped us off close to where we had chosen to stay at the International Youth Hostel in Cork.

We ambled around Cork for a day or two, took a trip out to Blarney Castle and kissed the Blarney Stone. It was then time for us to say goodbye as Roxy headed for the ferry to the continent while I continued on my way back towards Dublin. We clung together in a big bear hug, rocking from side to side. I closed my eyes and inhaled as much of her as I could. My emotions welled up in a lump in my throat and a flush emanated from my groin, spreading through my entire body. I opened my eyes to see Roxy blinking back tears. I struggled to speak. We locked eyes.

"I have to go," she waved towards the bus as she held my eyes with her own.

I nodded my understanding. "I know." I smiled at her and ran the back of my fingers down the side of her face. "Thank you so much, for everything." I leaned forward and kissed her on the cheek. "Safe travels."

With one last look she turned and walked to the waiting bus.

I want to make it clear at this point I had never had a real or imagined sexual encounter with a woman before. There were plenty of men in my past but I had never fantasised about a woman, never been turned on by a woman before. I grew up in a male-dominated society with a volatile father and a fearful and sexually repressed mother. A woman's sexuality was something to be ashamed of, to suppress and deny at all costs. Women were never taught anything about sexual exploration, how to pleasure themselves or their partner. As a teenager my parents had threatened me and stood over me to instil in me the need for me to "keep myself nice", to be bloody careful I didn't get "a reputation" or "get into trouble". Meanwhile, my brother was free to behave as he chose as "boys will be boys". It was a confusing, hypocritical way to be raised. How was a girl supposed to "find herself" sexually?

Faced with this unexpected same-sex attraction I felt like the Bonobo chimps I learnt about in psychology class. If raised in isolation without role models, both male and female Bonobos when faced with a horny "other" will sit and masturbate, because that's all they know. And that's about all I knew when faced with this unexpected same-sex attraction.

I moved on to beautiful historic Glendalough where I booked into the Old Mill Hostel. The ancient stone building had been a working woollen mill for many years before becoming a hippy commune in the seventies and a hostel after that. The place was being managed by a guy called Mark, a nurse from Dubbo, Australia, with a mop of red curly hair and a beard to match. Until he opened his mouth and spoke with his broad outback accent, you would swear he was the closest thing to a Leprechaun there was to see.

Glendalough was just what I needed. It was lush, super relaxed and had an abundance of interesting places to visit. In the valley below the hostel was one of the most important monastic sites in Ireland. Saint Kevin had established a monastery there in the sixth century. The site then grew until it became a Monastic City with most of the ruins being from the tenth to twelfth centuries including many ancient graves. Each day new busloads of tourists would rock up for tours around the ruins. The more enthusiastic would bring paper and pencils to do rubbings of the centuries old headstones. The wonderful sites gave me a welcome distraction from the muddle in my mind. On one hand, there was Jordi who I was excited to be meeting up with in London in a few days, then there was Roxy — what was I supposed to do with that? I couldn't find a box to put my experience with Roxy in. Unable to reconcile it I shrugged it off and focussed my mind on Jordi.

I spent my time wandering among the monastic ruins and hugging oak trees in the lush green forests. I returned to the hostel late one morning and bumped into Mark coming out of the office.

"Have you been hugging the oak trees?" His voice was light-hearted, teasing.

"Um, yeah ... How do you know?"

"The bark on your jumper is a dead giveaway."

I laughed and nodded. "Yes, I confess, I'm a tree hugger and this is a tree hugger's heaven."

Mark chuckled then his face became more serious. "What are your plans after you leave here?"

"I'm heading back to London, then across to the continent, why?"

"How would you like a job for the next few months? The boss needs someone to run a little tourist outlet in Kerry, I thought you might be a good fit."

"Hm, sounds interesting."

We went over the details of the job and I promised to let Mark know the following morning.

A job. That was a pull in a totally different direction. I loved Ireland and was so tempted. What was I to do? What would I choose? Looking back on that time I see I was at an incredible intersection in my life.

Six

I chose Jordi, if not the safest, at least the easiest, most well-trodden emotional path. We met up the next week in London.

We were both so keen we turned up at the hostel a day early. I saw him checking in as I walked in the door.

"Jordi!" I yelled in surprise and delight.

He spun around. "Oh, hello!" He gave me a broad quizzical smile, and we embraced awkwardly, both still wearing our backpacks. "You are early?"

"Yes, I am. And so are you!"

The following day we found a small hotel and checked out of the youth hostel. We couldn't wait to give into our longing for each other, ripping buttons off and tearing clothing as we gave ourselves up to our passion. We spent the next five days sightseeing, getting to know each other and having lots of sex.

Sex was wild, uninhibited and a bit loud. Jordi could at times be playful, serious and at others controlling and almost cruel. That was something new for me and I struggled to process it. The headiness of our relationship and the buzz from the cocktail of hormones being stirred up made it impossible to think clearly during that period. It felt like being in a drug fog. We couldn't get enough of each other. It was all-consuming, heady stuff. I had never made love with such complete abandon. I am sure part of this was the thought that after these five days I might never see this guy again. We would lie, bathed in sweat, spent from our love-making and share stories about ourselves. He asked me about my remaining travels through Ireland and suggested I was probably glad to see the back of Roxy when she left from Cork.

"What do you mean, glad to see her leave? She is my friend, we shared lots of good times together."

"Yes Laura, but she was, well, hopeless and scatter-brained so you are surely better off putting that behind you."

I was too bewildered to know how to respond; I didn't see Roxy that way at all. I am ashamed to say I chose silence instead of defending Roxy. I felt disconcerted and torn in my loyalties and that led me into my habitual loop of self-doubt. Jordi, meanwhile had picked up the map, charting our course through the Underground to the main destination for the day, the Tower of London. I shrugged and let go of the uncomfortable thoughts in my head.

Jordi was passionate about his country, his language, and his culture. He told me all about Catalan history, independence, the civil war, the dictatorship of Franco, the struggle of the Catalans to regain independence. It was personal to him. His paternal grandfather had been forced to flee to France after fighting for the resistance. He would swim out to the prison ships and try to free prisoners. He died in exile in Argentina while Franco had been still in power. He never regained the freedom to return to the country and the people he risked his life for.

In the mornings, in the dining room we found we were the only white lodgers there, the other guests being mainly from the Caribbean. I delighted in listening to their accents. They looked at us like they knew what we were doing, in fact they had probably heard us.

While exploring London we came across China Town and a memorial for the massacre of Tiananmen Square, Beijing. Over a million people had been involved in a peaceful protest. Peace ended when hundreds, possibly thousands, of students were shot or mown down by guns and tanks. Through the whole saga the world looked on in horror.

The days passed in a blur and soon the time came for Jordi to return home to work. He was catching the train at Victoria Station.

"Now, you've got my phone number and my address? Where did you put them?"

"They are with my passport."

"Good." He folded me in close in against his chest. "Oh Laura, I will miss you. Being with you has been such a wonderful surprise for me."

"Yeah, me too. I will miss you so much."

"Oh, my darling. You will visit me? Soon?"

"Of course. You will be on my mind every moment of the day till I see you again."

We embraced with passion and emotion before he pulled himself away and boarded the train.

We waved, made silly faces and blew kisses as the train departed. Then I was alone on the platform. It seemed like my life had just been turned upside down. I guess it was what you would call a "whirlwind romance". I had been in Europe less than a month. None of my vague plans held any value anymore. It was like my sole reason for existing had just departed for the continent. Life suddenly presented as flat, empty and meaningless. I returned to Earl's Court, to the hostel I had booked into, lay on my bed in the dorm and stared up towards the bunk above me. I barely registered what I was looking at, I was completely blank. After spending almost a week in such a passionate emotional storm I was becalmed, as if I was coming down from a drug high. I had no momentum, no desire to go out and explore anything, no need for conversation. Over the next two days I stirred a little, barely ate, only vaguely acknowledged the girls around me in our room.

On the third day I checked out and headed for Paris. I had organised to meet up with two different friends in the coming two weeks in London but I let them both down. Nothing mattered except seeing Jordi again.

And so, I skimmed through Paris, staying just four nights at a party-hard hostel called The Three Ducks. I had found it with the help of a French-Canadian guy I met on the ferry on the way over. He was a stained-glass enthusiast. He overloaded me with information about French stained-glass and how it differed from German stained-glass, etc. Having amazing examples like the beautiful glass in Notre Dame Cathedral in front of us as an example, made it easier to understand and appreciate.

From Paris I took the TGV south to the scenic feast that is Montpellier where a kind local woman rescued me while I was trying to read my map outside the railway station. I had started off in the wrong direction and she walked her moped with me at least half a kilometre until she had me on the right path. I was so grateful. I stayed a few nights, strolling through the medieval streets, soaking up hundreds of years of the best European art in the *Musee Fabre* and meditating beneath the huge sweeping oak trees in the oldest botanical garden in France.

But the restlessness would not leave me and soon I was drawn further south, moving on to the blazing white sands of Blanes on the Costa Brava in northern Spain/Catalonia. A sun-bleached hippy type from California I met in the *Place de la Comédie* in Montpellier had recommended it. We shared a few beers over travel stories and laughed together as we watched the world go by. A waiter across the square chased off a dreadlocked fringe dweller who had been scavenging the leftover food from the plates of departing diners. We had watched him stuff cold potato chips in his pocket as he chowed down on great spoonfuls of left-over chocolate mousse, obviously enjoying the treat.

I spent three days in Blanes, on a beautiful sunny beach among thousands of mainly local holiday makers. Then it was time to pack my bag and board the train for the two-hour trip south to Barcelona.

As the train pulled into the station in Barcelona my excitement and apprehension grew. I tried to calm my pulse as I lifted my luggage down from the overhead rack and joined the stream of people climbing the stairs up out of the platform. I tuned into the surrounding conversations. I searched syllables, sound patterns, signage and smells for anything common or familiar. The station building was busy. Unmissable large Arrival and Departure boards continually updated adding a low level click, click, click to the sounds of voices and footsteps. Trolleys weaved this way and that.

Most locals were easy to stereotype. Men and women had clear serious faces. Their hair was perfectly under control, clothes crisp, conservative and well-trimmed, shoes shined. Mixed among these were fresh eager backpackers like myself and life hardened, impoverished gypsies. A few tall ebony-black African men could be observed working hard to keep a low profile, staying out of the general throng, not making eye contact.

I emerged from the station into the hot, steamy, smelly streets. I detected a level of cigarette smoke in the air I was unused to. It was blended with the aroma of local cigars, diesel fumes, last night's urine and a vague whiff of sewage. My first taste of Spain. Dozy drivers waited in black and yellow taxis with doors open to catch any breeze. I would not allow myself the luxury of a taxi — my travellers' cheques had to work harder for me than that. I had consulted my travel guide, confident of finding cheap lodging in the *Barri Gotic* off to the left of the *Rambles*.

The heat and humidity were intense. I could feel the sweat gathering on my body, my hairline, cheeks and cleavage. I contemplated covering the distance on foot but instead dared to ask for instructions on how to get to *Plaça Catalunya* on the Metro. From there it was just a 10-15-minute walk down the *Rambles*. I was perspiring freely by the time I made my way up out of the Metro station into *Plaça Catalunya* but I was also beaming as I took in my surroundings. I managed for a moment to zoom out and see myself in the panorama that engulfed me.

Vehicles hummed anticlockwise around the perimeter but the square seemed strangely empty except for the pigeons quietly scratching and scavenging beneath benches and along pathways. Grand old buildings looked down over the square in all directions. Their windows appeared shuttered, their doors locked. Later I would learn that I had arrived during the midday dining and rest period — *la migdiada* as they called it in Catalan, or *la siesta*, as I understood it better. Not much was open for the tourist trade. I took out my map, determined the path that would take me in the direction the Rambles and set off.

I could have stayed longer in Blanes, or Montpellier or before that but I had been restless and unsettled. I needed to keep moving. The cathedrals, art galleries, river cruises and sunsets had all seemed two-dimensional, drained of colour and life. The music, the gaiety, the energy had not reached me. They were unimportant — they passed me by; they happened around me, not to me on my journey to Barcelona.

Just over two weeks after our heart filled goodbye on the platform at Victoria Station, I had made it to Barcelona, settled into the *Hostel El Pintor*, and was making an early morning call to Jordi.

Seven

"Laura! You are in Barcelona? I don't believe you are here! That's amazing. Where are you staying? I am working today but I can come and meet you after work. Do you want to come and stay with me, at my place?"

"Yes," I responded with breathless enthusiasm. "Yes, that would be great."

My whole body responded when I spied him striding confidently down the Rambles towards me. He laughed when he saw me, came forward and swept me up into his arms.

"Laura, Laura, you made it, you are here with me." He stepped back to look at me. "I can't get used to seeing you, here in Barcelona."

My mind went to mush as I allowed myself to be held captive by those intense blue eyes. Then he pulled me back in against his strong body, squeezing me so tight he took the breath out of me. "Yep, here I am," was all I could get out.

"Oh, it's so good to have you here with me. I've been quite distracted at work today, thinking of you."

"Hm, it's great to see you too, in your natural habitat."

He laughed. "Yes, there is so much for me to show you, so many things to do, starting with tonight. I have a surprise for you."

He had bought tickets to a theatre performance of *Mar i Cel* (Sea and Sky), a sort of Catalan version of *Les Miserables*. We had a walk along The Rambles and a couple of drinks in a bar while we caught up on what had been happening since we had said goodbye at the station in London. Then it was time for the performance which I loved but really didn't understand. Later we made our way to another bar where we dined on tapas and red wine as the sexual tension and the sense of anticipation grew between us. It was almost midnight before we arrived at his flat but the moment we walked in, before the door was even shut, he was taking my clothes off, steering me towards the bedroom.

I slept late the next morning, only half awake when Jordi leaned over, caressed my face and whispered in my ear.

"It's time for me to go. Have a good day beautiful girl." He kissed me slowly, deeply, lingering with his lips on mine and I reached up and locked my arms around him. "I'll see you this afternoon."

"Hmm, I'll be waiting." Reluctantly I let him go.

When I got up, I set about exploring his apartment on the third floor in the centre of the city. It was fitted out in a modern version of the typical Mediterranean style, polished tiles throughout, marble bench tops, heavy drapes and a small interior kitchen opening onto a central airspace. From the airspace the pungent aromas of local cuisine floated up in an endless sensual feast of garlic, virgin olive oil and seafood. The main bedroom and the lounge/dining room opened on to a balcony that looked out over the street. The whole place was immaculate, especially for a guy. His clothes were all folded and neatly stacked and the kitchen was sparkling clean and well-stocked with orderly rows of glasses, tinned and other foods carefully labelled and arranged. It impressed me, especially given he did not know I was coming which must mean he kept his place this way all the time. I realised I would have to pick up my cleaning game to fit in with him.

With each day that passed the intensity of our physical and emotional relationship deepened. In the beginning, we made love every night with almost the same passion and urgency as we had in London. It was exhilarating, exhausting all-consuming. He would serenade me with songs he had chosen from his vast music collection and read stanzas from his favourite poets as we drank local champagne and nibbled on delicious traditional pastries in bed. He suggested what I should wear, told me what to cook for dinner and ribbed me when I put something away in the wrong place. I had quickly learnt not to leave stuff around the house as it would just disappear. I caught Jordi throwing my notebook into the bin one day.

"Hey!" I objected with surprise and indignation, "what are you doing? That's mine!" I rushed forward to rescue the precious pages.

"Well, if you value it, don't leave it lying around like a piece of rubbish." He shrugged dismissively. "Not that there is anything in there that is worth saving," he added in an undertone.

"Excuse me, did you read my notebook?"

"Is that a problem, Laura, don't we share everything? We shouldn't have secrets you know." He cupped the back of my neck with his hand, pulling me to him, kissing my forehead.

I turned and walked out of the room with my precious journal, feeling vulnerable and confused but glad I had not written anything too personal in there, nothing controversial and nothing about my night time fantasies of Roxy. There was no point arguing with him or telling him he had invaded my privacy; he would not understand things that way. I resolved to keep my personal scribblings in a much safer place, if I could find one, and take extra care with my writing.

There was no love-making that night, in fact Jordi seemed out of sorts and hardly spoke. I felt the sun had just disappeared from my life. What was I supposed to do? I fluffed about, waiting for him to tell me. It didn't happen so I plucked up the courage to ask him after he had been sitting in an armchair reading for over half hour.

"Is something wrong?"

"No, why should something be wrong?" His manner made it clear he was not pleased.

"It's just that you are quiet, you don't seem quite yourself."

"Really Laura, what is 'myself'?" His voice seemed condescending, impatient.

"Well... I ... I don't know." I was lost for words. I didn't understand.

"Everything is fine. Stop making a fuss please."

"Okay, if you say so." I leant over him and kissed his cheek. That was all I could think to do to placate him. Meanwhile, I determined to make a better effort at keeping the place clean as that seemed the only reason I could find for him withdrawing.

A few days later we went to Valls and watched the "Castells", human towers up to 9 people high built to exacting patterns and rules all accompanied by traditional musicians. It was awesome but very scary stuff. The tension built and built as the tower grew higher and higher. Near the end I found I was holding my breath, with my hands to my mouth. When the little child raised their hand, showing the tower was complete, the climbers then had to descend quickly but in a strictly ordered fashion. Once everyone made it safely back on solid ground, the whole square erupted in wild cheering and clapping, fist pumping, back slapping and lots of hugs and kisses, especially for the children who had made the perilous journey to the top. It surprised me how it hit me emotionally as I breathed a big sigh of relief, clapped madly and swallowed the lump in my throat.

I turned to Jordi. "That's amazing! I have never seen anything like it. I had no idea people did this."

Jordi raised his head, appearing very proud and pleased. "Yes, this is Catalunya."

Later, as we joined what seemed like the whole village for lunch he continued. "Most of what people hear about Spain is actually Andalusian, from the south. Bullfighting, flamenco, what rubbish. The world does not hear about Catalunya because we are under the oppressor's shadow. We dislike bullfighting and flamenco. We are a different people. We have our own rich culture and traditions."

He never missed an opportunity to push the political line. I found it stifling, limiting, but kept my thoughts to myself and simply smiled and nodded at him.

In the evenings we often had a beer in a local bar, strolled through the surrounding neighbourhood or along The Rambles or joined the traditional folk dancing called *sardanes* in the street. We would then head home to eat or out for supper around ten. I found the late eating a challenge, but most of the food was great. We feasted on delicious fresh local dishes including lots of seafood, olives, fresh green salads and copious amounts of red wine.

I realised later that our life existed in a bubble. The rest of the world happened around us, our world consisted of just the two of us. Most of our conversation revolved around his culture, his country. One night over dinner I decided it was time to talk about me, about family, about something else.

I moved my fork through my dish of peas and bacon, wondering where to start.

"Laura, my love, what is the matter. Don't you like it?"

"Oh, no, this is delicious. I was just thinking of my brother, Jack, he hates peas. I haven't told you about my family, or my life in Melbourne."

He shrugged. "What do you want to tell me?"

I told him about my brother Jack and about the distance and dysfunction in my relationship with my parents. I also mentioned my theatre group, my other friends and talked about life in Melbourne. Jordi listened, but he didn't seem to have any enthusiasm, he didn't ask many questions.

"What about your family? You haven't told me about them. Do you have any brothers or sisters? What about your parents? Should we visit them sometime?"

"No. My mother died years ago."

"Oh, I'm sorry. Do you miss her much? Were you close?"

"No. She was ... she was hard to live with ... manipulative ... always looking into my things with her nose."

"What about your Dad?"

"My father has dementia. He is not himself."

Ok, brothers ... sisters?"

"Ok, if you really want me to tell you, it's not very interesting. I have a brother, Ferran, he is a doctor, he lives in Germany, and a sister, Alba."

"Hm, what does Alba do? Is she local, can I meet her?"

"She is ... wasting her life. She thinks she is an artist. She's not good. We are not close."

"That's unfortunate. It seems you really haven't had many people close to you in your life, many good people around you?"

He sniffed and turned to the topic of his previous girlfriend, Clara. He had talked about her before, in more detail than I cared to hear and with a level of anger and bitterness that was disconcerting.

"She pretended to love me, but all the time ... lying ... seeing other men." His lip curled. "She was obsessive, controlling, abusive ... always with the tears, the bad moods, the silence treatment."

"That sounds awful." I played along.

"Yes. I tried to leave her a number of times but she could be so manipulative. I finally got away from her when I did my military service when I had to live away." His face showed disgust, hurt.

"She sounds like a nightmare." He picked up my hand in both of his and kissed it. "Thank God I have finally found a generous, kind woman to share my life with."

I so wanted to be the person who helped him to build trust, who treated him well and allowed him to experience a healthy relationship. I was however, aware of the irony in this, having never had such a relationship before, but I believed in my potential. Perhaps we both believed we had found the right person.

Jordi never seemed to tire of showing, explaining, or encouraging me to experience different aspects of his country. I received a crash course in Catalonia, its history, language, culture, politics, art, cuisine and geography. Every morning I would have a new itinerary he had prepared for me for the day. It would be complete with places to go, things to see, where to eat and how to get there. Every evening, when he returned from work, he would go over the itinerary to see what I had done. Most particularly, he wanted to know what I had understood or gained from the experience. He readily filled in any misunderstandings or gaps in my knowledge. We also had daily Catalan language lessons. He talked a lot in Catalan, helping me to translate along the way. As a result, I could soon make myself understood in my daily transactions in life.

I had remained strong to my decision to stay only for three weeks but as the time drew nearer I weakened. How would I leave him? How could I find the desire or even the strength to pack my backpack and head to the station? As the time for my departure drew nearer Jordi had become moodier and easily upset. It left me feeling both isolated and guilty. I struggled with the notion of whether leaving would be right or wrong. Jordi almost convinced me I was a bad person for thinking of leaving, as if I was deserting him. The rest of Europe beckoned however, and the Eurail train pass I had purchased made it so easy. So, steeling myself for the backlash from Jordi, and with much sighing and a few tears I packed up ready to catch the midday train north to the border.

He rolled on his side and faced me in bed. "You could stay." His tone held a note of lightness, with more than a little tenderness. My skin pricked. I was awkward, fearful, caught in his gaze. My own eyes slipped from his face, down over his broad chest, and lower to his temporarily subdued manhood resting against his thigh. "It's been so great to share my life with you these last three weeks." He sighed. "And there is still so much I want to show you, so much for you to learn, to see, to experience here." He looked down, tracing the outline of my breasts with his finger, slowly, tantalisingly. He looked up, looked into my eyes with a certain solemn sadness. "And I will miss you. You have become so very important to me." His eyes flickered down to my breasts then up to my face again. "I think I am falling in love with you."

Tears welled in my eyes and I coughed through the lump in my throat as I returned his gaze. "I think I am falling in love with you too." My gaze slipped down over his chest, then back up. "These last weeks have been so great and I want to stay so, so much. I want to ..." I wanted to thank him for everything but thought it sounded like a farewell speech. "I never want to be anywhere but here with you. It's like anything that happened before this is unimportant except that it led me to you." I took a deep breath and looked down, steeling myself. "But I have to go. It's not time for me to settle, I can't, not 'til I've done what I came to do. I need to go and see the sights like I planned to or I know I will regret it." I paused, uncomfortable in my own skin as I looked for the right words. "I want to give myself to you, to be with you, with no reservations or regrets." Underneath I also knew better than to put myself in such a vulnerable position as to pin my life to a man I didn't know so well. Especially with so many of my travel plans still left unfulfilled.

"But I'm afraid you won't come back, that you will ..." He hung his head. "What would I do if you never came back? I know you have to go, I know you need to do these things, and I will go to work and go on living." He looked up again, into my eyes. How I loved those beautiful blue eyes. "I want you safe, here with me."

I smiled at him and caressed his beautiful locks. "I know, and I want to be here with you, and I will be here. I love being wanted by you. It's just three months, and —"

"You must be very careful. There are many things that can go wrong. You can ..." He ran his hand over his face, smoothed his hair where I had messed it. He moved over me, embracing me, covering me with feverish kisses and soft moans.

My own quiet tears flowed as we clung to each other in our longing and our despair. The mood changed when suddenly he grabbed hold of my hair and pulled my head back roughly. His face was just an inch from mine. "You will come back," he hissed. "You will come back."

I tried to nod but could not move my head. He was hurting me, frightening me with his intensity. I glimpsed a certain darkness in his passion that rattled me. "Yes," I choked out. "I will come back."

"Do you promise?" he spat at me, his face contorted with emotion.

"Yes, I promise."

I answered automatically from a familiar place of fear. My passion had dissolved. I was a little scared, a little panicky, trapped. He let me go and got up then, turning his back on me, pulling on his clothes. My heart raced, my head spun, and it freaked me out. Shit, that's too intense. I struggled silently to regain my composure. I realised my eyes were popping wide and dry, my mouth hung open. I quickly pressed my lips together.

He left the room without looking back at me. A trembling pit of emotion opened within me as the shock worked through my system. I struggled to blink back fresh tears, tears of outrage and confusion. I breathed deeply, trying to control my emotional response. All of a sudden, I feared him, I saw visions of my father screaming at me, my manipulative ex-lover. Dazed and confused, I did not feel safe, I needed to get away. I needed a refuge to process what had happened and work out how I should respond to it.

I heard Jordi in the kitchen, putting the coffee on, getting the plates and cups out. I took a few minutes to compose myself while I pushed my emotions down, down into a box, and shut the lid. Then I got up, dressed, and joined Jordi for breakfast.

"Come on sleepy head," he grinned at me, peace it seemed had returned to his spirit. "Coffee's almost ready." He presented his usual charming self, no trace of the frightening intensity of a few short minutes beforehand.

"Jordi, what . . . what happened in there? In the bedroom?" I hesitated, lacking in self-confidence and not wanting to cause a scene.

"What Laura, my love, what do you mean?"

"You hurt me when you pulled my hair. I didn't like that." I slipped into a familiar role, being cautious, afraid to upset him.

"Just being playful, my love." He raised his hands in a "what's the matter?" type of way. He came over and kissed me gently on the forehead. "Sorry I hurt your delicate little head beautiful girl. I must be more careful."

I smiled up at him as he ruffled my hair and caressed my face with his fingertips. Then he enclosed me in his arms, pulling me to his chest. "I love you my darling, oh how I love you."

Eight

I forgave him because he was Latin. Such a passionate man, his emotions overflowed easily. I needed to realise just how much he loved me and how upset and insecure he was about me leaving. He could not be sure I would come back. I held all the power in my hands. I reassured myself that he was not violent or unhinged; he was simply passionately in love. I decided that when I came back, and we really started our life together I would encourage him to feel safe. I wanted him to experience love, help him understand a gentler way to express himself.

We had our breakfast and a fairly low-key goodbye, Jordi had shut down emotionally again, then he left for work. I cleaned up the kitchen, made the bed and got ready to leave. Just after nine I pulled the door closed behind me and headed for the Metro.

Arriving at Barcelona Sants railway station I appreciated just how much had happened in the three weeks since my arrival. I looked about me with very different eyes. I caught and understood snippets of conversation around me, picked up body language cues. I walked into a bar and ordered a ham and cheese sandwich with tomato bread to take on the train, just like a local.

I settled down in my seat on the train, excited to be off again. The weeks ahead would be filled with new friendships, adventures and challenges. Bring it on, I thought to myself.

The first leg of my journey would take me to Port Bau on the French border from where I would take an overnight sleeper to Paris. *"Je voudrais un couchette a Paris ce soir, s'il vous plaît,"* I informed the man at the ticket booth. I giggled, quite chuffed with myself that I could pull out enough schoolgirl French to make myself understood. The Catalan I had been studying also helped, both being Latin based languages.

I didn't sleep much that night, enjoying the rhythmic rocking of the train. My mind roamed freely as it quietly processed my experiences from the last three weeks. There was a lot that would not fall into place. It was so all-consuming, so intense, so far beyond anything I had previously experienced, and also so unexpected. I had no answers, no idea what lay ahead, what path I would take. I needed time; I needed distance. Certain incidents that had happened and characteristics of Jordi's disturbed me. I pushed them away, not wanting to listen to what my insides might have to say about that. The dominant influence on my feelings was the tug of those strong arms, those beautiful blue eyes, that strong muscled torso. Above all, perhaps sat my desperate need to be loved. The draw was almost hypnotic. Reluctantly I conceded that maybe I was just kidding myself when I thought I had a choice at all.

The train pulled into *Gare de Lyon* railway station in Paris in the early morning. I stepped down onto the platform, groggy with sleep, and set about finding my way via the Metro to the *Gare du Nord* where I would catch a train to Brussels. After using the Barcelona Metro almost daily during the last three weeks, I was a lot more confident in navigating my way around than I had been the last time I was in Paris.

Back then, over a month ago I depended on Kyle, the French-Canadian guy, to get us around Paris. It was curious to see the nervousness and tension he and other French-Canadians showed when dealing with the locals, they were nervous that their accents would offend the French. I had almost lost my schoolgirl French and had no delusions about its usefulness. That first time in Paris I had accompanied hot headed Kyle as he tried to reserve his ticket onwards to Lyon. I noticed his stress rising as he tried to communicate with the man behind the glass screen. Then his tension overloaded, and he broke into English to be understood. At that point the French attendant stepped back from the glass, raised his hands and declared "No English!". He then turned and walked away from the ticket window into an inner room leaving

Kyle and a queue of people waiting. Kyle's response had been memorable. He took two steps back, raised his hands and let out a deafening "Well fuck you!" at the top of his voice before bringing his hands down in a truly dramatic manner. I found it quite funny and pretty embarrassing and turned my back as I cringed and covered my mirth.

This time I made it to *Gare du Nord* without a hitch and soon found my train, heading north.

I loved travelling by train, especially the sensation of the train pulling out of the station. It signalled escape, a new destination, a new adventure in the making. It also tasted like freedom, no one to answer to, no one to fit in with, no one to justify or explain myself to.

I spent my time in Brussels exploring the city centre and touring through the massive *Palais de Justice*. I fell in love with the amazing view of Brussels from the attached courtyard. I ventured further, catching up with local naughty-boy, the infamous *Manneken-Pis*. There were so many awesome sights to be found just by taking your curiosity for a stroll through the minor streets and lanes in the centre. I also included a day trip to Bruges which is about an hour away. Bruges, an almost fully preserved 14th to 15th century Flemish city, is one of the most beautiful cities in Europe. I strolled through the old streets, beside the canals and tried to allow myself to just be in the moment, immersed in the colour and the life around me.

It should have been so exciting, I should have been so full of awe and appreciation. Instead, everything possessed a slightly washed out appearance because of the constant underlying ache and confusion in my heart. Wherever I went during this time was referenced by the gnawing fact, I was not "with him".

From Brussels I booked a train north to Den Haag in the Netherlands. I was joined by two Finnish girls, Anna and Tina I met in the hostel in Brussels. They were fun and interesting, very sporty and clean cut. Anna was a pocket rocket, small, feisty with thick white blonde hair to her waist, Tina was taller and more pensive. I was intrigued by their language. I tried to catch a word or two but it was completely unfathomable to me.

The three of us bonded with three young Italian guys also staying in the hostel in Den Haag, and their soccer ball, they called *Marcus Spherico*. They carried Marcus around everywhere they went with great care and fondness. It was a lot of fun. The boys were only about 19 and this was their first time away from home. One of them, Paulo, almost had tears in his eyes as he spoke of his mother's pasta. We all made spaghetti bolognaise together one night at the hostel and they enjoyed it but of course it was "not as good as mama makes". One afternoon I walked down the beach, deep in conversation with a German girl, eventually sitting on the sand while we continued chatting. In a lull in the conversation we looked up and realised we were sitting in the middle of a nudist beach. We laughed quietly together then continued chatting. I learned to love the European attitude to nudity.

Den Haag provided a lovely peaceful space. All too soon it was time for Anna, Tina and I to say *ciao* and lug our packs back to the railway station and on to Amsterdam.

We arrived at Amsterdam Central Station and I allowed the girls to lead us to a youth hostel. Anna and Tina planned to stay just three nights in Amsterdam and I had decided to move on with them. They were going back to Finland and I would head into Germany. The hostel was warm and sunny and I was enjoying the company and having a break from finding my way. It was quite disconcerting at times, having to rely on my bad sense of direction. Once, back home, I nearly walked a group of bushwalkers off a cliff, all the time being relaxed and confident of my interpretation of the map.

The hostel was typical of the relaxed nature of Amsterdam. It comprised of mixed dorms and a central bar which dominated the atmosphere. It included a pool table, comfy booths and laid-back music. There were a lot more "cool backpacker" types hanging out there than in the average youth hostel.

One feature of Amsterdam which made it edgy was the relaxed drug culture. There was evidence of it everywhere, from coffee shops (the local name for a mixed bar where you can buy weed and drinks) to stoned Rasta or hippy types wandering or sitting about. I found the official Dutch attitude to marijuana or hash interesting.

It was not legal to sell drugs for personal use in a coffee shop but neither was it punishable. Therefore, you could buy weed but you could only consume it on site.

There was a darker element to the drug culture in the form of missing person posters, a lot of them. Have you seen this person, Tom Brown/Maria Green, last seen ... Nationality, etc. If you have any information, please call... Wherever Maria or Tom were there could be no doubt it was not a pretty story. The warning was there for all to see, don't lose yourself in Amsterdam. Still, it was Amsterdam, and in my opinion, drugs were all part of the experience. I knew how to look after myself. It was a box I wanted to tick though I wasn't sure how that would happen while I travelled with my lovely but conservative Finnish friends.

On my second morning in the hostel I connected with a few guys over breakfast. Describing them is like introducing a joke. An Australian man, a Scottish man and a South African man walked into a bar ... They were all clean-cut professional types. Dan, the Australian from Canberra sported a traveller's beard that was either recent or kept well-trimmed. Malcolm was a tall thin Scottish guy with pale skin and a mop of dark brown hair, and Henry was South African. Small, gently spoken he seemed the most street wise of the three. They met somewhere along the road and decided to travel together for a while.

We laughed and joked and told stories and I confessed, "I've been in Amsterdam for three days and I still haven't tasted the wares". I put it out there as a loaded statement, hoping they would pick up on my not-so-subtle suggestion.

"Really?" Dan grabbed the line.

"Well, I have no one to go out with except my Finnish friends who are not into that sort of thing."

Malcolm smiled at Dan and Henry. "Well, we can help you with that, can't we lads?" The other two nodded in agreement. "We'll be going out tonight, you can join us if you want."

"Sure, that would be great!"

We met in the hostel bar at 6.30pm and headed out. They were confident of our direction and I happily followed along. We were a team, I felt safe with them.

I thought we would get straight into it but instead we headed to a pub for a couple of drinks first. That made me wary. The old saying was one I had heard many times, "grass before beer, you're in the clear, beer before grass, you're on your arse". I had no intention of ending up on my arse that night, not in Amsterdam among all those missing persons' posters. I sipped my beer slowly while the others downed two or three each.

After the beers we were back out on the street, heading in a new direction and soon found ourselves in a strip of coffee shops. Somehow, we chose one and walked in. Just entering the bar was a rich experience for the senses. There was a strong Rastafari influence with more than a few head-bobbing dreadlocks among the patrons. Red, yellow and green flags and posters complete with images of Bob Marley, marijuana leaves and smoking paraphernalia covered the walls. The air was sweet and smoky with that attention-grabbing aroma of "MaryJane" in all her forms. Reggae music, Bob Marley at his best, played in the background. We headed for a table deep inside where we sat down and Henry and I waited while Dan and Malcolm perused the "menu".

We pooled our cash and Dan put our order through. Henry volunteered to be the joint roller, and we watched his progress with eager interest. He presented us with a long thick joint we passed around as we drank another beer and shared travel stories.

It didn't seem to take long before the effects started to hit me. I had smoked a little pot before, mainly leaf and not anything with any real psychedelic effects. This was a whole new experience. As the effects increased over time I looked around at the bar and my vision and movement were like a strobe light — everything moved in short bursts. As weird as it all seemed, I enjoyed it and I felt like I was still in control.

After we finished the joint, we all sat there, at times in our own little worlds, and at others grinning and giggling at each other. After some time, Henry started rolling our remaining weed into a second joint. We all watched him with great interest for what seemed an incredibly long time. He achieved absolutely nothing. Nobody cared. In the end, he gave up, and we all laughed. Nobody needed any more.

We got up and left, walking out into the clear fresh air. It had grown dark but other than that I had no thought what the time might have been or where we were going. We walked a lot in pairs except nobody wanted to walk with Malcolm. He was hard enough to understand at the best of times but by then his accent thickened. He also talked a constant stream of dribble, something about his brother, that no one was interested in. I was having a great time. My consciousness alternated between being lost in my own world, partying with imaginary friends in my head or laughing hysterically at my own hallucinations. I laughed so hard I grew hoarse. When I came back to the present from the party going on in my head, I would look around to orientate myself, reminding myself who these guys were and what the situation was. Ok, right, yes, I'm in Amsterdam. Yep, that's Malcolm beside me, rabbiting on, and Dan and Henry ahead of us. I wondered where we were going before disappearing back inside my own head.

Suddenly the scene changed. I came down from my head and looked about. Malcolm no longer jabbered away beside me and turning, I couldn't see Dan or Henry. Where was I? Where were my friends? Where was I going? I stopped and my mouth dropped open as I gazed about me. Oh fuck, oh fuck, where am I?

Nine

I struggled to stay focussed as I tried to assess my situation. I was faced with the stark reality. I was very stoned and very lost in a city I was completely unfamiliar with. I worried the hostel might have a curfew; I couldn't recall what street it was in or even the name.

Shit, shit, shit! I didn't want to be stuck out there all night. I turned my head about, attempting to get my bearings. I peered around me at the large square with people coming and going. I recognised buildings from earlier in the day sightseeing with Anna and Tina but that really didn't help me. For such an independent traveller I was incredibly unprepared. I had the sense to realise I was also very vulnerable.

I found a bench and sat down trying to think about what to do. I was terrified I would come back from tripping and find myself kidnapped in some hovel. I had heard about an underground operation where backpackers had been abducted and sold as sex slaves.

All I could do was sit there as time slipped by. I must have appeared desperate as a girl came over and spoke in accented English, asking me if I was alright.

I looked up, trying to make sense of the face before me. She had long dark hair and her big brown eyes were full of concern. "It's Laura, isn't it?"

I looked at her again recognising her face from the hostel. She had the bottom bunk, across from me.

"Yes, yes!" I thumped my chest, caveman style. "I am Laura, and you ... you are in my room ... my hostel ... in my room, from Sweden, or Chile or somewhere." I tried to stay present. "I don't remember your name."

"Yes, that's right. I'm Olivia." Her smile was warm. "Are you okay?"

"No, no, I'm, I'm not," I shook my head. "I'm not okay. I went out with friends and, and ... we had a joint ... and sssomehow, I got lost. I, I ... don't know... the hostel, where is it." I fixed my eyes on her face, I felt so lost. "I don't know." I was trying not to get upset.

"Oh, you poor girl ... but it's alright, it's alright, I will be going to the hostel soon. Do you want to come with me?"

"Oh, yes, please." I almost cried with relief.

"Okay, that's good. I am coming from a concert. I'm meeting friends in a bar, around the corner here for a little while. After that, I'll be going back. Are you ready? Come on." She extended her hand.

"Oh my God ... oh my ... you are a lifesaver. I ... I just ... what ... what a relief. Thank you, thank you." I stood up and took her hand firmly in mine. "Is there a curfew? Are we okay?" Once safe, embarrassment replaced the fear that had filled me. "I'm sorry, my head is everywhere, please don't let me go."

She grinned at me. "Yes, we are okay. Bob's Hostel does not have a curfew." Her voice sounded kind, reassuring. "I will look after you." We walked off holding hands. I giggled with relief, but not hysterically this time and Olivia laughed with me. We laughed so hard we had to stop so as not to lose our balance. I stepped forward and gave her a big bear hug.

"Thank you, thank you!" I cried over her shoulder. "You are my ... my guardian angel. Do you have wings, like angel wings?" I circled around her, all the time hanging on to her. "I didn't want to be a ... a sex slave in some ... somewhere." I gesticulated wildly with one arm as I stared seriously into her face. I shook my head to clear it and to catch up with reality. What a relief, what a rollercoaster of emotions.

She glanced at me sideways and laughed. "Oh, what a lovely sex slave you would be!" she teased before breaking into a cheeky grin, the tip of her tongue caught between her front teeth. I grinned back into those beautiful brown eyes and kissed her on the cheek before we continued on our way.

We made our way to the bar where a guy and girl played some relaxed folksy music. It was a more regular looking place. It had a huge rustic bar top made of a single slice of timber and mismatched seating, all drawn together by a heap of colourful cushions. Olivia introduced me to her friends and quickly explained the essence of our coming together. They nodded and smiled and sympathised with me while I sat grinning somewhat stupidly beside her. She bought me a cola and herself a beer and we sat chatting and listening to the music. Still tripping, I didn't contribute much of the conversation. I tuned in enough to realise that much of it wasn't in English, anyway.

"Do you want to leave now?" Olivia's voice close by and her hand on my shoulder brought me back down out of the party that still raged in my head.

"To go back to the hostel? Yes please, if you are ready."

"Okay, let's go."

We said our goodbyes to the group and headed back out into the street. She took my hand firmly in hers. "No wandering off now."

"Yes Boss, no Boss, thank you, Boss." I bowed in a playful subservient manner and we giggled together. I was still so relieved to be safe.

On our way back to the hostel, I tried hard to stay present while we chatted about ourselves. Olivia was three years older than me. She was in Amsterdam for a few days on her way back home after studying in Paris. It was something to do with her doctoral studies in reproductive biology.

We arrived back at the hostel safe and sound at about 1am and dropped down into the lounge chairs in the recreation room.

"I'm off in the morning, going north, I think. We catch the train at 8:30. Gonna be a struggle."

"I'm off too, to Stockholm but my train does not leave until 10:30, lucky me! It will be nice to be home again. I miss my little flat and my cat."

"You have a ... a cat? What's its name?"

"Smulan, she's a girl. My neighbour's looking after her."

"It's been good ... really good to meet you," I leant over in my drugged state and took her hand again. "Not only coz you saved me from ... from being a sex slave but ... I really like you." I held her hand to my cheek. "Thank you, thank you. I owe you." I was very aware of the dark possibilities that may have awaited me if Olivia had not happened by when she did.

We stood and embraced. "You don't owe me, it's been my pleasure," she murmured over my shoulder. "Perhaps we will see each other again. Maybe you will come to Sweden to visit sometime. You are welcome to stay with me."

"Thank you. That would be great," I responded enthusiastically. Meanwhile, my plans were taking me to Berlin and then to Munich and beyond, further and further from Sweden.

We headed to bed, tiptoeing into the dorm full of slumbering bodies. I was asleep the moment my head hit the pillow. It had been a big night.

It surprised me to find I was still high when I woke up. It slowed my progress as Anna, Tina and I packed up our bags ready to leave. They kept checking on me to make sure I was getting organised on time. I ran into Dan in the corridor as I came back from the bathroom.

"Laura! Jesus! Where did you go? Oh God, I'm so glad you are here, and okay, you are okay, aren't you?" He came close and studied my face as if searching for confirmation. He looked like shit.

"Yeah Dan, I'm okay. What happened? I just found myself on my own."

"We were all together, and I was trying to keep my mind straight so I could get us back here. That was some strong shit we had. I'm sorry, really sorry, I put you in danger. I've been worried." He shrugged apologetically before repeating "I didn't know that shit was so strong. I was trying to get us all back home but when I looked you weren't there, with us. You had just disappeared. We walked back and looked around everywhere but we never saw you. Did you have trouble finding your way back?"

I nodded dramatically. "Yeah, I had no idea where I was. I couldn't even remember the name of the bloody hostel, let alone what street it was in. I was shitting myself. I thought I was fucked, totally fucked. Then Olivia, the Swedish girl in the bunk opposite, she saw me sitting all spaced out and lost in some square and she rescued me. I was fucking lucky." We stood in silence for a moment, sharing the weight of what could have transpired. "So, thanks for the night out, thanks for coming back to find me, I don't know what happened but I don't blame you. It's all fine, thank God."

We stood, lost in our own thoughts for a moment.

"I'm still a bit loose in the head, how 'bout you?"

"Yeah," he raised his eyebrows. "Still spaced out."

We chuckled together and had a quick hug goodbye. "See you down under." I shot over my shoulder as I headed back to the room to finish packing my bag before breakfast.

I looked down at Olivia as I walked into the dorm room. She had been asleep when I had left the room and I had lingered just a few moments to watch her. Fast asleep, it had been her turn to be vulnerable. Seeing her had filled me with a sensation of warmth, fondness and gratitude all rolled into one.

She smiled at me sleepily. "Good morning."

I sat on the edge of her bunk and threw my arms around her enthusiastically. "Good morning, my handsome prince. It's great to see you." I grinned down at her. "I'm just about to go."

"Take this." She pulled a piece of paper out from under her pillow. "It's my address and phone number in Sweden. I'd love you to come and stay with me."

I took the note and read it quickly. "Thanks, I'd really like that, I just don't know when it might happen."

"That's okay," she shrugged casually, "at least you have my details."

I leant over her again and enfolded her, gently this time, in a soft warm embrace. As my head rested on her shoulder, I took in her scent, the feel of her soft silky hair. "Thank you so much for rescuing me. I'm so happy you found me." I stood up, holding her hand. "Bye, my prince, travel well." I kissed her hand and returned it to her. The drugs must have been giving me courage. I wasn't normally confident enough to be so touchy-feely, especially with a woman.

"And bye to you my friend, stay safe," she said with a stern face. Then she broke into a huge grin that crinkled up her eyes. I matched it with my own and we held each other's gaze for a minute before I turned and left the room. Her grin, showing just that little bit of tongue was truly infectious.

Ten

My next stop was Berlin. It was just months before the wall came down on 9th November 1989. I found it to be a depressing place with the wall and everything it represented. Then there were the scars from the Second World War bombings and the history of the persecution of the Jews. It was a cold mix of sadness and despair combined with stiff German authority and efficiency. So, I moved onto Munich.

Munich was like being in another country. The Bavarians were much more laid back than their northern countrymen. I found my way to the Hofbräuhaus in the early evening where I fell in with some Irish guys and a few Canadian girls. I did the chicken dance and laughed and chatted my way through two large beers. I knew I was a bit tipsy as I said my goodbyes to my new friends and headed home. They locked the doors of my hostel at midnight so I made sure I left by 11 to give myself plenty of time. I consulted my map and headed off, but my sense of direction was even worse after the two beers. I found myself, frustrated and desperate, walking down the median strip in the middle of a freeway. It was rather scary but at the time I couldn't see any other way to get where I needed to go. I made it back to the hostel just before midnight and sank into my bed with relief once more.

The next day I did a bus trip to the Neuschwanstein Castle. The view took me back to my childhood. Memories of Sunday nights by the fire, with my brother, in our jarmies watching Disneyland, eating tinned tomato soup and hot buttered scones. Later I agreed to go to back to the Hofbräuhaus with an American girl called

Silvia. I made her promise she would get us safely home before midnight. She laughed at me. "What, are you Cinderella? I think that castle is getting to you!"

I laughed and then related my navigational disaster from the night before.

I was just skimming through Europe, not staying long in any one place, not feeling settled. Underlying my drifting was a plan to return to Jordi. He filled my mind a lot and my hunger for him seemed to grow with each passing day. I wanted more of that heady passion that sparked between us. I moved on to Vienna where I had planned to stop and organise my Spanish visa.

Vienna, in mid-summer was breathtakingly beautiful. The great baroque buildings, arts festivals, and gorgeous lush gardens made it so easy to fill my days. What's more, with the ring road and tramways it was relatively easy to navigate my way around. During the day I visited the famous landmarks and even a fascinating Freud exhibition. I learnt a lot about the theories and treatments of female hysteria. I left feeling that true equality, freedom and a healthy sex life might have been what those poor women really needed.

I spent many evenings in Stadtpark, the large central park, at the classical music concerts. There was an official ticketed area with the orchestra set up and many tables full of beautiful people. Beyond this official zone were the scraggy backpackers such as myself, along with the rest of the "great unwashed". It was so magical. Everyone was happy, smiling, laughing, and dancing badly on the grass with complete strangers. I loved it.

Late in my second week there I took a Tramway out to Baden in the Viennese woods. There, in a rotunda in a large park was an orchestra playing the most heavenly classical music. Beneath huge inter-arching shade trees were many benches where locals of all ages were sitting, chatting and enjoying the music. It was a wonderful experience and so good for the soul.

After some time listening to the music and people watching, I walked up through the woods. The melody gently faded behind me as I wandered deeper into the forest. Alone, in a secluded part of the woods, I sat on a log and gave myself up to the turmoil inside. I had so many questions and so few answers. "What am I meant to do with my life? Should I go back to Spain? Can I trust my feelings? Is Jordi really the wonderful loving person I think he is? What did that hair pulling thing mean? How do I know what I am supposed to be doing?"

The path that seemed to hold the most promise was the one leading back to Barcelona. I admit, I didn't seriously consider any other possibility. I thought about visiting Olivia, sweet funny Olivia. I also thought about continuing on with my travels and not returning to Barcelona. In the end though, my need was too strong. I could not resist the yearning inside to return to Jordi, with his strong arms, soft lips and voracious sexual appetite.

My three-month Spanish Tourist Visa came through as expected the next week and so I said goodbye to the beautiful city of Vienna and continued on my way.

I spent a few days in Salzburg, the picturesque city that is home to The Sound of Music. While there I went for a day trip out to the salt mines in nearby Germany. Following this I joined a "free armchair tour of the Sound of Music", also known as "watching the movie" in the recreation room. Salzburg is so enchanting it is no wonder that Julie Andrews kept breaking into song. I skipped and sang softly around the fountain, through the streets and along the "Convent" wall.

From Salzburg I caught a train towards Italy. On the train I met a university student called Matteo who, in broken English gave me a few salient facts about Italy. The country had a population of 60 million but only 6 million were registered as employed and paying taxes. The rest of the economy operated on an informal and untraceable cash or barter basis.

"Italy," explained Matteo spreading his hands wide, "Is a festival of imperfection."

I stopped at Verona, home to Romeo and Juliet and stayed in a lovely little rustic hostel. On my way down for breakfast, I bumped into a guy as we both tried to go through the door into the dining area.

"After you." He smiled at me and waved his hand forward.

"Oh, sorry, thank you." I smiled back at him, appreciating his bleached blond hair and the little dimples that played around at the corners of his mouth.

"Where are you from?" he asked as we lined up for our plates.

"Melbourne Australia, and you?"

"Vancouver, Canada. I'm Mitch."

"Hi, I'm Laura."

We had breakfast together and teamed up for a day trip to Venice. Mitch was sweet and indecisive and had the sexiest legs beneath his close-fitting frayed denim shorts I had ever encountered on a man. We had a great day. We laughed, joked and shared our lives in a simple relaxed way.

That night we shared a beer in the hostel gardens, enjoying the chemistry bubbling between us.

"I've really enjoyed spending today with you."

I nodded. "Yeah, it's been a lot of fun."

Our eyes met, lingering. We held each other's gaze with increasing intensity over the top of our beers.

It's just a kiss I told myself. But just a kiss became just a fondle which led into just a night together in Mitch's tent, hastily erected in the dark in the gardens.

The next morning, we said our goodbyes as our paths led us in different directions. Mitch wanted to stay in touch. I wanted to get the hell out of there before I became too emotionally conflicted.

I travelled to Rome with three Americans I met on the station platform in Verona, two girls and a guy. We shared a room in Rome and went out each day exploring the popular tourist spots. I found myself whizzing by "yet another Roman ruin" with rising impatience. I had a constant sensation of life being elsewhere that made it hard to connect with the present moment.

A severe heat wave set in at this point. There were reports of people dying in Greece and Rome had become very oppressive. This spurred me on to see everything I could in a few days before jumping on a train and not getting off till I reached Switzerland. I missed all of Greece, southern Italy, Florence, Pisa, Milan. I had money; I had time, but I had no peace of mind, no heart for it. Like the Buddhist conundrum: "If a tree falls in the forest and no one sees it, does it really fall?" so it was with me. If I experienced something but had no one to share it with, did I really experience it? This made me question why I had come to Europe on my own. Had I set off to "go" somewhere or to "escape" from somewhere?

I thought of Olivia as I travelled north and remembering that night together made me smile. The desire to visit her increased as I got closer to my return to Spain.

I left the train at Interlaken where I hired a moped for the day and rode around the stunning lakeside scenery. The weather was clear and sunny and the water in the lakes presented such a clear icy blue, or pale turquoise, it was just breath-taking. The following day I hitched up into the mountains above Grindelwald with two young American guys. We jumped up and down excitedly when we got picked up on the edge of Interlaken by a big black super shiny stretch limousine. The driver, a chauffeur (in fact "our chauffeur" for the morning) was on his way up to a resort to pick up his boss. He appeared happy to have the company. We were careful not to leave dirty footprints in the back and refrained from exploring the minibar though we helped ourselves to a few mints. The countryside was stunning. I was blown away by the snow and ice-capped mountains, lush green hillsides and gentle fluffy-eared Brown Swiss cows complete with cow bells. That night we cooked up a huge mound of spaghetti bolognaise and auctioned off the leftovers to other hungry residents. We covered our cost, fed the masses and even made a tiny profit.

And then it was crunch time. I had to decide whether I would go north to see Olivia or straight south back to Jordi. I had a few days travel left on my Eurail pass and I knew once I settled in with Jordi, I would be content to stay put. So finally, after changing my mind several times, I mustered some courage and decided to visit Olivia.

Eleven

My journey north from Interlaken would take over 24 hours, travelling through Frankfurt, Hamburg, Copenhagen and on to Stockholm. Doubts crept in and I hummed quietly to stop the negative chatter in my head. It was a long way to go on a whim, a long way to go to find Olivia wasn't the wonderful person of my first impressions. I nearly backed out. I considered calling her but chickened out. I had also told Jordi in an expensive phone call before I left Rome that I would probably be back within ten days or so. I didn't want him to be worried about me or be pissed off when I didn't turn up as expected. I sent him a postcard with brief details. I gave a new ETA of a week or so later than expected. I hoped that would suffice. It gave me about two weeks to play with. I would finish with a train journey from Stockholm to Barcelona of almost two whole days at the end.

I was so nervous, possibly more nervous than I remembered being on the way to visiting Jordi in Barcelona. Women were much scarier to me than men, I understood them much less.

I kept telling myself that I was simply going to see a friend. It would be fun. I would only stay for a couple of days, that's all. I didn't need to stay any longer. I was looking forward to seeing the city sights in Stockholm, which I had been told were breathtakingly beautiful. If it turned out to be uncomfortable, I could always go to a hostel. Uncomfortable? Why should it be uncomfortable? My mind kept chattering on, pulling the future apart from every possible direction.

I finally arrived at the massive Stockholm Central Station and walked out into the street to get my bearings. I double checked the map in my guidebook and made my way down, over Central Bridge to a hostel on a former Swedish Navy ship, the Gustaf A/F Klint. I settled in, had a walk, some dinner and an early night, pulling my towel over my head to block out the seemingly endless twilight.

I waited until 9.30 the next morning before dialling Olivia's number from a pay phone in the street. I wanted to make sure I didn't wake her, but I was also anxious to get the phone call over with. I was so churned up I almost backed out even at that late stage.

Ring ring, ring ring. Nothing remarkable about the Swedish ring tone. It kept ringing. I prepared myself for disappointment.

Finally, it picked up. A man's voice answered sleepily "Halla?" For a moment I struggled, unable to speak as I quickly checked the number. I had not expected that. Shit, I thought, what do I say?

"Um, this is Laura, is Olivia there please." I hoped he understood English.

"Yes, just one minute please." He said thickly. I listened intently as he put the phone down and spoke to someone off in the distance. The phone was picked up again.

"Hallo?" Olivia's voice, also sounding a bit sleepy. I could not detect any note of recognition. My hopes fell. I resisted the urge to hang up.

"Hello, Olivia?"

"Yes," Her voice held a note of interest this time.

"Um, it's Laura. We met in Amsterdam ..." In the phone box I grimaced, shook my head. This was the moment of truth, salvation or mortal wounding. There was silence for a moment as I held my breath.

"Laura!" she responded after a moment, laughing. "Yes, of course. Lovely to hear from you. Where are you calling from?"

Time for another deep breath before the 'great reveal'. "I'm in Stockholm. I arrived yesterday, I'm in a hostel." There, it was out.

"In Stockholm? Really? I can't believe this. Do you want to come to my place, do you want to stay with me?" Her voice became warm and more than a little excited.

I exhaled. I was so relieved. I felt joyous and a little light headed. "Yes please, that would be great, if it's okay, if, if you have room ..."

"Yes, yes, there is room for you. My place is not big but we will be fine."

We agreed to meet up a couple of hours later in the Kungstradgarden, a public park in the historic royal gardens. My heart leapt as I saw her in the distance and I found I was smiling. She laughed when she saw me and hurried forward.

"Laura!" She wrapped me in a bear hug. "It is you." She held me at arm's length and looked me up and down. I just stood there nodding and grinning. "It is really you, here in Stockholm! But I thought you were in Spain or ... or somewhere like that. How are you? Are you hungry? Have you had breakfast? Do you want some coffee or something to eat?"

All of my doubts and insecurities vanished in the face of Olivia's genuine warmth and enthusiasm. I was so glad I had been able to overcome my fear and get on top of the urgency to return to Jordi. I was in the right place, where I was meant to be. I had made a good decision.

"I had breakfast at the hostel but that was hours ago, so yes please, especially coffee." I made a mock desperate face and we both laughed. I would soon learn that Swedes were very keen on their coffee, which suited me fine.

I shouldered my back pack and she insisted on carrying my day pack along with her own bag. We chatted gaily as we walked to a nearby bar. I followed Olivia's lead and grabbed a coffee and a plate of cinnamon buns. She paid for us both and we headed for a table in the corner.

"Having coffee and cake is a very Swedish thing to do."

I nodded my understanding.

"In Swedish it's called *fika* and Swedes loved their *fika*, especially with cinnamon buns." She chuckled and added "Seriously, I hope you like cinnamon. Swedes are in love with cinnamon."

I assured her I did.

We were both hungry and for a start there was silence except for a few appreciative mm's and ah's as we chowed down on the yummy buns.

Once the warmth from the food started to hit my stomach, I slowed down enough to talk. I had spent quite a bit of time working out in my head how I would ask her about the man who answered the phone. I didn't want to look nosey.

"When I heard a man's voice on your phone, I thought I must have dialled the wrong number." I followed up with what I hoped was a casual little laugh.

"Oh, that's Lucas, my brother. He sometimes sleeps on my couch if he is partying in the city with his friends. The telephone is right by the couch so it probably woke him up." She rolled her eyes. "He came in late, he was drinking a lot so he is a bit hung over."

"Okay," I nodded. "I see. I thought it might be your boyfriend, and I didn't want to intrude."

"No, no, not at all. I was seeing someone, Oscar, on and off, but he is actually in Australia just now for one year."

"Really? What's he doing? Where is he?"

"He is a marine biologist and is working on a project at a place called AIMS ... umm, the Australian something of Marine Science. It's near a place called ... umm, Townsville, I think that's it. Do you know it?"

"I am not familiar with AIMS but Townsville, yes. It's up North, in Queensland. I haven't been there."

"Okay. He will not be home until December so there is just you and me. Sometimes Lucas stays although I can tell him to go stay with another friend if he wants to party while you are here."

"I didn't know if you were working or busy ..."

"I'm on Summer break from my studies. I work three days a week. Fortunately, not today." She leaned forward across the table as she spoke and put her hand on mine, gently squeezing it.

I felt the warmth and the energy coming from her. It was like liquid love on my skin and I surprised myself by my emotional response. A lump came into my throat and my eyes started to prickle with tears. To avoid detection, I quickly looked down, blinking rapidly, pretending to dust crumbs off my lap.

Olivia just sat smiling calmly at me while I fluffed about getting my emotions under wraps. "Let's go home. You can get settled in and then we can decide what we will do with our day."

"Great, let's move. You lead the way, as usual."

"Yes." She grinned at me playfully. "Maybe I will buy a little rope to tie to your arm so you cannot get lost."

She took my hand as we left the bar. We skipped our way down the path for a few steps before I sagged under the weight of my backpack.

I expected Olivia to lead us to the Underground but instead we walked south, across the bridge past the Royal Palace and on to Sodermalm. I recognised the street that led down to the ship-hostel and told Olivia about my night aboard. Moving on, we arrived at the front door of her apartment building less than ten minutes later.

She led me up the stairs and I smiled inwardly as she came out with the usual things we say when bringing someone home for the first time. The "Please excuse the mess, it's not normally like this, I've been so busy, I can't remember when I did the dusting last..." Culture and language may change but some things are the same the world over.

The door to her fourth-floor flat was painted in thick black glossy paint to hide many years of scuffs and scratches. A decorative peephole at eye level sat like a slightly tarnished crown on the worn surface. Olivia unlocked the door and swung it open.

"Välkommen!" she said dramatically sweeping her arm in through the doorway.

I gave a clumsy curtsy before walking in still wearing my backpack, my legs a bit wobbly from the walk up.

I dropped my pack in the small hallway and walked through into what was essentially a studio apartment. To the right at the back, the bedroom was screened off from the sitting room area. Indian print material in rich purple and gold hues had been hung as a curtain. To the left was the kitchen with windows looking out onto an internal airspace. At the back of the kitchen was a door I presumed went into the bathroom. The sitting room took up the rest of the space. It was furnished with an old worn beige couch covered in bright cushions, an old stiff-backed arm chair and a pair of well used velour beanbags. Old wooden framed windows looked down onto the street below. A plate with toast crusts was still sitting on the large low coffee table that seemed to double as a dining table.

The walls were dotted with artwork, among them, were early Parisian burlesque posters and some amateurish seascapes. A couple in black and red in a dramatic tango pose covered most of the bathroom door. Meanwhile, potted plants filled the window sill and corners in a way that blended and harmonised the small apartment. It all combined to give an impression of warmth and comfort despite the mismatch of themes and textures.

The other important element for me was the aroma of the place. A home does nothing for me if it doesn't smell welcoming. Olivia's place smelt like Olivia—warm, slightly floral but with earthy notes of patchouli and sandalwood. I loved it. I closed my eyes for a moment and breathed slowly and deeply, committing the scent to memory. I knew that the longer I stayed there the less I would be aware of it. I needed to grab that impression and etch it into my brain as soon as I could.

I turned to Olivia who was standing by, watching me and waiting for my response. "Great place." I gave her a broad smile, spreading my arms wide. "It's relaxed and homey yet practical and well set out ... a little arty and a little green. Thank you so much for inviting me." I gave her a big hug. When I stepped back, I realised she had become a little flushed and uncomfortable. I pretended not to notice and turned and walked over to study a large lush-green parlour palm in the corner.

"What a beautiful specimen!" I exclaimed. "Can I take it home?" It was a silly thing to say to get us away from an awkward moment.

"You would have to take me too." Her look was appreciative. "We are good friends, this palm tree and me. We have been together for many years now. In fact, I have had that tree for longer than I have had my cat."

"Oh yes, your cat! What was his name? Smollem? Smoggom?"

"Smulan, and she is a girl." She corrected me lightly. "She is probably asleep on my bed."

My energy changed as we passed through the curtain into the bedroom. A person's home is personal and I was honoured to be in Olivia's. Her bedroom however, was her sacred space and I felt humbled, more than a little nervous and curious to enter.

She had a queen-sized bed with a generous assortment of pillows. Curiously, there were two single duvets spread over it. The bedside tables had quaint mismatching lamps and there was a small bronze Buddha statue in the Tibetan tradition sitting on a chest of drawers.

We found Smulan, a gorgeous ginger cat curled up in the middle of the bed as predicted.

Olivia picked her up and the cat hung docilely from her hands as she brought her to her chest. "Smulan, this is Laura. Laura, this is Smulan."

I shook Smulan's paw attempting a little theatrical flair. "Pleased to make your acquaintance Smulan. I will do my best not to crowd your space while I am here." The cat was completely unfazed at having her paw pumped up and down. We both chuckled and Olivia gently placed Smulan back on the bed.

Olivia did a great job at making me comfortable and welcome. She showed me through the kitchen, the bathroom, the sitting area, explaining where things were kept and how everything worked. She also cleared a shelf in her wardrobe, in the corner of the bedroom for my stuff and gave me a shelf in the bathroom cupboard for my toiletries.

"Wow! This is so great, I may not want to leave!"

She just smiled and shrugged.

The elephant in the room, for me at least, was — where am I going to sleep? I know lots of women who wouldn't think twice about bunking in with a friend and I sort of assumed that would happen. Still, I waited for it to be raised. The experience of sharing a bed with Roxy recently allowed me to feel more comfortable, but also more nervous than I may have been in the past. A door to new possibilities had been unlocked.

Twelve

I sat on a cushion on the floor, near the coffee table while Olivia made us more coffee.

"You can sleep on the couch if you want or you can sleep with me. My bed is much more comfortable. Also, there is a chance you may have a drunk Lucas trying to get into bed with you if you are out here. It's up to you."

"Well, I guess I'll choose option 'a' and sleep with you if that's okay." There, that was settled.

We drank our coffee and ate biscuits, lounging on the cushions on the floor.

"So, where have you come from, what have you been doing?"

I filled her in on my travels, leaving out the bit about spending a night with Mitch, but explaining in detail how I got lost in Munich.

"Oh, you poor girl. I must look after you. I don't want you to get lost in Stockholm."

"I'm sure I will be fine." I followed her with my eyes as she rose and fetched a bottle of wine and chocolate. "I like the look of this." I sniffed at the wine then looked back at Olivia. I was trying to remember what she had told me about herself in Amsterdam. "Now, you weren't born in Sweden, were you? Your dark hair and your brown eyes where did they come from?"

"No, I am from Chile. My family left Chile, like many other people, in 1973, first to Germany then to Sweden to escape the military coup."

"Ah, that's right, Chile. Gee. That must have been frightening."

"Yes, it was very frightening, and so confusing." Olivia looked down at her glass of wine. "It was a crazy time. We were desperate. We were coming to a new life, a better life." She gave a brief wistful smile. "Or so we thought."

"So, how many brothers and sisters do you have?"

"Apart from Lucas who is older, I also have a younger sister, Isabella."

I searched her face as she took a long swallow from her glass, my curiosity piqued by her words and the emotion I saw in her.

"What about you? Do you have a family?" Her smile was brave but her eyes were still sad.

I grinned broadly. "Just wait, I'll show you." I darted off to get my little photo album. I told her about my parents, about Jack, the farm, the animals and life in Australia.

She poured over my pictures, delighted at the mug shots of my furry/woolly friends. I really enjoyed her interest, Jordi had not seen them, not shown any curiosity or desire to know about my life.

Later, she glanced at her watch. "It's after six o'clock already! I'm sorry. I said I would take you out ... but we haven't done anything except talk, talk, talk. What do you want to do?"

"That's fine, really, I am happy right here, unless you want to go out?" I shrugged. "I'm really enjoying just chatting."

"Good, me too." Olivia lit some candles and threw together an impressive platter with cheeses, pate, cured meats, rye bread. She brought it back to the coffee table with another bottle of wine.

As the time whizzed by, we waded deeper and deeper into the flow of each other's stories. Olivia seemed to understand the weight of my outpourings and my feelings as I shared them. She wasn't dismissive and didn't judge me or react with shock or disdain when I "aired my dirty linen".

The whole experience was deeply rewarding and I loved getting to know Olivia. Into our second bottle of wine, I returned to the question of her family.

"So, what about your parents? Are they here?"

She took a swig of wine, played with the cheese knife. "No. They are both dead."

"Oh, I'm so sorry, I shouldn't have asked."

"It's okay, really. My mother ... she got cancer not long after we arrived in Sweden. She died. My father died some years later."

"How awful, I'm so sorry." I didn't know what else to say.

She nodded sadly then smiled. "It's okay, it was years ago. I have Lucas and Isabella. We stay in touch ... support each other."

"That's great, to have that bond. I would like to have a sister." I cut myself a piece of cheese and changed the topic. "What about your studies and your work? What do you do?"

"Well it's all the same thing, really. My doctoral studies are looking at ways to improve women's fertility. You know, their ability to conceive and bear a child."

"How interesting. And your work?"

"Yes, I work in a fertility clinic. You know ... with in vitro fertilisation and that sort of thing. The clinic is like a part of the university. I really love it. But what about you? What do you do?"

"Nothing, I'm a bum." I laughed. "No, I studied accounting, worked in professional offices but really, I don't enjoy it. I am a people person, not a money person, and I have a problem with the whole nine to five sitting at a desk thing. I don't know what I'm going to do. I wouldn't mind going back and studying something new ... Psychology or something like that."

Later, we moved on to the problems of the world. We shared a tub of raspberry ice cream and some local port as we sat together resting against the sofa.

It was late and we were more than a bit drunk when we finally crawled into bed in our shirts and underwear and fell asleep.

I woke the next morning to the strange sounds of a new city, my throat parched and my head throbbing. Olivia's arm was stretched out towards me, her fingers just under the edge of my ribs. Her deep regular breathing told me she was still deeply asleep. I carefully extricated myself from the bed, stood up and turned to look at her. Scenes from the night before flashed across my mind. I saw much laughter, a few tears and a deep, growing connection. I smiled down at her tenderly as she lay on her side, knees curled up, her long dark hair partly covering her face. She was so beautiful. I was full of a deep appreciation and a desire to protect her and resisted the desire to lean over and caress her cheek.

After drinking nearly a litre of water and downing some paracetamol I checked out the kitchen. I boiled the kettle and made myself an instant coffee without too much noise. With cup in hand, I browsed the crowded bookshelf under the sitting room window before sprawling on the mat on the floor to thumb through some titles. A couple of hours went by before Olivia joined me.

"How long are you here for?" asked Olivia, prepping the coffee machine.

"I can stay with you for seven nights, if that's okay." I wasn't sure, as I looked at her if that was going to be too long.

"Great, we will have time to talk all we want and go out and explore the city."

Her attention was on the breakfast preparation so I was free to observe her for a moment with relative freedom. She was a little shorter than me and had a lovely soft figure, a little plump, voluptuous, perfect for cuddling.

I shook my head as I realised what I was doing. I brought my thoughts back on track and hastened over to the kitchen to help her.

"Yes. Then I have to take the train back to Barcelona. The trip back will take about two full days and nights." I rolled my eyes.

She winced in sympathy as she plated up the poached eggs on toast. "You will meet Isabella tonight. She is coming for dinner."

"Okay, that will be nice, what does she do?"

"She is studying to be a Social Worker."

Over breakfast we worked up a rough plan for the next week. Olivia had to work the following three days so we would need to squeeze in our time together when we could.

We headed out into the varied weather of a late Summer day in Stockholm, equipped with coats, sun hats, beanies and water. Let the weather do what it would, we were prepared, and Olivia proved to be a great tour guide.

Given we were both hungover we took a relaxed pace and stopped early for coffee, including more of the delicious cinnamon buns we had had the day before. We were in high spirits, playing about, dancing to the beat of a reggae-styled busker, waltzing to the classical violin offering from another. Our hands connected often, and our bodies brushed against each other. We seemed to both delight in the warmth and intimacy of our growing friendship. In the evening we had some wine and a large pot of Fettucine Carbonara we had prepared. I stopped grating the parmesan cheese and looked up to see Olivia looking at me with a small smile on her face. I met her eyes but looked away when I realised I was blushing.

"I am sorry I have to work. What will you do?"

"Just relax, take a walk around the Old City, maybe find a nice park to sit in."

I heard a key in the door signalling Isabella's arrival. I admit the moment produced a touch of "meet the family" anxiety in me which was weird. Did I need to pull back from the physical intimacy that was growing between us? I decided to take my queue from Olivia.

"Issa!" Olivia wiped her hands on her apron and gave her sister a hug. Turning, she beckoned me with an outstretched arm that she placed about my shoulders as I came close.

Just 20 years old, Isabella was taller than Olivia and very slim, but the family resemblance was unmistakable. Her hair was dark, messy with blue tips. Her heavily made-up eyes were almost the same, but her face was longer and not quite as soft as her sister's.

"Isabella, this is Laura, my friend from Australia, the one I met in Amsterdam."

Isabella looked at me with a bright welcoming smile. "Hallo Laura, it is nice to meet you. Liv told me about your scary experience in Amsterdam. I am happy you are safe."

I smiled and rolled my eyes self-consciously before stepping forward and extending my hand to her. "Hello Isabella, thank you. Good to meet you too. Yes, your lovely sister saved my life."

We all set about getting the food and wine onto the coffee table then settled ourselves around it.

Isabella, wiping sauce off her chin, turned to me. "So, what is your life like in Australia? And your family?"

"She has a big family, and photos." Olivia put her hand on my arm. "Show Issa your photos."

"Mmm," I nodded with my mouth full. I jumped up and fetched my album. "Here's my Mum and Dad." I turned the page. "And here's my brother Jack."

Isabella looked closely at him. "He looks like you. Is he older or younger?"

"We are twins."

"Oh, how special."

"And here are the other members of my family." I turned the page again to show the animals.

She threw her head back and laughed. "I love it, I love it. Oh, I have never seen a sheep with so much personality. So cute!"

"Yeah, it's not fair. Chester's the only family member to get curly hair." I paused for comedic effect, then continued, "So, Olivia said you are studying Social Work."

Isabella nodded as she chewed through a mouthful of fettucini. "Yes, this is my last year."

"And what are you hoping to do?"

"I want to work with youth. Young people on the street, broken families, homeless, that sort of thing."

"That's a tough job. I'm not sure I could handle that. You must be very strong."

"Yes, she is, strong and determined, and well ... very stubborn." Olivia's mouth was set and she frowned across at Isabella.

Isabella made a face at Olivia, fending off her attempt to mother her. "Ja, ja." She turned to me. "I love my sister but she can be a pain, you know, worrying. Like 'Isabella, put your shoes on, Isabella, put your hat on, stay home, be safe,' ... and all that. She thinks sometimes I am still five years old." She smiled at Olivia.

"Oh Issa. Stop exaggerating, I just want you to be safe, you know that." Olivia replied a little impatiently.

"I know, I know. I'm sorry, but I'm a big girl now Liv. You don't have to worry." She put her fork down. "Now, where was I?"

"Telling me about what you want to do."

"Okay, so, I've been volunteering at a shelter for two years now." Isabella's face was serious. "I want to help these young people. It's so hard, and so complex. Many of them have been through so much shit in their lives they aren't really capable of a 'normal life'. So ... we must work with them where they are. We can't judge them, I mean society has no right to judge them because most people have no fucking idea what their world is like ..." She stopped, took a deep breath. "Sorry, sorry, I just get so mad sometimes."

"That's fine, well it's not really, is it? It's all pretty sad."

We fell silent for a moment.

"I'm sorry but I can't stay late." Isabella rose and started clearing plates. "Some friends are dropping in to pick me up at about nine to go out for some drinks, but thank you both for a delicious dinner. It has been nice to meet you Laura."

"Yeah, and you. It's been really nice to see you two sisters together. Maybe I will see you again before I leave."

Just on nine there was a knock at the door. Olivia opened the door and greeted each of Isabella's friends with a hug. There were three of them and it was clear it wasn't the first time they had been at Olivia's. She introduced them to me as Isabella readied herself to leave. They were in a very jolly mood, probably all a bit drunk.

When they had gone, we finished cleaning up the kitchen, then collapsed on the couch with a herbal tea. "That was lovely, I really liked Isabella, you must be proud of her."

"Yes, I am. I am very proud and a little concerned, it is tough. She goes out into the street at night to help the homeless. I worry about her. She is so ... so passionate. I am sure that part of this is her own ... trauma." She grimaced. "What can we do?"

"I'm sure it helps to have loving support around you."

"Definitely, if only she would listen to me. She works too hard, puts herself in danger sometimes." She reached out her hand and fluffed my hair. "Thank you. Thank you, Laura, for being here, for sharing my little life with me. You are good company and I could see that Issa liked you."

"Ta. You're welcome. I am really enjoying my time here."

"Good, I am happy to hear this. Also, I need to tell you, Lucas is going to come in tomorrow morning ... some time before nine o'clock to pick up his jacket. It's in the corner there. Will you be here?"

"Yeah, sure. Gotta meet the whole family, hey?"

"Ha ha, yes, that will be good. I will call him and let him know you will be here, okay?"

"Sure. I'll go out after he's been."

"Good, I hope you will enjoy your day, just don't get lost," she frowned with mock seriousness.

"That's okay," I said raising my eyebrows. "I know my prince charming will save me." I turned away, a little disconcerted at my own words, was I flirting with her?

I shook that thought out of my head as Olivia scoffed. "Ja, but this is Sweden, you may freeze to death before I find you."

We finished our tea, put the cups in the sink and headed to bed early. I felt surprisingly comfortable in bed beside her, each of us wrapped in our own separate duvet. I was tired from our big day and drifted off to sleep as we lay spooning through the covers.

Thirteen

The next morning it was Olivia's turn to be up and out of bed while I slept. I woke to the wonderful aroma of fresh-perked coffee. I slid out of bed and headed for the bathroom.

"Hello, my darling, did you sleep well?" Olivia greeted me as I came out of the bathroom into the kitchen. She was in her work uniform, her beautiful hair neatly swept up in a bun high on the back of her head.

"Mmm," I answered, nodding as I stretched and yawned.

Five minutes later she gave me a big hug and picked up her bag to go. "Now, you have all you need? Food, money, a key, maps, emergency contact numbers ...?"

"You forgot the string. You do have some string, don't you?"

"String?"

"Yeah, so I can tie it to the door handle when I go out ... you know, follow it home at the end of the day. So much better than breadcrumbs."

She rolled her eyes. "Crazy girl, I thought you were serious."

"Sorry, bit of Australian humour for you. Yes, thanks, I think I have everything I need."

"Okay, good. Have a wonderful day. Do anything you want, Sweden is very safe. I will call Lucas when I get to work."

"Thank you, I will. Have a great day at work." I hugged her close to me, breathing in her scent. "See you tonight." Then I stepped back.

"Mmm." She smiled at me, reached out and caressed my cheek.

I felt a jolt go through me. I'm not sure if it started in my brain or my groin but I was instantly hot and wet. I felt flustered and looked away as Olivia grabbed her bag and keys and headed out the door. I stood there for a minute or two, dazed and disorientated. What was that?

I shook my head and looked at the clock in the kitchen. It was just after seven thirty. I had plenty of time to shower and have breakfast before Lucas arrived. After he left, I would be alone. Precious alone time. That wonderful space where I had nothing to do, no one I had to please, and almost all day to do anything I wanted.

At 8:45 I heard a key in the door. I was sitting on the floor by the coffee table studying my map and finishing my second cup of coffee. My eyes darted towards the door a little nervously, waiting for Lucas to appear. He came through into the room amid a rustle of plastic bags that he placed on the bench in the kitchen.

"Hallo, you must be Laura, I am Lucas." He smiled at me.

I stood up out of politeness, and to get a better look at him. Lucas was about six feet tall. He had the same dark hair as his sisters only he wore his shoulder length and it was wavy. His dark brown eyes twinkled as he spoke. He was a little haggard, in a way that suggested he lived hard and drank too much. Still, I thought, if it wasn't for the odour of stale cigarette smoke, he exuded he would be an attractive package. I stepped forward and offered him my hand to shake. Some people are a bit confused by this, especially from a woman, but I liked to touch people when I met them.

"Hello Lucas, it's lovely to meet you."

He stepped forward and took my hand, peering into my face with curiosity. "You are from Australia?"

"Yes, I met Olivia in Amsterdam and she generously invited me to stay. I just arrived two days ago by surprise, she didn't know I was coming."

"Ja, she told me the story. I answered the phone when you called."

"Oh, that's right. I forgot. I am sorry if I woke you up."

"That's okay, I had to get up, anyway. It sounds like you had a crazy adventure in Amsterdam."

"Oh yeah, how embarrassing. It certainly was crazy. I was just so lucky that Olivia came by."

"How long are you staying?"

"I'm here for seven nights. Then I take a train south to Barcelona."

"Barcelona? Hmm, nice city. Good bars. Well I hope you enjoy your stay. I passed by the market on the way and bought something for you girls to share."

I peaked in the bags. There were fresh strawberries, ripe pears and a decadent looking chocolate cake. "Oh wow, yummo," I chirped with enthusiasm. "That looks delicious. Thank you, Lucas. I will put everything in the fridge before I go out."

I poured him a coffee and we sat and chatted for a while and after a slow start the conversation flowed fairly well. Olivia's English was better but Lucas could still speak with fluency. He worked for a transport company, driving long haul trucks so he was either away working, driving all over Europe, or enjoying some leisure time when he was at home.

"So, where do you live when you are in Stockholm? When you are not on the couch here?"

"Well, I am house-sitting for a friend who is away. Has Olivia said anything about our friend Oscar? I am looking after his house, while he is in Australia."

"Okay, yes, she did mention him. He is a Marine Biologist?"

"Ja. That's him. I spend so much time on the road, you see. But ... Oscar's place is ... not close to the city ... so, if I have a big night out with friends it is easier to ... to crash here."

"I see. Well, don't let me stop you. If you want to stay while I'm here, that's fine with me."

"Thank you but I have to leave in the truck tomorrow morning. I won't be back for more than a week."

"Wow."

He stood up. "But it has been nice to meet you. Olivia was excited when you called. Maybe I will see you again sometime."

"Thank you, I hope so. It has been great to meet you too. Olivia is so lovely. I'm really enjoying being here."

"Ja. That is good." He smiled wistfully. "I think ... er ... she likes you ... she thinks you are special." He gave a funny little shrug, almost embarrassed it seemed.

"Thanks Lucas." He put his hand out and we had an awkward little handshake while we smiled at each other.

After I closed the door, I stood there with a happy grin on my face. Both of Olivia's siblings seemed to be warm, friendly people who were nice to be around. As I washed the cups and tidied the kitchen, my stomach flipped as Lucas's words swum around in my head. "Olivia was excited when you called ... she thinks you are special." What did that mean?

My mind wandered back over the last couple of days. My memories were full of little intimate moments. Olivia kissing me on the cheek, taking my hand out in the street, her eyes, soft and dark, following me around the room. "Olivia was very excited ... she thinks you are special." Special? Special how? What does this affection and warmth really mean? I want it, I am loving it but what does it really mean? She was in a relationship with Oscar but, is she also into women? Does she want more than a friendship? Is that what all of this means? Or is she just affectionate? I didn't know what Olivia wanted, I didn't know what her warmth and affection meant, but I knew I liked it, I wanted more of it and that sent my head into a spin.

I grabbed my things and wandered out into the light morning mist. I needed to catch up with what was happening to me. I wandered through the Old City, lost in thought, trying to understand the conflicting feelings that struggled for attention within. As much as I wanted to deny it, I had to confess to myself, I was becoming physically attracted to Olivia. I had left plutonic friendship behind, was racing right past a "girl crush" and was entering the perilous realm of infatuation - or as I labelled it then, love. When I held Olivia in my arms, when we locked eyes, when she touched me, my whole body responded. Every sense, every cell. I had been trying hard not to listen to the stirrings inside. My sensual responses were alien to me and I fought against them, mistrusting my own being.

I asked myself how I could have romantic feelings for both Jordi and Olivia? Being in love with Jordi fell within the realms of my lived experience. Girl meets boy, girl falls in love with boy. Girl and boy marry and live (more or less) happily ever after — but what do I do with my feelings for Olivia? I was back identifying with the Bonobo chimp again. Nothing made sense. Thinking of Jordi, my heart swelled. I looked forward to seeing him, to being with him, building a love nest together. It seemed right, like the "normal order of things". My feelings for Olivia were totally out of the box. It scared me so much I wanted to forget it, push it away. My mind gravitated towards the negative things that people would say if I chose to have a relationship with her. "Really, she's a lesbian? Never would have picked that." I shivered at the sound of the "L" word. Am I a lesbian? If I fall in love with a woman does that necessarily mean I am a lesbian? Or am I bisexual? I shook my head and screwed up my face with aversion and distress. The "B" word, sounded weird and not something I sensed I would ever be comfortable with. Where had my open mind gone? Where had the "falling in love with a person", no labels bullshit gone? All that was intellectual, this was real.

I found some trees and a patch of grass, protected from the weather, in a small park. I sat down. I studied the ground, the way the grass grew, the small sticks and seeds that lay on the soil between the roots. My eyes followed the occasional small ant that busied itself foraging for food. It was an effective practice I had, of calming and centring myself by focusing on a microcosm.

I soon calmed down, my emotions settled, and I was able to think more clearly and logically. It was interesting how much scrutiny I put these feelings for Olivia under. With Jordi I had just jumped into a hot sticky sexual relationship. Like with most men in my life it seemed more a case of attraction then jump in and ask questions later. I started to see how that approach had not really worked so well for me. The problem being that once I had become sexually involved, my emotions engaged and they just took over. Out came my neediness which would override my better judgement and I would be screwed — literally and metaphorically.

"Shit, shit, shit!" I whispered to myself. "What a mess." For a split second, I had an urge to grab my stuff and run, not back to Oliva, not to Jordi but on to a new location where I had no ties — somewhere where I could start again, free from my current screw-ups. The urge didn't last. I couldn't just keep moving on when life got challenging. I grabbed out my trusty notebook, took a deep breath and faced the situation with my logical left brain.

The Facts
1. I am in love with Jordi
2. I have a level of commitment to Jordi
3. He's expecting me back in about a week or so
4. I may go on and spend the rest of my life with him
5. This is the course I am familiar and comfortable with
6. This is the course I choose
Okay, so far, so good.

7. I have a very strong physical, sexual, emotional attraction to Olivia (there I said it)
8. This is totally unfamiliar ground and I am not comfortable with it
9. The fact that something is different is not a reason to reject it, or nothing new would ever happen
10. Whatever happens between Olivia and I, I am still going back to Jordi (my happily ever after)
11. I admit I am imagining what it would be like to have sex with Olivia
12. I am more than a bit freaked out about having sex with a woman, emotions are one thing, I can do emotions but the other ...
13. I recognise that having a physical sexual relationship with Olivia may deepen my feelings for her or may "cure" me, making it harder to leave or easier
14. Whichever it is, I am still leaving
15. Olivia has a boyfriend, on the other side of the world
16. I don't know if sex with Olivia (whatever that means) is even an option

The fundamental question was therefore, did I want to pursue a short-term physical relationship with Olivia, if it presented as an option? My answer, as scary as all hell, was an unequivocal "Yes. I do."

I spent the rest of my day analysing the various twists, turns, and possible outcomes of this decision. I returned to the apartment at about three o'clock and tried to have a nap. Not possible. I paced about restlessly, my heart racing, my stomach in knots. At one point I found myself in the bedroom staring at my backpack, wondering how long it would take for me to load it up and leave. Then my mind turned to Olivia's kindness, her genuine warmth, she deserved better than that. I forced myself to stay.

When Olivia arrived home, I had dinner organised. I tried my best to be relaxed and happy, like nothing had changed. I talked about my day in what I imagined was a light, breezy fashion but her quizzical look made it clear she wasn't fooled. Rats! Men are so much easier to hide from.

She came over to me, took me by the hand and led me to the couch. After sitting, she studied my face a moment before asking, in a voice that was both casual and full of concern, "What's the matter?"

I was almost jittery with fear as I looked into those beautiful eyes that were starting to feel so much like home to me. I choked, tears came to my eyes and any game plan I had flew out the window. I withdrew my hand, stood up, walked about the room, tormented, panicky. When I turned, she was still sitting, patiently watching me, her brow furrowed but otherwise calm.

For a moment I felt stuck, full of fear. I opened my mouth to speak, I needed to say something, but no words came out. I raised my hands, shrugged, closed my eyes, breathed deeply, imagining myself in a deep forest. A small sense of calm returned, and I found the courage to move forward. I sat back down on the couch and faced her. With painful self-consciousness I slowly reached one hand out and gently caressed her cheek. Then I reached out with my other hand and cupped her face in both of my hands. Even now my mouth moistens and the warmth spreads throughout my body as I remember that moment. I leaned forward searchingly and was alarmed and excited to see her lean in as well. When our lips met an overwhelming surge of energy ripped through my soul. I thought my heart or my brain might explode, or maybe I would have an orgasm right there on the spot.

Her lips were warm and soft. I smelt her fragrant skin, her breath, a touch of saltiness. Her tongue tip brushed against my lip, against my tongue, gently caressing, exploring. We tumbled onto the mat. The energy was electric. We were oblivious to everything around us. Nothing else mattered except this overwhelming desire to be one.

There were tears on both sides, muffled cries, broken buttons. I felt like an awkward teenager. I was all arms and legs, not knowing what to do, what to touch but I realised that Olivia knew what she was doing. I was not the first woman she had had sex with. This raised my desire to new heights. She guided me with her hands, her soft whispers, her moans.

She called in sick the next day, even saw the doctor. "I have the next two days off with the flu," she announced, grinning cheekily as she tossed off her clothes and joined me once more in the bed that had become our love nest. That was fair. In her place I couldn't have worked anyway. I was so lost in the maelstrom of our lovemaking. She looked down at me as I lay naked in the rumpled mess of the bed.

"My poor sweet girl, what can I do for you to make you better?" I teased up at her.

She stretched out her soft voluptuous body beside me, smiling seductively. "Hmm, let me see ..." She brushed her finger tips across the tip of her tongue before applying their moisture to my already erect nipples, teasing, tantalising. I moaned and writhed beneath her touch. I reached out to stroke her stomach, her hips and the luscious curve of her buttocks before circling back to her dark wiry bush.

We only slept in the exhaustion and sweet chemical cocktail after sex, naked and entangled together. Waking, the burning hunger would be there again, and our love making would start all over. But there was no quenching the fire. Morning, afternoon, evening, night, sunset, sunrise, all slipped by in a haze of love making, intimate conversation and deep satisfied sleep. We devoured Lucas's chocolate cake and fruit, ate left overs, scavenged what we could eat with minimal preparation from the pantry then ordered in pizza as one day slipped into the next.

The Secrets We Keep

Fourteen

By the afternoon of our third day of love-making, we were getting desperate for supplies. We dressed and went out for coffee, cinnamon buns, and some fresh air. I was due to leave the day after next but until that point, we had avoided talking about the future. In a safe, neutral space it was time to face the reality of our situation.

"It is almost time for me to leave." I focussed on pulling apart my cinnamon bun, not able in that moment to meet her eyes. "The train leaves at 1pm, Central Station, the day after tomorrow."

Olivia didn't respond straight away. She picked up the spoon and stirred her coffee even though it was half finished. "Ja," she said, looking up at me. "You must go," answering the unstated question.

"This has all been so unexpected. It's less than two weeks ago that I was in Interlaken, deciding whether to come see you or not."

"Yes, it has all happened very quickly."

"Yeah, I had no idea if you really wanted me to come. I had only met you when I was stoned, I didn't know what to expect but I never expected all of this to happen." With these last words I spread my hands wide as if indicating something in front of me.

She looked at me sadly. "What is 'all of this' that has happened?" She too spread her hands, imitating me.

"Well," I started steeling myself, pulling back and closing off in preparation for my exit, but then I changed my mind. She deserved the truth and an open heart even if it hurt like hell. I couldn't just give her a cold, distant farewell. "Bloody hell," I blurted out and leant across the table into her face. "I've never met anyone like you before. 'All of this' is finding you, getting to know you, sharing so much with you, making love with you." Suddenly I was filled with guilt, unsure of myself and tears were filling my eyes. I sniffed and wiped my face on my napkin. "I'm sorry, I'm so sorry. This is so hard."

I waited for her to respond. "Are you sorry you came?" Her voice was husky with emotion.

"Sorry I came? Shit no. Sorry I have had this time with you? Sorry I developed these feelings for you? Shit no!" I took a moment to calm down. "I am so, so glad I decided to come. It has been incredible. I will treasure it forever. But I see the pain in your eyes and I have to put my hand up and say, I caused that." I covered her hand with mine. "You are so precious. I don't want to ever see you suffer and yet because of me you are suffering. And that makes me think ... maybe it would have been better not to come, not to hurt you. I am so sorry." I was so full of guilt. "I hate myself for hurting you."

Anger flickered across her face and she withdrew her hand. "Laura, stop it! I am not some helpless deer caught in the headlamps of your car. I am an adult, just like you. You are not responsible for my choices. You have not been dishonest with me."

My whole being began to relax a little as she continued.

"I make my own choices. I chose to invite you, knowing I was attracted to you. Okay, yes, I was aware in Amsterdam that I liked you, I wanted to see you again. You are a beautiful sexy, generous hearted woman and I love spending time with you. I understood you had someone in your life already but I still wanted to see you." She paused, looked down at her cup. "Maybe I am the bad person for this. Maybe I am the one who must be guilty but I did not have any idea what would happen between us ... maybe some laughs ... a friendship ... maybe a kiss ... maybe not even that."

Time and space disappeared as I lost myself in what she was saying.

"I chose to invite you, I chose to hold your hand." My chin wobbled and two large tears fell down my face as she reached over and took my hand in hers. "I chose to kiss you, to make love to you. I did not choose to develop such feelings, I didn't know that would happen." She looked down at her coffee, her anger spent, then looked up again. "I did not choose to fall in love with you but I know I could love you so easily."

She gave me a small, sad smile. "How wonderful and how sad that we are falling in love."

How could she shape things in such a way that united us and strengthened us in such a time of distress? "Thank you. You have done nothing to feel bad or guilty about, don't think like that. I'm a big girl too, I make my own decisions." I pressed her hand to my lips. "Oh, shit, I love being with you. How am I supposed to get on that fucking train and leave you?"

"You will because that is your life, the same as my life is here." She was so much better at that stuff than me.

Olivia had planned something special for my last day. It was a day out at the beach, nude bathing at the popular Agesta beach, south of Sodermalm.

Though it was certainly not hot that day, the sun had come out and warmed us through the train window as we travelled south. I was excited and apprehensive. I had never been to a nudist beach before, except by accident in Den Haag, never swum naked anywhere since I was too little for it to matter.

We made our way from the railway station down through the green grassy parklands to the beach area. Like most of the waterways around Stockholm the water that lapped against the sandy beach was a deep dark blue. We had brought a decadent picnic lunch, including a quality bottle of champagne and a flask of coffee. We plonked everything down on the picnic rug in our chosen spot on the grass by the water's edge. There were quite a few other people there, some wearing clothes, some not. It was still a popular place even though it was early Autumn. I could imagine it would have been very crowded in the middle of Summer.

We had agreed on the train to having a swim before lunch and Olivia started straight away to strip off. I followed her lead as she removed her clothes layer by layer. Half a minute later I was standing there completely naked and shivering both from excitement and from the cool breeze that danced around us.

"Let's go!" Olivia grabbed my hand and started to run down onto the beach. As we were getting closer and closer to the water we ran faster until the moment we splashed together into the dark rippling blue expanse. Four steps in, the chill of the water registered, and I stopped, almost hyperventilating. Apparently, the water at that time of the year was about 12 degrees Celsius but to me, I was surprised there were no icebergs floating by.

Olivia encouraged me. "It will be cold for a moment, but your body will get used to the temperature. Close your mouth and breathe slowly through your nose."

"Shit, shit, shit, that's bloody cold." I shot back as I stood in water almost up to my navel, my arms wrapped tightly about my body. I fought the urge to panic and recoil from the cold. "I'll get used to it in a moment, my arse. I'll get used to it when my body turns numb and I get bloody hypothermia." My teeth started chattering as the cold took possession of my genitals and lower stomach.

Olivia laughed at me. She swam over, the water glistening off her face and shoulders. She took me by the hand and grinned at me. She looked deep, almost hypnotically up into my eyes. "What have you got to lose? Let go Laura, give yourself over to the experience. You will not regret it, I promise you."

Her words worked on me like a spell, cutting through my fear and filling me with courage and strength, and so I let myself go. I took a couple of deep breaths before diving under the water and swimming close to the bottom for a few strokes. The sensation of gliding through that deep icy cold water completely naked was an amazing sensual experience. I opened my eyes just a little which allowed me to appreciate the clarity and the colour of the water. On resurfacing I was breathless but also invigorated. As my body acclimatised (became somewhat numb) I enjoyed it more and we frolicked and swam about in the water like a pair of kids.

We spent about fifteen minutes in the water before agreeing it was time to warm up. We ran up to our picnic rug, rubbed ourselves down briskly with our towels and scrambled into our clothes. It was too cool for sun baking.

We ate lunch, washed down with steaming cups of coffee as we sat on the rug in the intermittent sunshine. The champagne was not so attractive in the cold so we saved it for when we got home. We both laughed at our swimming experience and especially at how precious I had been. Olivia did a wonderful theatrical impression of me, freezing to death in the water that had us both rolling on the rug with laughter. I rejected the suggestion of another swim after lunch. By then I was warm, dry and very comfortable and not at all interested in diving into those icy depths again.

Our bodies were awash with the happy chemicals such a chilly dip will bring and the sense of wellbeing that filled me meant everything. As I lay there, pressed up against Olivia's side, feeling her breath enter and leave her body, and the growing warmth between us, I found what was possibly the most peaceful, contented moment I had ever experienced in my life. I felt so blessed. My world was perfect. I lacked nothing. I could have died right then and been completely fulfilled. In the darkest moments of my life, I have almost wished I did.

Fifteen

Rather than making me feel guilty, Olivia strengthened me, she made everything okay. She was the one who made sure I was on that train two days later, travelling south to Barcelona, to the man who was my future.

I did not know if I would ever see Olivia again. We didn't sugar coat our goodbyes with promises to visit, to write, we knew that wasn't what we wanted. Maybe in many years to come, but the pain of separation was too great to want an intermittent, drip fed connection. We promised to always let each other know our permanent address and agreed to always be there for the other if we could be.

We both tried to hold back our tears at the station. I, in my usual way attempted to lighten the air with a few lame jokes. Olivia was kind enough to play along and laugh with me though neither of us found anything funny. We had said everything we needed to say. It was time for solidarity, and in our last minutes, before I boarded, we stood in silence, looking at the train that would tear us apart.

"I think it is time." Olivia laid a gentle hand on my shoulder.

I nodded, unable to speak through the lump in my throat. I turned and embraced her, inhaling her scent one more time. I stepped back, blinked back tears and gave her a sad smile. She returned my smile and gave a little impatient nod of her head and wave of her hand, hurrying me onto the train.

I turned from her then and boarded the train. I didn't stop and wave from the doorway, she didn't follow me down the aisle from the platform. I glanced up once after stowing my luggage. She was still there in the same place, but not looking in my direction. She turned and left as the train began to pull out of the station. For a long time, I sat, stiff, staring out the window. I held on to the image of Olivia receding on the platform as I struggled to rise above the emotional storm within. I settled down further into my seat, glad now that the trip south would take so long. I wanted that time to get a handle on myself. I desperately needed to cry, to dream, to reflect on everything that had happened in Stockholm and prepare myself for my life ahead with Jordi.

I did a lot of thinking on the way down, some quiet sobbing, a lot of self-analysis. How the hell did I get into that situation? So typical of me. I couldn't seem to get anything right. I always screwed everything up. I was so dysfunctional I should just crawl away in a hole and die. What possessed me to ever think I had it in me to build a successful relationship with anyone? Look what a bloody mess I'd made. I was a bloody basket case. I didn't deserve Olivia, I didn't deserve Jordi, why would I think either of them would love me? Holy crap!

I ran a negative commentary on my choices and actions to the point where I crumbled inside. I suffered intense anxiety and self-loathing. I felt poisoned by it. I tried to shake it off by eating, humming, reading, but it was so hard to budge. Through this process I came to understand how I could be my own worst enemy, sapping my strength and my life blood with my venomous thoughts. I had to stop or I would kill myself, one way or another. I had to learn to support myself, be my best friend, not my own personal executioner.

The subconscious is such a slippery cowardly fawning fuck. It whispers, tugs, placates us. It makes us focus on what it wants then retreats into invisibility. We are left deluded, held in the mistaken belief that it was us, in our rational mind who had the thoughts, who made the decisions.

Was I so certain I had made the right decision? Was I only sitting on that train because it was what I previously planned? Was I on the train simply because I was too shit scared to stay? Should I have been more flexible? Should I have stayed? I really didn't know Jordi much better than Olivia, in fact, maybe I knew Olivia better. Did I have the confidence in him, his character, his love, that I did in Olivia's? Could I really be in love with two people at the same time? Could they really be compared? Or could one be dismissed as an infatuation? Maybe they were both infatuations. What the fuck was love, anyway? How does anybody realise when a relationship is the beginning of love and when it is infatuation? Is it really just happenstance? At such a crossroads is there ever really a right and a wrong path? If it was Olivia in Barcelona whom I had met first, and Jordi whom I had just been with in Stockholm would I still have been on that train at that moment?

That last question pulled me up. I confessed to myself that had it been Jordi in Stockholm I probably would have stayed. I realised that in choosing Jordi I had chosen the familiar, the known, even if you will, the more socially acceptable — male dominance. The "hetero" model. Man and woman. I told myself I wanted children, a family, for that I needed a man. A long-term relationship with Olivia really wasn't a valid option. I didn't even question it. It's not that I held prejudice against same-sex relationships, not at all, it was a question of self-perception, self-identification.

But was it really so clear and straight forward as that? My heart said no. Opening my mind, I admitted, maybe a legitimate, long lasting relationship with Olivia was a valid option. Perhaps I was bisexual, maybe my ability to love another woman was a legitimate part of me. Maybe it would have worked, maybe, with Olivia, maybe ... When I recognised this, I was filled with grief, longing, despair. For a while as the train sped on I allowed myself to explore the possibility of a life with Olivia. What would it have been like? What would time have done to Olivia and me? In my mind I saw so many happy times, so much love. It filled me with sadness to reflect on what I had walked away from. What have I done? What have I done? Silent tears fell like raindrops at the realisation that I would never have a chance to learn the value of what I had left behind.

As the hours slipped by and my tiredness grew, I let my grief rest. I sought distraction in the changing scenery as the train made its way south. I watched as we travelled through Copenhagen,

Hanover, Frankfurt, west to Paris, south again through Montpellier and finally, at two in the afternoon, Barcelona.

Two days would never be long enough to make the transition back into my life with Jordi. Somehow, I had to throw off the grief and put behind me the intense intimacy and heady fragrance of my relationship and love-making with Olivia. Perhaps six months would do it but how I thought I could pull it off in a little over two days seemed crazy. It showed my stubborn strength, my lack of regard and consideration for my own needs. It provided a great example of the inane iron fisted self-denial that characterised my life. I was also nervous about how life with Jordi would be. There was a chance he would have moved on, perhaps the bubble had burst in my absence. He seemed excited that I was coming back, had made it very clear before I left that he really wanted me to return. I tried to focus on this rather than thoughts about whether the relationship would work out. I had decided that Jordi would be my future and I clung to that, confident that if I put enough work into making what we had together great it would be.

I also decided not to tell him anything about what happened with Olivia. My time with her would remain a secret. Telling him would be an unnecessary complication in our already intense relationship. I wrestled with the question of what I owed him, was I in fact unfaithful given the early stages of our relationship? Of course, the answer was a resounding "yes" and I sank beneath all the guilt that knowledge brought. I told myself I would tell him sometime in the future when we were well and truly settled as a couple. Someday, when my trip around Europe faded to a dim memory, including my night with Mitch.

I had called Jordi from Copenhagen as I waited for my connecting train. He didn't sound excited to hear I would be back. He sounded petulant. I wondered if he intended to put a guilt trip on me for being away so long. I had missed a concert the previous night by the reclusive Catalan folk musician Lluís Llach that he had really wanted to take me to. He appeared to be a bit miffed about that as he wouldn't be playing publicly again for quite some time. It worked, I filled up with guilt. I apologised for not getting back sooner and placated him by asking him about the concert. At least this way he would see my interest and also that I had retained some of the Catalan culture he worked so hard to instil in me.

I arrived at Jordi's flat just before three. Jordi wouldn't be home from work until after five. I retrieved the spare key and let myself in. The place appeared just the same as when I left, except for a flower in a vase and a bright flowery card sitting on the kitchen table.

> *To my beautiful Laura. Welcome home. I love you so much and miss you even more. I can't wait to hold you tight and never let you go!*
>
> *Love Jordi.*

I smiled as I read it. It helped me to realise I made the right decision, I was in the right place. I stripped off, chucked a pile of clothes in the washing machine. Reluctantly, even the clean ones went in as everything smelt like Olivia. I buried my face in a handful of clothes, closing my eyes, allowing myself just one more time to connect deeply with the headiness of our time together.

I emptied the tiny hot water service as I washed and rewashed to rid myself of the dust and grime of the last two days. In the back of my mind I also wanted to ensure I removed the smell of Olivia. Whilst in Stockholm I enjoyed carrying the subtle aroma of her sex around on my skin. Now I was frightened to think what might happen if Jordi got a whiff of it.

Sixteen

Jordi arrived home as I finished hanging up my washing. The rest of my things were spread out on the bedroom floor. I heard his footsteps at the door and as I listened to him fumble with the key my stomach lurched. I thought I was ready for this moment but my anxiety shot through the roof. How the hell was I going to hide what I had been through from him? He would ask questions about every part of my life since I had left.

"You're back!" he said in his lovely sing-song voice.

He threw his keys on the kitchen table, swept me into his arms and kissed me deeply and passionately. I noticed for the first time how scratchy his dense stubble was. I fanned my own embers, trying to stir the fire that had been in me just months before.

"Hello my beautiful girl." I gave him my biggest smile. He looked deep into my eyes and I'm sure he was searching for my secrets. I dropped my eyes first and fussed about finding the gift I had bought him in Sweden. It was a small traditional figurine of the Norse Warrior God Thor, son of Odin and master of the weather.

He loved it, and as I expected, had more knowledge about Norse mythology than I did. I had successfully navigated my way through that first awkward moment and I found myself relaxing a little inside.

Once he had placed Thor the Thunder God in pride of place on the bookshelf, he turned to me. He approached quickly, sweeping me into his arms once more while at the same time sliding his hand up my dress. I did my best to respond with equal passion. I unbuckled his belt and unzipped his pants to reveal the swollen pulsing bulge in his shorts. I did a quick double take as I mentally processed how different this would be, with a throbbing, thrusting penis back in the mix. With some effort I let go and lost myself in our lovemaking.

Lying spent in bed, we talked about my trip, comparing our impressions of places we had both been. I didn't tell him about my adventure in Amsterdam, except that I had a night out with a group of friends from the hostel. He took me out for pizza and beer to celebrate my return and I got into bed early. I was light-headed, worn out from having spent the previous two nights on the train. It was so nice to lie down and go to sleep in a real bed.

The next morning Jordi got up and off to work while I was still dozing. He kissed my cheek and stroked my hair and told me he had left me a note in the kitchen.

When he had gone, I got up and dragged myself out to the kitchen for coffee and breakfast. I saw the note, folded, sitting where my welcome card had been the day before. I opened it and read:

> *Good morning Princess, there is plenty of food for you to choose from for breakfast. Get yourself organised today because I have a surprise ready for you for tomorrow. Go to La Boqueria, you remember, the market near Les Rambles. You can have some lunch there and buy us some things for a picnic tomorrow. Buy some sausage, cheese, pate, fruit, olives. We will get bread in the morning. I will see you after work my darling.*
>
> *Love J*

I headed out midmorning, happy to have a direction and a purpose that got me away from my inner turmoil. I loved *La Boqueria* market. The stalls were so colourful and full of all sorts of delicious fresh fruit, vegetables, amazing cheeses, wine, so many types of olives, hams, fish and much more. I had lunch at a rustic vegetarian restaurant just nearby. I had been there before with

Jordi. They made a zesty carrot salad that was amazing and unlike anything I had ever had before.

On entry to Spain this time I had been given a three-month visitor visa. That gave us three months to work out where our relationship was going. Often, I was able to look forward and see the probable trajectory of my life, but at that time, I had no clue where I was going. I couldn't legally work in Spain during those three months though Jordi had assured me he would find me some students for English classes, paying cash. That would give me a bit of an income and something to do. Otherwise, I was, in a way, marking time, just in Spain to be with him. I had to admit, the idea didn't look nearly as rosy as it had when I had taken off around Europe. I told myself it was only day two, I was tired and still "hungover" from Olivia, everything would settle and fall into place.

The next day Jordi took a day off and we hopped a train south to a city called Tarragona. They were having their annual Festival — *La Festa de Santa Tecla*. The trip down in the train followed the coast with a wonderful panorama of sun-drenched beaches and rocky outcrops right beside the train. I was surprised to see so many bronzed nudists. Most of them comprised of older men with pot bellies and sagging testes taking a morning dip or stroll along the beach quite close to the train.

Tarragona proved to be a fascinating place. In the time of the Romans, it was the most important port in the whole of the Iberic peninsula (Spain and Portugal). There was an old amphitheatre, a Roman forum, underground dungeons some of which had in recent times been turned into pubs. I also enjoyed walking on top of the old Roman wall. The old city was definitely worth a wander around even though it was jam packed with festival goers. We were entertained by traditional music and dancing and large puppets dressed in traditional costumes. There was also free local food and generous amounts of beer and red wine.

Santa Tecla, the patron saint in whose honour the festival is held, was a catholic nun who apparently died in Africa. After her death, her body was cut into several pieces and sent to various catholic communities around the world. Tarragona, so the story goes, received an arm. Consequently, each year, as part of the procession a box containing Santa Tecla's arm is paraded solemnly through the street. I found the whole thing a bit macabre and giggled and waved as the arm went past. Jordi did not appreciate my silliness. Even though he was not religious, he took his culture and celebrations very seriously. Too seriously I thought. That was one train I could not get aboard.

We had our picnic on the steps in the old amphitheatre. A cool breeze stirred around us as we gazed out over the Mediterranean Sea.

"I do not like your attitude towards the *festa*." Jordi's manner seemed hostile, accusatory. "It's like I don't even recognise you. You do not have respect for what is happening, for my culture."

My mouth opened in surprise. He was rather precious about it all — but really?

"Well, I have told you I am not religious, and Australia is pretty relaxed about its customs and festivals. Some of it seems a bit over the top for me." I shrugged. "It's interesting, some things even fascinating but I can't get super excited like you and everyone else here does, sorry." I tried to find the right words to explain my position. "Everywhere we go we see the virgin of here, the virgin of there, who knew Spain was so full of virgins?" That was a private joke of mine. That was the first time I shared it. It didn't go well.

"Laura!" Jordi rounded on me. "Why are you so disrespectful? I make a special effort to bring you here today to show you this traditional festival and this is how you repay me? And I know you are deliberately provoking me by calling this Spain." His voice rose with emotion. "This is not Spain, this will never be Spain. This is *Catalunya*, not Spain. We are an occupied nation. I have taught you that. Are you dumb or something that you do not even remember this?" His face reddened, his eyes narrowed and he gesticulated wildly as he spoke.

"No, no, of course not. I remember." I paused and wiped his spittle off my cheek as I attempted to regroup. "I'm sorry, it's just all foreign to me and as I said, it's interesting but I'm not connected to any of it. I don't understand how so many people can turn out every year, year after year to see the same thing." I waved my hand back up at the crowd. "The same procession, the same dances and displays. I find that weird and very restrictive, sort of claustrophobic." My emotions were rising, my voice becoming higher pitched as I spoke.

"Weird? You think my people are weird? You do not understand because you have not tried. You have no respect. Did you come back here just to insult me? You are the weird one. It is not our fault if you Australians have no appreciation for culture!"

I was confused, genuinely confused. I really did not understand. I felt hurt and unfairly judged. Worse, he seemed to be rejecting me for who I was, like he considered my feelings to be invalid. I shrugged and got up and walked off down the crumbling stairs to the base of the amphitheatre. I wiped away hot angry tears as I replayed our conversation in my head. When I looked up the half-eaten picnic still sat spread out where we had been sitting but Jordi was nowhere to be seen.

"Ah fuck." I had just arrived back, and we were already arguing. It was not pretty. Jordi had done so much to teach me about his world, but I was starting to feel it was all a bit bossy and controlling. The daily Catalan lessons recommenced as soon as I arrived as well as him quizzing me on what I understood of their politics and culture. He tried so hard with me, I determined to try harder to make it work. I needed to if I wanted to build a future here in Catalonia with him.

I packed up the picnic and found Jordi not far away, staring out at the Mediterranean Sea from the balcony at the end of Rambla Nova. The view was awe inspiring and something I could easily appreciate.

I walked up to him, put my hand on his arm, looked into his face and said "I'm sorry. My culture is very different. We do not have the same traditional values that you have. I did not mean to be disrespectful."

He was more settled but still angry. He grudgingly accepted the apology I offered and we headed down Rambla Nova through the market stalls.

We looked about for a while before heading back to the railway station. The air was still tense and there had been few words between us. We arrived home earlier than expected, the day having "turned to shit". His flat became claustrophobically small with the tension between us. I retired to bed early without peace having been restored.

When I woke the next morning, Jordi was already up. He had suggested, before things turned bad the day before that we would go out to a local village market and have lunch in a bar. That idea did not get brought up again, Jordi was still not talking to me. I was relieved when he announced that he was going out to catch up with a friend and I had time to do whatever I liked. I breathed a sigh of relief when the door closed behind him.

I grabbed my day pack and headed out for a walk through the old part of the city and took refuge in the cool dimness of the cloisters of the Barcelona Cathedral. I sat on a stone bench, relaxing in the peaceful stillness and tried to make sense of yesterday's mess. It was just three nights since my return and here we were fighting like an old couple. It disturbed me but I saw it as a problem I could fix if I just worked harder at myself and our relationship. And so, I did.

I walked down to the market, bought ingredients and prepared delicious meals, but even here my efforts fell short. I prepared an authentic shepherd's pie with fresh steamed vegetables and Jordi appeared to really enjoy it. When I brought out fruit to finish the meal on, he complained there was no second main course. In Spain they always have two distinct main courses for their large midday meal, the main meal of the day. I responded that, there were two dishes, shepherd's pie and vegetables, they were just on the one plate, but that didn't wash.

I studied my Catalan lessons more earnestly. I learnt the words to Lluís Llach's *Abril 74*, the stirring ballad about the Portuguese battle to free their country from dictatorship. I tried to be happy, to be agreeable, interested. I stopped voicing my opinion unless it agreed with his. I showed enthusiasm for all the cultural outings he took me to, tried to ask intelligent questions about the local politics. I initiated sex often and faked my orgasms loudly.

Whatever I did though, it never seemed quite enough. Jordi often expressed disappointment in me. He was always able to find a weak point in my efforts. This led to more and more pointless arguments after which Jordi would be moody and withdrawn for days.

Seventeen

One day he came home from work while I was on the balcony reading. His key sounded in the lock and I stirred uneasily in my seat. I quickly scanned around me to make sure there was nothing amiss, nothing obvious to complain about. I thought I was safe until I heard him coming towards me, and the tone of his voice as he called my name.

"Laura ... Laura." My stomach flipped at the sound. Something was wrong.

"Yes, Jordi, what ... what's the matter?" I dropped my book on the chair as I jumped to my feet.

"There are ants in the sink."

"Yes, I saw them. They're so annoying. I have wiped them up a few times to—"

"Wipe ... wiped them up? Are you stupid as well as lazy? They will not go away just because you wipe them up!"

"What? Excuse me? I am not stupid or lazy. You don't get to say that to me. I have—"

"Yes, I can. This is my home — and you are! This place is always a mess when I get home."

"It is not! What's messy about it?"

"You are!"

"What? Why don't you just go listen to some music ... cool down for a while." I attempted to squeeze past him, heading for the bedroom but he took hold of me by the upper arms, stopping me in my tracks.

"Do not walk away from me when I am talking to you." His voice was cold, hard and hateful.

I tried to free myself as I glared up at him. He was hurting me. "Let me go."

"You listen to me."

"I am not listening to you unless you let me go." I struggled in his grip. "Let me go."

He let go and laughed. "Or what Laura? What will you do?" He pushed me with both hands in my chest and forced me to step backwards onto the balcony. "Go! Go over the edge for all I care." Then he turned and walked away.

I watched him go, hot tears filling my eyes. "Why are you like this? What have I done?"

He stopped at the other end of the lounge and turned. "What have you done? You deliberately provoke me, you leave your mess everywhere. I have been very patient with you but you just want to upset me, you have no respect."

"What? What are you referring to?"

"Don't pretend to be innocent with me. You are so full of lies. I know what you do while I'm at work all day, huh?" He looked about the room. "Who is it? Who has been here?"

"What?" I struggled to understand what he was saying. "Nobody has been here. What are you talking about." I tried desperately to stop the tears from falling, knowing his response.

"So, now the crying." He shook his head impatiently. "You don't fool me. You are a liar. Who are you fucking while I am at work?"

"Jordi, how can you say that? I love you."

"You don't know what love is. You will say whatever to manipulate me and get what you want."

I was so shocked at his words; my mind would not engage to respond. I stood there shaking my head then ran past him into the bedroom sobbing. I shut the door behind me and sat down in a corner on the floor.

My mind raced. I didn't understand, didn't know what to think. How did everything suddenly go so badly? Where did he get such ridiculous ideas? How could I get him to see he was wrong, and prove my innocence? Why did he think all that about me? What had I done to make him think those things? My heart was breaking.

I drew my knees up, dropped my head and silently bawled my eyes out.

I didn't leave the room for the rest of the evening except once to go to the toilet. I stopped in the kitchen to get a drink of water and grab a packet of biscuits. He didn't come in. Eventually I climbed into bed, still half-dressed and tried to sleep.

Jordi came in the next morning, got his clean clothes for the day and walked out again, closing the door. I pretended to be asleep. In truth, I don't think I had slept at all.

After I heard the front door shut, footsteps down the stairs, I started to feel safe. I let out a long slow breath and got out of bed. My eyes had grown puffy from crying and my body felt heavy with grief. I winced as I raised my arm to open the door. Lifting my shirt sleeves, I found finger shaped bruises making a band across each upper arm. I cautiously opened the door and stepped out into the lounge. The neatly folded rugs on the end of the couch told me he had slept there.

I had a shower then toyed with breakfast as I tried to understand what had happened and what it meant. I had no one to turn to, there was no one available to talk this over with, no one I could go to for help. I still had not met any of Jordi's family and few of his friends.

I wandered aimlessly through the day, dreading the sound of his key in the lock. When he did come home, he looked through me as if I were a ghost. He didn't speak to me, didn't respond when I spoke, didn't even seem to see me. He went out in the evening. I had something to eat and crawled into bed early.

He came home late and (I suppose) slept on the couch again.

The following afternoon, when he came home, he looked at me, looked into my eyes for a brief moment. He had a wounded, haunted look. I had the impression his suffering was not much less than mine.

I decided to try to reach him. I waited until he settled on the couch with the music going then came and sat on a stool opposite him.

"Jordi?" My voice was soft, hesitant. "Jordi, can we talk?"

I tried to read his eyes as he looked at me but they were flat, unresponsive. "What would you like to talk about?"

"Us ... what happened? ... what is going on here?"

"Okay."

"Jordi, I love you. You said some awful things, untrue, very hurtful things. I don't know why. Is that what you really think of me?" My lip trembled, but I was determined not to cry.

"And you said very ugly things too."

I couldn't remember saying anything so bad but perhaps I did. "Jordi, I'm sorry if I said anything that hurt you. I don't want to hurt you. I love you, I love you so much ... I don't want to fight with you." My words ended in a whisper as emotions closed my throat.

He looked across at me. "Thank you, Laura, I needed to hear that from you. I don't want to fight either. I am also sorry." His face softened. "I love you so deeply. What would I do if you left me? I need to know you love me."

"Okay." I met his eyes with a small smile. "Maybe I need to tell you more often so you don't forget."

He nodded. "Maybe you do."

"Can I have a hug?"

He gave a brief, small smile and opened his arms to me.

We ate out that night, drank a fair bit of red wine and had passionate heart wrenching make-up sex after stumbling back home. We fell asleep naked entangled in each other's bodies.

The next day, when he returned from work, the sun came out with no sign left of the storm that had raged. We laughed, joked, talked about the future and snuggled on the couch before heading to bed for an early night.

By late November, having been back in Barcelona for over two months I was exhausted and starting to become unwell. I turned myself inside out trying to please Jordi with less and less success as the days passed. I had so severely neglected my own needs and suppressed my thoughts and feelings that I was becoming despondent and depressed. Despite his early assurances, he had thwarted every attempt I had made to gain some English students. This meant I had no income and no one to talk to. Stressed and run down, I caught the flu which left me housebound for over a week.

Late in the week as I started to get better, there was a knock at the door. It took me by surprise as Jordi was at work and there had never been any visitors in the whole time I had been there. I hesitated, my hand on the knob, and peaked through the spyhole to get a glance at whoever was there. It was a young woman, glancing about her. Cautiously I opened the door.

"*Si?*" I enquired.

She had a friendly somewhat alternative look about her, but seemed hesitant, unsure, even nervous. "Are you Laura?" she asked, in a husky voice. She pronounced my name in the local manner with a heavy Catalan accent.

"Yes," I nodded, curious.

"I am Alba, Jordi's sister."

"Oh, hello." Surprised, I just stood there looking at her as I tried to remember what Jordi had said about her. The perception I had formed was that she was a bit of a ratbag, not to be trusted. A little rattled, I wondered what she wanted.

"Can I come in?" Her hands fidgeted nervously with a cigarette packet she held in front of her.

I stepped back, on my guard, making way for her to enter. "Of course, Alba. Please come in."

"Thank you." As she moved forward into the light in the small hallway, I could suddenly spot the resemblance. She had the same blue eyes, the same curly hair though hers was badly dyed and rather unkempt.

I led her through to the lounge room.

"I'm sorry, I hope this is not a bad time for you. I am friends with Magda, who lives downstairs. I have been visiting with her and she told me about you. I do not meet with Jordi often, but Magda said that maybe you were unwell." She looked enquiringly at me.

"Umm, yes, I've had the flu, been a bit sick but I'm getting better, thank you." I was still cautious, wondering why she was there.

"Magda's study looks over the street, you see. So, she has seen you coming and going, but lately she said she only hears you coughing and ... em... using the tissues. I told her I will stop in and, um ... check if you are okay."

I was a bit disconcerted to learn the neighbours were so aware of my presence. I had not thought about the people around us in any tangible way. I nodded and smiled when I passed them in the foyer or joined them in the lift. Also, I was starting to question Jordi's dismissive description of his sister. It had led me to form a very different picture of her to what I was now seeing. I decided to drop my guard, push away that early impression so I could be open to the young woman in front of me.

"Thank you, Alba, that's kind of you. I'm happy to meet you. Thank you so much for thinking of me. Please take a seat." I motioned towards the couch. "Can I get you a coffee or a beer or something?" She was sweet and natural and she seemed genuine. How odd that I hadn't met her before.

"Do you have some tea?" she asked smiling at me.

"Yes," I nodded. "Of course."

"Great, I will help you make it if that is okay."

I accepted her assistance and we chatted lightly about ourselves while we made the tea and settled back in the lounge room. It turned out that Alba was an artist and a musician. She played the keyboard and sang in a successful Catalan rock band that had toured across Europe and Canada over the summer.

"So, you have done much travelling? Do you miss your family?" She still seemed nervous, glancing towards the door from time to time and chewing on her nails.

"Well, I am not used to seeing my family very often, so not really. I do miss my country a bit. I miss my friends, the way of life in Australia. It's much more relaxed than it is here."

"You do not find our country relaxing?"

"Well, it's just that ... in Australia we are free, socially, culturally free to spend our leisure time as we like. Here, everybody must go to the festival, everybody has to dance *sardanes*, follow a certain political line ..."

"Hmm," she responded pensively and chewed at the corner of a nail. "Perhaps ... you do not have ... er ... the best introduction to our country."

"What do you mean?" An odd uncomfortable sensation was starting to creep up my spine.

"Well ... how do I say this? It is ... it is only ... Jordi can be very intense. He is not a typical Catalan boy." She shrugged and looked at me, her eyes searching for signs of my understanding. "It is true that many peoples like to follow traditions. But there are many

Catalans as well, they do not go to the religious festivals, do not agree with the ... the ... the political line as you call it. There are independent, free thinking peoples here. They create, explore ... er ... things through art, music and so on."

"Really? I don't know any of these people. Well, the truth is, I haven't met many people here at all."

"Yes, really. This part of our society is growing. It is exciting. Some peoples have enough of tradition. It can kill creativity." She put her tea down and looked at me. "This is my world, it is not perfect but ... it is there."

"Oh, I see." I didn't really see at all, or better said, for the first time I was able to glimpse how limited my understanding was. "Yes, Jordi is intense. I put that down to being Latin and all that. I have been trying hard to fit in," I confessed.

"Have you met many of his friends? I don't think you meet our parents, did you?"

"Your parents?" I asked quizzically, trying to remember what he had said. "Jordi said that ... your mother died years ago, and ... your father is in a home with dementia ...?"

Alba took a quick breath, shook her head and covered her mouth. "Is that what he told you?"

"Yes, are you telling me that ... is that not true?" I could sense the colour creeping into my face as I became even more disconcerted. "Alba, please excuse me for asking this but ... please help me, how do I know who is saying the truth, you or Jordi?"

"Our parents, our mother and father are both alive and healthy and living just half an hour from here." Indignation and hurt showed in her face and voice. She shook her head sadly. "What did his friends say to you?"

"I really haven't met any of them — except in passing in the street. We keep to ourselves a lot. I thought it was because of ... of the intensity of our relationship." I felt self-conscious, silly even. "You know, we are so wrapped up in each other. I've met almost nobody."

Alba was gently nodding, her expression suggesting it was more or less as expected. This made it easier for me to relax a little and just let it out.

"To be honest, it's pretty lonely. I've bumped into a few other Australians passing through, but I don't have any friends here." Relief began to seep in as I unloaded. "All my life is revolving around Jordi. I met two girls, from England, teaching English here but Jordi didn't like them. He made a fuss, so I stopped seeing them." As I said this, as I heard the words come out of my mouth I flushed with embarrassment. It didn't sound right. It didn't sound healthy. It left me with an uncomfortable tightness in my stomach.

Alba must have registered my emotion. Quietly she said, "I ... I ... this is how Jordi likes to live. I love my brother but ... he is not easy." She shifted uncomfortably and glanced towards the door. "Perhaps I say too much. I must go. You need to rest."

We stood up. She put her hand on my arm. "Take care of yourself."

"Thank you. I won't tell Jordi you were here." I tried to smile but my emotions were rising in my chest.

Then she was gone. I checked the clock. I had about an hour until Jordi came home. I washed the dishes and put them away. I wanted to ensure there was no remaining evidence of my visitor. After that I went into the bedroom and collapsed on the bed. My stomach churned, my head was throbbing and my mind was confused. I lay there, curled up on my side, staring at the wall. I stepped back from my busy thoughts, allowing my spirit to digest my meeting with Alba. I needed time. I wouldn't try to analyse and process anything until I had slept on it.

Eighteen

Jordi came home, perhaps in a better mood than usual. He fussed about, showing concern for my welfare and even joking a little. He played me special songs and filled me with pills and potions. It was almost the old Jordi, the one before I had left on my trip around Europe. Perhaps it was and it was just me who had changed. I managed to smile and appreciate his efforts. He seemed a bit more forgiving of me while I was sick. Was that why I was unwell? Did I make myself ill to get Jordi off my back, to get myself off my own back and lighten my load for a while? It was certainly possible.

The medications Jordi gave me made me drowsy. That worked in my favour as it meant he held few expectations of me. I wanted to ask him something to cross reference with what Alba had said. I started by mentioning my brother Jack and a funny story he would tell from his outback shearing experiences. Then, playing on my fuzzy headedness I asked him, "What did you say your sister does? I don't remember."

He sniffed and shook his head. "She is an artist." He responded with evident disdain.

"Does she paint?" I asked. "I like art."

"Not her sort of art, it is not good, she has no talent. She is wasting her time painting and singing in some sort of band."

"What's she like?"

"Like someone who is wasting their life trying to be an artist. Really Laura, please don't waste my time asking these silly questions."

I understood more clearly how evasive and dismissive he was and how he attempted to control me by belittling my questions. I noticed an inner discomfort and despite my foggy head I realised that the knot in my stomach was not a new condition.

Thanks to the drugs Jordi gave me I slept solidly and woke after he had already left for work. I yawned and stretched and headed for the kitchen. I needed food and some time to ponder.

After breakfast I opened the lounge room doors onto the balcony and sat in the sun. I had my notebook with me. I had been very careful to keep it in my daypack or somewhere else safe from Jordi's prying eyes. I did not want my privacy to be violated again. I flicked through the past entries, mostly problem solving or emotional issues. It read like a summary of my growth points. I reread the earlier entry listing the "facts" of Olivia and my relationship. At the time I was deciding whether to pursue something physical with her. It seemed so long ago. I pushed the presence of Olivia from my mind, my plate was filled with enough mess already.

I poured out my feelings and my confusion and I asked questions of God, the Universe or maybe it was just my intuition. I found if I was relaxed, patient and open-minded enough the answers would come. I started getting an insight into how unhealthy my relationship with Jordi had become. I had deserted myself in order to please him and keep the peace. I didn't spend much time analysing what Alba said. I didn't need to. I had enough from my own experiences to ruminate on. Alba had simply been a catalyst, someone who assisted me to view my life from a new perspective. I realised how lost I had become and was able to see the toxic dynamic between us. I thought of everything I could to find a way for the relationship to be turned around.

When I finished writing I made myself a cup of tea and sat down to review my outpouring. I spent time contemplating my predicament and my feelings before finally it was time to ask the logical questions.

1. *Do I believe Jordi's behaviour is acceptable? No*
2. *Do I think he will improve? Possibly, maybe, ... actually no.*

3.   *Do I want to continue to live with him the way things are? Reluctantly, no.*

4.   *So, does this relationship have a future? No, it doesn't.*

5.   *What do I need to do? I need to leave.*

6.   *When? As soon as possible. I can't fake a relationship, I can't. Even if I tried, he analysed me so much he would soon know something was up.*

When I arrived at that point I was gutted. I believed in us. I so wanted the relationship to work. I trusted in our future. I thought this was my happily ever after. I exhausted myself trying to make it work. But it didn't work. I was embarrassed, really crushed at the realisation I had chosen another arsehole to get involved with. I had fucked up again, what a loser. Oh God, when would I ever learn. Words my brother Jack said after I told him about my torrid affair with the married jerk rang through my head. "How can someone who is so intelligent be so dumb when it comes to men." How indeed? How many more times did I need to hit my head against that wall before I learnt my lesson?

I allowed myself to wallow in the full weight of my grief. I let go and sobbed into my towel ensuring no trace of my snot and tears would be left to be discovered later. I tried to process it all. My head throbbed with exhaustion. I had no strength left to work out my next move — when to leave or where to go. I needed to rest. I crawled into bed and fell into a deep sleep.

I woke about an hour later, my head feeling much calmer and clearer. I started planning what I would do in my mind while I had lunch. I decided to go to Edinburgh. I could work in the UK and I really wanted to experience Scotland. That settled that. The next big question was whether to leave while Jordi was at work or to tell him I was leaving and have it out with him. That was not an easy question. I didn't want to take the approach of packing and going while he was out. I didn't want to treat him so badly nor did I want to give him anything further to blame me for. That was a hard one. I envisaged myself writing him a note then packing guiltily and leaving while he was at work. I saw his devastation and heart break when he arrived home and found my belongings gone and my note. Then I looked at the other option. I imagined myself explaining to him how I felt and why I had to leave, why this relationship wasn't right for me. My head filled with his angry response. I saw him argue against and dismiss every point I had made. He made fun of my feelings. I had seen him do these things too often already. I realised the end result may be that I would be out on the street without my stuff. More importantly though, I feared for my safety, afraid he would become violent. With considerable reluctance, I chose option one.

The evening went by as normal. I was much improved physically, and I made more effort to be cheerful. We even had sex and afterwards I lay in the dark beside him, listening to his gentle breathing. I cried, silently telling him everything I lacked the courage to say to his face. Jordi, I loved you so much. I truly believed in us and our future together. I sincerely appreciate all your efforts to integrate me into your way of life. You've been so generous in allowing me into your home, trusting me with your feelings. But, you see, it's well, it's so hard to live with you. You are rarely happy with what I have done to try to please you. I've turned myself inside out, lost touch with my inner being trying to please you. As a result, I don't even know who I am anymore. This is not your fault, I don't blame you for how I have chosen to respond to you. But at the same time, I confess I am afraid of you and your rages. I can't live with you attempting to control me all the time. I'm so sorry for not being able to make it work and for leaving. I am so heart broken and I'm grieving for the lost illusion of our future together. I want to thank you for all you have given to me, for your love, your care. I had so desperately wanted it to work, but it didn't. I'm so sorry Jordi for the way I am leaving. I know it will be tough on you. I wish there was a better way, but I am too fearful of you to face you. Finally, Jordi, I just want to say goodbye, I wish you all the best of everything. I will always remember you and cherish the good in what we have shared. I just hoped that somewhere in his spirit he received what I told him.

I timed my "waking up" so I could give him a sleepy hug and a kiss before he left for work. He told me he loved me and I told him I loved him too. Then he left. I watched him walk out of the room. He pickup his keys and wallet, walked to the door. I heard the creak as the door opened and finally, the bang and click of it closing behind him.

I realised I had been holding my breath. My body was tense. For a moment I felt overwhelmed. "I can't do this, I can't, I just can't. I don't want to leave him, I want the future we talked about. I don't want it to end, I want us to love each other. I want us to get along, to build a future together, can't we? Can't we do that please?" But when my emotions had quietened down, I knew despite my grief I couldn't stay.

I waited a little while, in case he had forgotten something. Then fuelled by nervous energy I quickly prepared myself to leave. I didn't have breakfast, I couldn't stomach food. My heart was racing the whole time. I was shit scared he would come back unexpectedly and catch me out. I showered, packed and when I was ready, I wrote him a goodbye note, trying to stop my hand from shaking as I wrote. I left it propped up against a small vase on the kitchen table.

Dear Jordi

When you get this note, I will have left Barcelona. I love you and I have tried so hard to make this relationship work, but it seems whatever I do is not enough. I realise we are not ultimately very compatible and so I have decided that it is better we part sooner rather than later.
Please forgive me for leaving like this but I know you would be able to talk me out of going if I discussed it with you.
You have been so kind and generous, and I really appreciate everything you have done for me. I will always treasure our time together.
I wish for you a life filled with love and happiness with the right person.

Laura

Then I shouldered my backpack and walked out, pulling the door locked behind me.

Nineteen

I experienced intense anxiety as I left Jordi's place. The whole time descending the stairs of the apartment block, my legs were like jelly. Out on the footpath I looked about me furtively. I scurried down into the metro and made it to *Estacio Nord*, the major bus station in the north of Barcelona. I fidgeted with my bag, sat down, stood up, all the time surveying the area as if there were a chance that Jordi would turn up. My heart pounded, and I avoided the eyes of friendly faced backpackers, not wanting to be distracted by conversation.

I bought a ticket, found my bus and handed over my backpack to the attendant. I watched his bald patch shine in the morning sun as he threw my bag into the hold beneath the bus. It was a large modern carrier. Carrier was an apt word. It would carry me away from Barcelona, away from Jordi, away from yet another mess my bad choices had gotten me into. I saw myself as a failure. I felt guilty, cowardly. I wondered what showed on my face as I made my way down the aisle. In that last morning I appreciated the fact I had not met many people Jordi knew. It was all the better for the success of this deep betrayal I chose to play out.

I slumped down in the seat and stared out the window. My pulse raced, and my stomach churned with anxiety and fear lest my flight be detected. I waited impatiently for the bus to move off. Time seemed to stand still. I half stood in my seat, swivelling my head from side to side, hypervigilance making it impossible for me to sit still. The attendant continued to stand beside the open hold. He was staring from his load sheet up and down the depot, to his watch and back to the paper in his hand. I directed a tirade of frustrated and impatient thoughts at his polished dome hovering below me.

"Come on, come on, let's get out of here, we are late already. What are you waiting for? Shut the bloody door and let the driver get on with the job, come on man."

Finally, after what seemed like an hour a chubby dishevelled backpacker puffed up to the bus. She handed her oversized pack to the attendant. The poor guy busied about pulling out and rearranging baggage items to make room for the massive pack. I exhaled with relief as he finally slammed down the hold cover. Once aboard the doors snapped shut, the driver quickly revved up the engine, engaged the gears and we smoothly left the scene. As the bus finally pulled away from the terminal, I closed my eyes and breathed a long sigh of relief.

Of course, Little Miss Huffy Puffy sat in the vacant seat next to me. She smiled at me through her thick glasses. She then pushed her lank auburn hair out of her eyes and wiped the beads of sweat off her face and neck with the sleeve of her jacket. I tried to return her smile, but I was still too anxious and too pissed off that we were late to give her any warmth. I sat there staring out the window, fuming with impatience and indignation.

As we left the northern outskirts of Barcelona behind I said a final silent farewell to Jordi and apologised again for the way I was leaving. Only then did I let go of my battle readiness and allow myself to relax a little.

I turned to the girl beside me and confessed "Sorry, I was a bit stressed and impatient before. I've been through a few dramas and I was itching to get going. My name is Laura." This time my smile was warm and generous, and I rolled my eyes and chuckled in a self-deprecating way at my preciousness.

"Hi, I'm Jade," she responded with a Canadian accent and a genuine smile. "Ah, yeah, sorry I held the bus up. I've had my own dramas." It was her turn to laugh and roll her eyes.

The bus cruised through coastal Catalonia into France moving ever northward. I settled in and enjoyed the chit chat with Jade. The change in the scenery zooming past the window was also a pleasant distraction from the turmoil in my mind.

As we travelled towards Spain's northern border, I craned my neck to the right to catch the last glimpses of the Mediterranean Sea. To my left the foothills of the Pyrenees rose in jagged, inhospitable rock faces. Small villages dotted the landscape and olive and almond trees filled many of the surrounding stone walled terraces. These gave way to lusher, greener scenery as we continued motoring up through France the scenery and I relished the lush damp greenness and thick forests that flew past my window. Spain seemed so crumbly, dry and dusty, I welcomed with enthusiasm and increasing optimism the arrival of everything misty and moisty and green.

I allowed my thoughts and feelings to drift, like clouds through my consciousness. I checked the time on my new Swatch Watch, waiting for the moment when I knew Jordi would be arriving home. I pictured him climbing the stairs, unlocking the door, walking in and calling for me. In my mind he noticed the tidiness, the bareness. Then he walked into the kitchen and saw the note. He shook his head in confusion and disbelief. He turned the note over in his hands as he looked about for more clues that would help him make sense of the situation. He would walk into the bedroom and scan the room as he called my name. He would register the missing backpack, the empty shelves where I stored my clothes. He would then walk into the bathroom, spotting the gaps where my toiletries normally sat. By this point he would be getting quite upset.

He might call out impatiently, "Laura, that's enough! Where are you?"

He would eventually realise I wasn't there, I was not attempting to manipulate him with the note, that I was really gone. Then he would collapse on the couch and allow himself to sob, to grieve. I saw him asking "Why? Why Laura, why?" Then he would get angry and abusive, calling me names I care not to imagine. He would make the transition in his feelings for me from love to hate. I saw him conjuring up all the times I had hurt him or fucked up in his eyes. The idea that I had ever loved him would be dismissed. In its place I imagined him spinning a web of hate and bitterness to contain our story.

I could not grieve for him at that moment, too much had happened and it was all too raw. I was desperately sad that it had not turned out to be the wonderful relationship I had first believed in. The harsh reality of my predicament however meant my feelings for him had already begun to evaporate. My grief was more for the illusion I had lost than for the man I had abandoned. I had started my grieving while I was still there, at night, crying silently beside him in bed at the hopeless situation I had found myself in. I shuddered and moved my thoughts to a healthier place.

I checked in to the Walkabout Club in London for a couple of nights, sorted through some old mail and retrieved my suitcase out of storage. There was no sense of inferiority any more. I no longer needed to measure my self-worth against other backpackers. My travels, adventures and life experiences had somehow given me a new sense of self-confidence. Or maybe I just realised that travel did not make anybody worth more as a human being. The thought gave me a taste of self-satisfaction that was new to me. The irony was, one large benefit from the roller coaster ride of the previous months would be the valuable learning and growing it provided me.

London had so many wonderful places to go and sites to see and I was determined to make the most of my time. After dumping my stuff in my room, I rugged up and headed out for an energising walk through the damp and chilly afternoon. I crossed into the park noting where I had sat in so much despair beneath the oak tree when I had first arrived. There were no squirrels scampering about this time, and the grass, faded and boggy, no longer invited an afternoon of contemplation. Instead, the trees were releasing the last of their bronzed leaves, the air full of their earthy, composting aroma and the sound of the leaves rustling under foot. The whole scene was somewhat sombre, and I chuckled as it occurred to me that this time, I was the more chipper. I felt like I had left my winter behind. I was sprouting new shoots. I believed my days of fading and wilting, of being bogged down, were receding into the past. I walked on with a newfound spring in my step as I contemplated the sunshine and roses that lay ahead of me in my life.

The next morning, after breakfast, I settled down on the floor of my room to enjoy the fun of rummaging through my case. I discarded some of the clothes I had packed (over packed!). In Barcelona I had been able to smell the approach of winter and I wished I had my warmer clothes with me. Moving forward, I really needed my winter woollies if I was going to live and work in Edinburgh in the winter.

I went shopping around Carnaby Street and later took myself off to see Agatha Christie's The Mousetrap at St Martin's theatre. I had loved Agatha Christie since first finding her novels in my early teens. For just a short while I lost myself in the magic of the stage performance.

I was up early the next day. I checked out and headed for the bus station. As the bus for Scotland pulled out, I started to feel truly safe. No one could trace me, not even Jordi. I allowed myself to relax more deeply and get just a little excited about my new adventure.

Twenty

What better place for rest and repair than beautiful old Edinburgh? I loved it from the first moment I arrived. As usual, I focussed on the people around me, their dress, their accents, their hair and faces. I amused myself with imitating some of the sounds, the phonetics, common in their speech. I felt like Henry Higgins as he studied Eliza Doolittle. The difference being I had much more respect and no desire to change anything about those lovely folks. With so many variations in pronunciation this would be an ongoing source of fun and curiosity for much time to come.

I made my way to the privately-owned High-Street Hostel, ironically, in Blackfriars Street. My guide book assured me it was one of the best deals in town for those okay with sleeping in multi-bed dorms. That suited me. Walking in, the hostel impressed me with its homeliness. The guy on the front desk (who I found out later was from Peru) seemed friendly and casual. The décor was rustic, slightly hippy and I could detect the strains of "Love Shack" by the B-52's playing from the dining room further down.

I booked in, paid my first week's fees and made my way upstairs to my assigned room. It was a busy, messy dorm room, sleeping about 26 girls. The colder it got, the more they cranked up the radiators. With so many bodies in the room, snoring and snuffling at night, it got very stuffy. As the heaters were turned up and the windows closed against the chilly night air. I felt quite uncomfortable, slightly claustrophobic and struggled to sleep.

I lined up some work the very next day through a local labour hire agency, to start in about ten days' time. I was happy about that.

I had found a home and I would have some work. I breathed a relieved sigh, stability at last! I went out then and bought myself a super warm snow coat, woollen scarf and beany. Then I was ready for the winter."

Hostel management was kind enough to allow me to hold over the fees I had paid in advance and store my luggage. This allowed me to take off for a quick trip up north before I started work. I tried to hitchhike but got nowhere, it was so different to Ireland. After wasting far too long on the side of the road, I caught a bus. I travelled north over the odd sounding Firth of Forth up through a patchwork of farming land, and quaint little villages. I got off the bus in St Andrews, home of the first golf links, the third oldest university and some truly awesome ruins. From there I continued up to Inverness, taking the tour out to Loch Ness with a bunch of other tourists. It was a fun day. We listened to all the legends surrounding Loch Ness and the monster. Then they taught us a few old Scottish songs. All the while, we took turns to have our photos taken wearing the red-wigged tartan Tam o' Shanter, the traditional Scottish men's hat.

From Inverness I travelled south east to Fort William. I loved the highlands with their wild, rocky crags and the heather, brown and dormant as it prepared for the snow falls of winter. I stopped in Fort William a couple of nights to climb Ben Nevis, the highest mountain in Scotland. This was not as impressive as it might sound. It was easily achievable in a day in normal bush walking clothing. Even more so as there was no snow yet on the popular Pony Track from Glen Nevis. It was a lovely and at times challenging walk. I arrived back to my lodgings at the end of the day exhausted but glowing with a great sense of achievement.

I caught a bus back to Edinburgh the following day and this time I managed to snaffle a bottom bunk by the window. I opened the window a fraction at night to get some fresh air, yey!

My new job was a clerical position at the huge Scottish Widows Insurance company. It was reached by an easy walk through central Edinburgh from my lodgings. I had walked it already, before my trip north to make sure I had my bearings.

I was a little unnerved to find it still almost totally dark as I set forth in the morning. The darkness gave the walk a somewhat gothic edge as I hurried past twinkling street lights. I would not have been surprised to see Mr Hyde scurrying home after a night of madness. Possibly even Sherlock Holmes in his deerstalker hat, examining a spot of blood on a doorstep with his magnifying glass.

I arrived early. I introduced myself at reception and a woman showed me through to my seat at a large table. I read through the introductory information and waited, as instructed, for my new work colleagues to arrive.

They soon turned up. There were four or five lads, mostly younger than me, with sports bags on their shoulders and they sauntered in, chatting away together. In a moment of near panic, I realised I hardly understood a word of what they were saying. I tried hard to follow the gestures and tones and guessed they were talking about the weekend sports results. I stood up as they came over and introduced myself. They nodded and smiled quizzically at me, before one of them stepped forward, shook my hand and introduced himself. I stared back blankly, not understanding anything he said.

"I ... I ... I'm sorry, what's your name?"

He gave a little laugh and a couple of his companions giggled nervously. "My name's Angus." He repeated more slowly. "Where ya from?"

"I'm from Australia, Melbourne," I responded with my warmest, most charming grin, hoping to establish a good connection. The rest of them had been standing back, amused by our attempt to communicate. They came forward then and each took his turn to awkwardly stick out his hand and introduce himself. They were mostly from Fife, to the north. The accent was a lot stronger than I had grown accustomed to in the short time I had been there.

I seemed to make slow progress getting a handle on their pronunciation and idioms. Fortunately, they were quite patient with me, showing me where everything was and what I had to do. On day two I had to ask one of them, Jimmy, for instructions about some paperwork I had to complete. He explained the task but I didn't understand a single word. I didn't want to guess or make a mistake and I looked back at him blankly as my mind raced. I scanned and rescanned the sounds I had heard, trying to comprehend what he said.

He tilted his head, laughed softly and said, "ya dunna ken wha' I min, eh lassie?"

I pieced together what he was saying this time. I shook my head and looked at him in a pleading manner. "Sorry, not really, sorry to be a pain, can we start again please."

With good natured patience, confirming my understanding every few words he conveyed what I had to do.

Over the days the awkwardness diminished, and they moved from their initial "best behaviour" to their more natural selves. They joked and teased and pushed each other around. They also started asking me about Australia.

"Do you really have those kangaroos down there?" which sounded completely different when they said it.

They taught me some Scottish words and adapted a traditional Scottish song they would sing to tease me: "Laura where's ya trousers" (pronounced troosers, rhymes with losers). I liked the way my name sounded when it came out of their mouths. We traded lessons in slang and traditional insults. I even learnt a bit about soccer though first I had to learn to call it football.

One Monday morning in the middle of December, I woke to see snow on the window sill. I jumped out of bed, raised the window high and stuck my head out in disbelief. Everything was covered in snow! At least eight inches of snow had fallen softly overnight. I got ready for work quickly and headed out into the new white wonderland. It was gob-smackingly awe inspiring. The beautiful old city of Edinburgh glistened under a blanket of soft snow. It was so white and pure it looked like a giant had covered the city in fondant as we had been sleeping.

As I gazed about, I noticed the snow was still falling lightly. That was the first time I had ever been in falling snow. I danced about, beside myself with excitement and happiness. To my good fortune was added the bonus of having this winter wonderland almost to myself. The streets were largely deserted. The snow had come by surprise with the salt trucks and ploughs not yet ready for action. There would be no traffic access until later the following day. I spread my arms wide and watched the fluffy little flakes gently land on my jacket and gloves. The experience of walking to work in

Edinburgh, beneath the street lights, through glistening virgin snow was a delight and a privilege that will stay with me always.

Two days later the snow was all melty, dirtied, trampled and pushed aside by the snow ploughs. It presented a much less spectacular sight but I still enjoyed the new experience.

Most of the people in the hostel would stay a week or two and then pass on. Some would come and go a number of times while I stayed there. I made a few friends, mainly girls. We enjoyed getting together to cook up a storm or talk about the changing European political climate. A lot happened in Europe in 1989.

The revolution started in Poland and spread throughout the eastern bloc countries. We started to hear about countries that we had no idea existed. A good example of this was the three Baltic states of Lithuania, Latvia and Estonia. On 23rd of August 1989 they formed the Baltic Chain. Approximately two million people across the three adjoining countries coordinated to join hands, forming a human chain 675.5 kilometres long. The amazing feat was performed as a peaceful protest and to raise worldwide awareness of their fight to regain their freedom from the Soviet Union. Within seven months Lithuania became the first Soviet state to declare independence with all three gaining recognised independence by the end of 1991. Meanwhile, the Berlin wall finally came down, after increasing tension and bloodshed on the ninth of November 1989.

Much closer to home, Newcastle, New South Wales experienced an earthquake on 28 December. It measured 5.6 on the Richter scale and was recognised as one of Australia's worst natural disasters. 13 lives were lost and the damage bill was estimated at four billion dollars. There was one girl, Catherine, staying at the hostel who was from Newcastle. We all waited for news as she desperately tried to get in touch with her family. Fortunately, they were all unharmed, but the shock affected the whole city. Catherine worried for several days trying to decide whether she should go home.

We were all excited about the daily news from the continent and blissfully ignorant of the impending earthquake in Australia as we busied around preparing for a massive Christmas lunch. We had a few chefs and cooks among the residents to handle the technical side of things, and that left us minions to do the chopping, stirring, napkin folding and endless washing up. We served Christmas lunch with the juke box blasting out current hits and golden oldies. We all shared stories from home, we ate, we drank, we sang, we laughed, we danced. We all fuelled the festivities and appreciated each other in a spirit that could only come from being united in being far from loved ones. There was no rancour, apathy, jealousy or sarcasm, no mind games, no dysfunctional family shit.

The next day, Boxing Day, a large group of us set out on an expedition to nearby Arthur's Seat in Holyrood Park. The view from the top looked across Edinburgh with spectacular views of the Firth of Forth. I climbed with a dozen others while those less adventurous (or more hungover) crammed into cars and drove up to meet us at the top. A few had done the climb before and knew the best paths to take. Despite that, it still required quite an effort and a bit of a scramble as we got higher. There was a slight rain blowing almost horizontal, but I remained snug and warm in my snow coat. We laughed and joked and took in the incredible views. The truth is, I think we all just felt so privileged to be alive and to be right there in that amazing place.

I believe what was happening in Europe gave us all a greater appreciation for our own freedom. I certainly appreciated mine. I looked back on my flight from Spain with relief and happiness to be where I was. It had been a wild ride and an incredible learning experience. I promised myself I would never again allow a man to manipulate and control me as Jordi had. But for that to be possible, something fundamental inside me had to change and this was soon to be brought to my attention in no uncertain terms.

Twenty-one

There was one particular person I met in Edinburgh who really helped me sort myself out. Her name was Fern and she was several years older than me. She was from New Zealand and was travelling with her Kiwi boyfriend Dave. She wore a Maori tattoo on her upper arm, black patterns with a large frangipani flower in the middle. I was immediately drawn to her tattoo and then to her. Fern and Dave had been working in Edinburgh for a couple of months before I arrived. After a long wait they had recently managed to snaffle one of the very highly sought-after double rooms at the hostel.

Dave appeared to be all whitey, but Fern was clearly part Maori. Apart from her beautiful brown skin and thick blue-black hair she was also pretty ballsy, some would say downright rough. She swore a lot. She was loud and opinionated and prepared to push her point. But despite her rough edges, she was also generous to her friends, intuitive and very grounded. On top of that she possessed a fantastic sense of humour and a roaring laugh that could frequently be heard through the hostel.

I had a bit of a run in with Fern not long after I started work. I forgot to set the alarm. Fortunately, the general noise of the others in the dorm woke me. I looked at the time, jumped out of bed, grabbed my things and raced to the bathroom. There was only one shower free. I raced into the cubicle, noticing a towel hanging on the hook. I chucked the towel out onto the vanity opposite and turned the water on.

"What the fuck? Who's stolen me fucking shower?"

I froze, half way through washing my hair as I realised my mistake. Oh, God, was I in for it.

She banged on the door of the cubicle. "Bitch! My towel was in there. Now its half fucking wet and covered in fucking germy wet shit where you chucked it out. You're not the only one who has to be somewhere! Stupid selfish bitch!"

Should I respond? She might be able to identify my voice. To stay quiet seemed cowardly. I didn't mean to drop her towel in slops. I sighed deeply.

"Fern? Shit, I'm sorry, I'm running really late, my alarm didn't go off. I didn't realise the bench was wet. My mistake, sorry." I felt genuinely remorseful.

I didn't see her before I left for work. I would need to find a way to make it up to her. I decided to buy her a new towel. I picked up a luxury travel towel out of the camping store down town. I gift wrapped it and left it with a note at reception the following afternoon for her.

> *Dear Fern*
> *I'm sorry I stole your shower and messed up your*
> *towel. I would hate it if someone did that to me.*
> *Here's a backup plan in case some halfwit (like me)*
> *screws with your stuff again.*
> *Laura*

Fern tracked me down in the common room later that evening.

"Laura, you stupid bitch, you didn't have to buy me a new fucking towel."

I stood up. "Hi Fern, sorry, I screwed up. I didn't know the bench was wet. I can imagine how pissed off I'd have been to find my towel all wet and germy. Even worse when I'd left it in the shower. I felt really shitty. Sorry."

"Bloody hell girl, it's alright. Yeah, I was pissed off, but still ... a new towel? I'm gonna keep it, ya know. It's a bloody good towel." She smiled at me.

"Thank you." I smiled back.

"No, thank you. You coulda just kept quiet. I wouldn't even've known it was you."

"That's not my style."

After that Fern and I became friends. She invited me out to the pub with her and Dave and a group of friends. I thought it might be all a bit rough for me — I didn't drink much — but we had a lot of fun. I relaxed more than I had in ages, letting my hair down and just enjoying myself.

I started to go out with them regularly and Fern and I would sit and chat about all sorts of things. Some of it was just the beer talking, but we also shared our personal stories. It was a bit like having an older sister. She was supportive, straight forward, listened well, asked probing questions and called a spade a fucking shovel.

I told her about Jordi as we shared a few pints one night. A mediocre covers band blasted out tunes and we either put our heads close together or shouted to be heard. She listened closely as I gave her the lowdown on my time with Jordi then sat back and stubbed out her cigarette.

Through a cloud of smoke, she yelled back at me. "Fuck that. He sounds like a psycho."

I shrank just a little as everyone turned to look at us.

"Well done Lor for getting out of that one." She put her hand on my shoulder. "You gotta take better care of yourself girl. You had a shitty childhood." She shrugged. "Me too, but you gotta get past it!" She shook her head. "No fucking guilt and no pissy excuses coz it follows you around like a bad smell, fucking up your life. That shit'll kill you if you don't deal with it."

I nodded, not knowing what to say.

"Do what you gotta do but just get it outa ya system and move on."

"Okay, but that's easier said than done."

"Yeah, sure, but for Christ's sake, at the end of the day, whether your folks belted ya, raped ya or spoilt ya rotten, you gotta deal with that shit. Leave it behind. That's what growing up's all about." She paused while she lit another cigarette. "You know, there are bloody 70-year-old's running around still fucked up inside coz they haven't dealt with their old shit." She raised her shoulders, spread her hands, palms up and peered into my face. "Who wants that, hey? Do you want that? Do you want to be bloody 70 and still be making shitty choices? Still having shitty relationships and being all screwed up inside coz your old man was a prick to you? Do ya?"

I quivered like a rabbit caught in the headlights. Her manner was so direct, her argument so logical, the choices so clear even in my beer induced brain fog. I had the choice. I could continue to make excuses and shrink away or find the courage to face my own demons. I nodded gravely at Fern before shaking my head in resignation.

"Bloody hell, that's tough, but it makes sense. Looks like I'm going to have to grow some balls!" I said and rolled my eyes.

She laughed loudly and punched me in the arm. "That's my girl! You're scared?" she shrugged, "You're afraid? Fucking deal with it." She said this last bit with real venom and an aggressive wave of her arm. It left me in no doubt that is exactly how she handled it. "You're depressed, tell that fucker in your head to piss off, you're not interested. Just like it was the Johos at the door."

As I lay awake in bed, the next night listening to the gentle snoring and snuffling around me I reflected on Fern's words. I had a fair bit I needed to deal with. Living in a hostel and sharing a room with twenty-or so other girls, it was all too easy to bottle things up, to live in denial. After all, where do you go to let off steam? For the first time in months I let my guard down and allowed myself to peek inside the box labelled "Olivia". The pain and the grief that rushed out were physically and emotionally overwhelming. I turned my face into the pillow to muffle my sobs. I pulled the bed covers up over my head as I worked at getting the lid back on. Holy shit! It was like being hit by a freight train. I had no idea what I was carrying around inside.

I couldn't keep moving on. It was time to deal with the muddle of emotions that was polluting my life and decision making. I asked myself, what might help and my mind wandered back to my last counselling session.

Some months before taking off on my big trip I went to see someone to help me cope with breaking up with my married lover. The counsellor kept trying to get me to express my anger but all I could do was sob. In the end I was able to break through and found a stinking cesspool of rage and bitterness within. This would have been overwhelming if I had not been in such good hands. The counsellor was a straight-talking middle-aged woman called Joan. She had set up a heavy old arm chair in front of me, placed a large cushion on it and told me the cushion was "him".

She handed me a broom handle. "Now hit him," she said.

I backed off and sobbed. "I can't hit him, I love him."

Joan was unimpressed by my tears. "It's not time for crying, it's time for justice. Think of what that bastard has done to you. You tell him exactly what he has done to you, leading you on, promising to leave his wife, screwing with your life. Tell the bastard what he's done."

Hesitantly at first, I revisited our story. "You pursued me, you wooed me, you told me I meant more to you than life itself."

Then it started to pour out from my gut where it had all been swirling around for months. "You promised ... you promised to give me the earth ... when you could get away from your wife. You ... you held me so gently, made love to me ... So, so tender." I took a moment to let my emotions settle. "You told me I was special. You said ... more than anyone you ever met before." I looked about me, collecting my thoughts. "Fuck, what an idiot I was. You even called me your soulmate, you said we were meant to be together." I was focussing more and more on the cushion. "You painted such a beautiful fucking picture of our future ... the white picket fence, the family, growing old together as we played with our grandchildren." I sobbed my heart out. "I trusted you, I ... I believed in you. I gave you my, my everything. I put you above everything, everything in my life — including my own fucking health."

I sobbed and sobbed, letting out the pain I had been keeping inside for so long. "Do you know, you prick, I would drive past your house at night just to see if you were home. How pathetic is that? And here's the biggy, the secret you will never know. The one that fucking burns me up inside. I ... I got pregnant, you ... you didn't know that, did you? But I did. I did it, deliberately, I stopped taking the pill. I wanted you so bad, I just wanted us to be together like you said. So, I got pregnant. I was so happy when I found out. We could be together. We would be a family." I shook my head, bitterness welling inside me. "But I lost our baby, I lost it. I never got to tell you. I never got to tell anyone. I was all alone. Nobody knew, fucking nobody. Do you ... do you know what that's like? Fucking nobody knew. I was all alone, all a-fucking-lone."

I tightened my grip on the broom handle. "I needed you. I needed to tell you what had happened, but you wouldn't come to see me. You said you had to go with your fucking wife to ... to choose the paint for the spare room, for the spare fucking room!" I felt myself grow steely cold inside. "I saw her, you don't know this, but I saw her not long after that, I saw she was pregnant. Yeah, I knew. I stared at her in the supermarket aisle and she turned my way. I coulda told her then. Your husband's a fucking pig whore. You are a pig whore. I really wanted to tell her so bad, she's married to a total prick but I didn't. I don't know who I was protecting, her or you, you fucking prick."

And then I hit him. At first it was a light tap but then a torrent of rage surged up inside and I screamed and swore. I struck the cushion again and again with such force that the broom handle broke in the middle. At this point I lunged forward, like a foot soldier on the front line of battle. I started driving the splintered end of the broomstick into the cushion. I was stabbing and screaming and cursing him to hell with his predatory ways, his fucking lies, manipulation and massive cock-sucking ego. I told him I would ram his balls down his throat if he ever came near me again.

I had no consciousness of time but eventually I slowed, my rage spent. I was breathless, disorientated and emotionally and physically exhausted. I sensed the wildness in my eyes and the pounding in my heart receding. I looked down at where the cushion sat on the chair. It was destroyed, bits of fluffy white stuffing lay scattered about the floor. The chair, still standing showed bruise marks on the arms.

I had been largely unaware of Joan's presence as the rage came out of me but I turned to her in that moment. She was standing back, observing it all with her eyebrows raised and a small amused smile on her face.

"Wow," she said coming forward, reaching out cautiously for what was left of the broom handle, which had become a dangerous weapon in my hands.

"Well done, how do you feel?"

I sighed and handed over the stick, still quite overwhelmed by the flood of my emotions. I shook my head to clear it. "Oh boy," I said. "That was awesome! Oh my God, I had no idea that was there."

"Do you still have that pain in your chest?"

"No."

"Do you still think you love him?"

"No."

"Do you think you can get on with your life now?"

"Yes, I do."

"Good," she seemed satisfied as she stood studying me.

I turned gesturing towards the chair. "I ... I ... I'm really s ... sorry about your cushion," I said apologetically, at a loss to know how to deal with the fallout from my rage. "I am happy to pay you for it or replace it. And the chair—"

She cut me off with a wave of her hand. "Don't be sorry for anything that has happened today. You're not the first and you'll certainly not be the last to make use of that chair. Though I must admit you are the first person to break the fucking broomstick and stab the cushion. You really needed that." She laughed a rattling smoker's laugh that ended in a cough. "Forget about it. Tools of the trade, easily replaced."

She gave me a hug. I gave her eighty dollars and I walked out a lighter happier person.

I really needed to do that again. I had to get rid of the emotional load sitting on my chest. I needed to clear out the crap with Jordi and the grief of leaving Olivia. While I was at it, to move forward I wanted to clear some crap from my childhood. I'd been avoiding facing that stuff but I knew, doing it would help me have more confidence in my decision making and not be such a shit magnet. I needed a private room with a sturdy chair, a big cushion and a broomstick. Where could I find that? Or what could I replace it with? I considered going to a bed-and-breakfast but envisaged myself being kicked out for trashing the joint. I thought about climbing the hill again but I knew from experience that the sound of my cursing and screaming would travel for miles. I went through each day with growing impatience, searching in my mind for an outlet. I had to find somewhere or somehow to vent in safety.

Twenty-two

I decided to write a letter to Jordi. I wanted him to understand what he did to me, to let him know how fucked up our relationship was. I also wanted to apologise. It took me several days as I allowed myself to wallow in the mental effluent of our time together. I kept a notepad in my pocket and scribbled in it as thoughts and feelings came to me. I continued at this until I reached a day when there was nothing left inside. I searched through my feelings, relived some of the best and worst moments. I even encouraged myself to get upset about it all. Then I captured everything on paper that came up until the well of grief and anger ran dry. Finally, I was ready to forgive him and to forgive myself for choosing a man like him, and for leaving as I did. I wrote everything down in the letter and then I let him go. When this process finished, I sealed the letter up in an envelope. I penned a simple "J" on the front and put it in the bottom of my daypack. I found a new patch of peace within.

I gave myself up to a few days of levity then. A dozen or so of my friends at the hostel were heading off for a weekend trip to Glasgow and I joined them. We took off Saturday morning, catching the train in a boisterous, multicultural group. We booked into a guest house, three or four to a room. We were all used to not having much privacy.

The highlight of the trip was a night out in a nearby pub renowned for its traditional folk music. Everyone was in high spirits, the beer flowed, and we danced silly drunken dances and attempted to nail the Glaswegian accent. We staggered back to the guesthouse as one rowdy group at about three in the morning. It felt good to be alive.

As we travelled back on the train the next afternoon, many among us, like myself, were sleepy and hungover. Despite this, I felt great — lighter, happier with a fresh appreciation for the world and the people around me.

I had planned to do continue digging out the roots of my disfunction the next day after work. My sense of peace and wellbeing though, made it hard to bring my attention back to the emotional baggage I still carried. The seductive appeal of denial was strong and I put it off a few more days. Eventually I started the process of writing down my thoughts, feelings and memories of my father. This took much longer to write than the letter to Jordi. Most of it was written late at night and often in one of the toilet cubicles. I didn't want my anger and distress to be observed. I took my towel, so I was able to sob or scream without waking everybody or worse yet, someone calling the cops or the ambulance.

I recalled a half-buried memory of how, when I was eight years old. I had tried to get out of doing some chore on the farm. In a flash, my father raised a shovel over my head. He cursed me and told me he should hit me over the head with it for being so bloody lazy. He told me I was a useless piece of shit. I cowered in terror. I internalised every word and every horrific moment of the experience. It imprinted heavily on my brain, including how my mother looked anxiously on, making no attempt to come to my rescue.

I drew out another memory of him taunting me. He called me a conniving, manipulative little bitch, telling me it was all my fault that he and my mother argued so much. He asked me if I was satisfied, was it enough for me? His face was crimson, spittle flew as he spat out his words and the look in his eyes terrified me. I never managed to look at him after that day without remembering the scene, seeing the drops of venom fly from his mouth and those crazed, hateful eyes.

I wrote all of it down, everything he did that hurt me. I poured out every nasty ugly thing he ever said to me that I still carried. I let out all the arguments, insults and retorts I was never game enough to say to him. I cursed him, swore at him and insulted him.

I let him know every time and every way that he damaged me over the years. I told him what I wanted from him but never got. I confided how I prayed that he would become a good Dad, how I longed to have a Dad like some of my friends. I wanted a Dad who nurtured and supported his kids, a Dad who I could rely on, who was there for me.

I described how much it hurt me that he failed me and instead raised me with violence, fear and a deep lack of self-worth. I talked to him about how that fear and self-hatred still kept me prisoner. I opened up about the bad decisions I made because of them. Finally, I told him how I was going to let him go. He would hold no power over me ever again. I would no longer be shaped by what had happened during my early years under his care. And, after many hours and many tears, as far as I was able, I forgave him and let him go from my heart and my mind.

The experience was awful, but it was such a relief to get it out of me. It was like releasing poison. When I was sure I had finished, I folded the sheets of paper — there were quite a few. I placed them in a series of envelopes, sealed them and wrote a simple "D" on the front. I also put those letters into the bottom of my daypack.

The process changed something deep inside. The thought of those letters sitting in my pack was like written validation of myself as a person. They gave me a new spring in my step and a sense of freedom. I carried them with me for a while, opening and rereading them, scribbling more on them, swearing at them. Then, just as with a flesh wound, my psyche healed. I was finally ready to say goodbye to the trauma and emotion of those old experiences. As everyone else busied about their evening dinner preparations, I re-read each of the letters in turn. Satisfied that there were no emotional lumps left within I quietly ripped up the pages. I stood by the hearth and fed them piece by piece into the blazing open fire in the dining room. I watched each shred of paper turn to ash as the flames devoured it. At the same time the scars of my own traumatic feelings softened and disintegrated, leaving fresh, clean, sensitive space in my heart.

I was not naïve enough to think that I could erase all the effects of my childhood through my letter to my father. I was also aware that I had yet to deal with any mother issues but a weight fell from me. My confidence and general happiness grew. I became less fearful. I laughed and socialised a little more easily and I started to see more positive aspects in the people and life around me. Overcoming all that shit was truly like peeling one layer off the onion at a time. With each step forward there would be joy, relief and newfound energy.

Fern noticed my new chirpiness. "What's happening Lor? I've hardly seen you for weeks and now here you are, all light and breezy. I watched you go by last week with a real hang-dog expression but here you are, all rainbows and fairy floss."

I grinned at her. "Yeah, I avoided people for a while, sorry. Been cleaning out my shit, getting over my bad potty training, like you said."

"Really? Good for you, girly. It looks like it's working for you." She studied my face, making sure I was being straight with her. "You tell me, won't you, if you need anything, need to talk or something."

"Thanks Fern, you really helped. Thanks to you, I finally bit the bullet and faced some demons. I just want to stop making shitty choices in my life. It's been bloody hard, but the difference is amazing."

It really did feel great, but it wasn't over yet. I still carried the big box inside labelled "Olivia". I hadn't written to her. In fact, there had been no contact with her at all since our tearful farewell at Stockholm Central Station all those months before. I had tried hard to stop thinking about her.

I realised the letter technique would not work for Olivia. She did me no wrong. I held no anger towards her just a mountain of grief. As soon as my thoughts turned towards her, my chest swelled with pain, choking my airways and my eyes swam with tears. I no longer needed a chair, a cushion and a stick. These would not ease my grief. I tried other ways to ease the burden, but every way ended in tears. Finally, I realised that there was no other way forward but to release those tears. So, I set about finding a safe way to do that.

In the end I decided to head back up the hill, back up into the wilderness of Holyrood Park. I took a sick day from work to avoid the weekend trail blazers even though it was early February with an expected top of just five degrees Celsius so I was probably being over cautious. Most Importantly, I wanted the privacy to just let myself go. I needed to experience the full weight of my feelings, to sob or curse or scream without self-censorship.

I packed my daypack the evening before, complete with my travel towel and a giant wad of toilet paper to catch the expected flood of tears and snot. I included a few plastic bags to place underneath me on the damp ground, paper to write on, matches, some fruit, nuts, water and a map.

I set out just after nine o'clock in the morning. The main path led almost right by the huge Scottish Widows building. Fortunately, I was so rugged up it was not that difficult to be "incognito". The sky was clear, and the air freezing cold, ice puddles lay about the pavement ready to catch distracted passers-by. I had full woollen thermals under my clothes and a hot coffee and some warm porridge in my belly to start me off. The walk up the hill if I went to the top would take me a bit over an hour at a decent pace.

As I started the climb, I opened my mind and invited in images of Olivia. They played before me in small vignettes: Olivia peering down at me in the square in Amsterdam as she asked if I was okay (it surprised me that I still remembered that one); Olivia, the next morning, all sleepy, handing me the note with her contact details; laughing so hard she snorted over coffee and cinnamon buns, and holding my hand and guiding me through the streets of Stockholm. Olivia's hand. I saw her pale naked body as she swam towards me through the icy cold water at Agesta beach. Etched in my brain were her words as she encouraged me to make the plunge into the freezing water.

"What have you got to lose? Let go Laura, give yourself over to the experience. You will not regret it, I promise you."

I stopped my ascent and closed my eyes. I sensed the strength and soft warmth of her hand, and tears sprang immediately into my eyes. I remembered it so well. I reached out beside me to take her hand. I felt it and I saw it, the golden colour of her skin, the little wrinkles around her knuckles, the shape of her nails. I held her hand the rest of the way until I found just the place I was looking for. Off one of the wilder tracks, there was a bit of a hollow, screened by an old dead tree and gorse and other scrubby bushes.

I spread my plastic on the damp ground. There was enough space for me to lean back against the overgrown rocky wall behind me with room out in front for my legs and my pack. I made a place beside me for Olivia. In my mind I sat her down, asked her if she was comfortable, if she needed anything. And I talked to her. I told her that I loved her that I loved her so much it hurt.

When I opened the inner depths of my heart, the pain throbbed like an open wound. It spread rapidly, infecting my whole body and I sobbed and sobbed into my towel. Great chunks of pain shot up through my chest and out my mouth, stealing my breath, causing my stomach to convulse. I moved quickly forward onto all fours and vomited my porridge and coffee into the bushes.

My stomach now empty I sat back, breathing deeply, temporarily subdued as I reached for my water bottle to rinse my mouth. "Oh, my sweet girl. What am I to do? I miss you so much. I don't even know how you are. What are you up to? Are you happy? Do you think of me, like I think of you?"

I wiped my face and the sobs came again as large hot tears flowed down my cheeks. I closed my eyes and mentally placed myself in her sitting room. I breathed in the aroma I had committed to memory. My mind responded by taking me deeper. I let myself be filled with the treasure trove of scents I had explored on her body — the scent of her hair, her breath, her armpits, her secret places. This brought a fresh burst of pain and heavy sobbing and I covered my face in the towel. I rolled into a ball on my side as my heart threatened to burst out of my chest. My stomach went into spasm again with the overwhelming strength of my grief.

I lost touch with time as I lay there. At some point, exhausted by the emotional outpouring, I fell asleep, curled up in the foetal position right there on the ground. I woke some time later, cramped, cold and disorientated. I sat up, wiping the leaves, dirt and dribble from the side of my hair and face. I gazed up through the overhead bushes at the fluffy grey clouds moving slowly across the sky as the fog cleared from my mind. I reached out and plucked a blade of grass, bringing further clarity as I examined this microcosm of nature. I was able to look at my relationship with Olivia more calmly.

"This is fucked," I said to myself. "This is not dealing with something from my past that I need to get over. This is not a bloody childhood issue or an arsehole boyfriend, this is now. This is how I feel right now. I love Olivia. She is the kindest, sweetest, funniest person and I am crazy about her."

I realised that I had been trying to deal with the "problem of Olivia". Trying hard to move on and leave her behind as a past trauma or a travel fling. I had attempted to label it as the girl on girl experience to add to my growing file of adventures. I had put the lid down tight on my feelings for her. Inside, I didn't connect with the idea of being in love with a woman. That was something that had never been on my "to do" list and yet, I had first been physically attracted to Roxy and then Olivia. What did it all mean? Had I always had the potential to be a lesbian? Did my love for Olivia make me a lesbian? I didn't want to be a lesbian. Was there any way I could love Olivia and not be one? How could I get past my concept of the label?

Yeah, I returned to that, I didn't want to be labelled. If I were to be with Olivia, people would label us as lesbians, as dykes, "carpet lickers". We would be "batting for the other side", "in need of a good root". My mind overflowed with the ignorant, cruel, judgemental comments that people make. I really struggled to reconcile my feelings with my social identity. Who and what was Laura Maree Cassidy?

I realised I was operating out of fear, fear of the unknown. I was afraid of being seen as a lesbian, anxious about what my friends would think. I didn't even know how to act like a lesbian. I had short hair, and since being in Europe had let my body hair grow where it would. But that didn't qualify me to be called a dyke, a hippy maybe but not a dyke. It was like someone wanted to hand me a certificate, giving me a vocation, I hadn't studied for. "Congratulations Laura, you are now a midwife, your first patient is waiting for you in the birthing suite". Or, "Here you go Laura, congratulations on being chosen as the new fast bowler for the Australian cricket team, you'll lead the charge for the match against England tomorrow."

That's how it all presented in my mind. I had been raised to be hetero, there had been no other option. I was what society called a "normal woman". Suddenly, at the age of 25 though my heart was telling me that maybe, that wasn't me, or not all that I was. It suggested I too could fall in love with a person, regardless of their genitals. I sat and mulled this over for a long time, breathing in the rich earthy dampness of my surroundings and relaxing into the nurturing energy of the earth.

I had the wisdom not to push myself to make a decision or reach an outcome. First, I would sleep on it, giving my brain a chance to sort all of this stuff out in my absence. In a moment of indulgence, I imagined myself as Virginia Woolf's Orlando and drew some comfort from this. Possibly, I just needed to sleep for a very long time.

A little before two thirty in the afternoon I packed up, returned to the trail and finished the climb to Arthur's seat. I loved the view out over Edinburgh and the Forth. There's something about looking down on the tiny cars and the little ant-people that helps me not take myself so seriously. I am sure there are many people who, in my situation would have given a single shrug and moved on in one direction or another. Not me, I had to spend hours and hours agonising over my life. Growing up, my Mother always told me "Your problem is you think too much". Is that possible? I don't know.

My head crowded in again with more questions as I descended. What about kids? If I settled into a relationship with Olivia how could I have kids? Would I even be allowed to stay in Sweden legally for more than a few months? Was that long enough to know if it was to be a "forever" thing? What about the language? What would I do with myself? Could I have a sexually fulfilling relationship without a penis — ever? Are same-sex relationships even legal in Sweden? Where are they legal? Did I really want to do this? How cold does it get in Sweden? I stopped and shook my head, amazed and frustrated at my own propensity for analysis and over thinking. I was getting way ahead of myself. I reminded my overactive brain that Olivia could be all loved up with Oscar. He had been due to return from Australia late last year. Or she could be all loved up with someone else. I said good bye to her in September and it was then February.

Was I too late? Had I lost my chance at discovering the love of my life? I had discarded it the first time, not recognising the potential of what I held in my hands. Did I deserve a second chance? I didn't know but I had to try, I had to find out.

Twenty-three

When my alarm sounded the next day, I jumped out of bed with a new sense of purpose. I got up and went to work, assuring my colleagues that I was much better, thank you. My boss Bev, a kind Scottish woman in her forties, peered into my face with concern. She told me I looked rather peaky and if I wasn't up to the day's work I could go home. I thanked her. She had been wonderful to me. In fact, the position at Scottish Widows had worked out really well for me. The relaxed work environment, the subsidised staff canteen, the location close to the hostel, everything had all worked out really well. I had also managed to save a few thousand pounds. That would serve me well once the gig finished, whatever I decided to do.

I walked down to the pub with a group from the hostel the next Friday night to enjoy some live music. It was a great night and I got a bit drunk. Late in the night, Fern and I were talking. She asked me what I was planning to do after my job finished in a few weeks.

"Well, I'm not sure." I looked down at the dregs of my beer to avoid her eyes. "Really not sure."

"Why do you look so sad?"

I met her gaze. Fern was studying me through slightly narrowed eyes.

"What's going on? What are you sitting on girly?"

I opened my mouth, took a deep breath, "I'm mulling over whether to go and visit someone." My gaze slid south again as I spoke.

"Visit someone?" She frowned. "What are you talking about? You're not thinking of going back to that loser Jordi, are you?"

I smiled broadly and shook my head. "No, I wouldn't do that."

"So, what's going on, come on, fess up."

"Well, when I was in Sweden last year, I had a fling ... with someone. We met in Amsterdam." I saw her eyebrows raise. "Yeah, I know, I know, didn't I have enough on my plate already?" I rolled my eyes. "I didn't plan it. It just ... happened. But the truth is, I can't get them out of my head. Yeah, it sounds strange because of the whole Jordi thing, it wasn't supposed to happen ..." I found it really awkward trying to explain. "It's like I just didn't possess enough awareness or confidence to change course. It was ... it was bloody confusing. It's taken all this time for me to be able to clear the shit from the water and determine what I want."

"Jeez. So, what's he like? Do you think he might have feelings for you too?"

Another big breath. "Well, you see, it's actually a woman, Olivia, and yeah, at the time the feeling was very mutual."

Fern blew out a big cloud of smoke and ashed her cigarette. "Christ, so what are you gonna do?"

I sat back out of the smoke cloud and shrugged. "Well, I'm not sure. It's taken me a long time to get used to the idea that I could be in love with a woman. I mean, it's never happened before. I mean ... well, you know, just never." I held up my hands, palms raised. "I'm struggling, really struggling with what it all means. The whole thing is very much unchartered terra ... territory. There may be a guy on the scene. I have no idea. I'm trying to work out what to do about it."

"How strong are your feelings?" Fern leaned forward, studying my face.

It only took a moment of reflection for my emotions to rise into my chest. "I've been in denial, kept pushing my feelings down. I thought my future was with Jordi, so I shut everything else up in a box." I shook my head. "But, like I told you, I've been sorting my shit out and eventually I had to face this. That's why I took yesterday off. I hiked up the hill, had a good bawl and just let it all out."

"Shit, hey." Fern shrugged her shoulders. "Never been in that position meself, but I reckon it's possible, you know. I don't reckon you'd be having those feelings if you didn't have it in you."

She leaned forward and put her hand on my arm. Then she looked into my face with her bloodshot eyes and said, "Whatever you do girly, you be sure you make your decision from a place of love, not fear, alright?"

I nodded. "Yeah, I will. This is too important to be chicken shit about it all."

When she put it so simply there really was only one choice. Attempting to connect with Olivia was a choice based on love. Ignoring or denying my feelings, analysing and rationalising why I shouldn't do it was fear based. It was time to put those big girl panties on and write to Olivia.

Once I had made the decision to write I became excited, almost school girlish. It took me ages to compose a letter. I agonised over exactly what to say. Should I tell her everything that had happened? Should I confess to her that I loved her? Or should I just turn up? She had cared for me all those months ago, but what about now? Had she moved on? Did I really want to upset her life again?

I mulled it over all the next day and finally sat down late in the afternoon with pen in hand. I chose a postcard so I could be brief. Then I put it in an envelope for privacy, in case somebody at her end picked it up before she did.

Dear Olivia
How are you and Smulan? Sorry I haven't written. Things didn't pan out with Jordi and I've been living and working in Scotland since November while I sorted myself out. I think of you and our time together often and would love to see you again. I finish my work contract Friday 3rd March and was thinking of taking the ferry to Gothenburg and travelling across to visit you.
Please let me know how you are and if it would be okay for me to come your way. I will understand if

you are busy or it doesn't suit. You can reach me at
the address on the back.
Love always
Laura

My stomach was churning as I sealed the envelope. I dropped it into a letterbox on my way into the gardens at Dunbar's Close on Sunday morning. I watched it disappear from my fingers into the blackness within, whispering "God speed."

I gave myself up to the pleasure of the landscape, delighting in the sight of the tiny buds emerging on bare tree limbs. Nature was about done with winter. Further on, I sat and observed the "pigeon woman". Arms outstretched, seed in hand, she was covered, like a human perch, in pigeons, all cooing, pecking, flapping.

The week dragged by as I followed the letter across to Stockholm in my mind. I watched it being delivered. I imagined Olivia picking it up and studying it with curiosity. She turned it over and read my name ... but how did she respond? If she was contented in her life, I didn't want to intrude. If she was happily in a relationship, I would accept that, go through my grief process and move on as best I could. More than anything I wanted her to be happy, or so I told myself.

I had an answer on Friday of the same week. The Canadian girl, Rowena, on reception duty called out to me as I came in. "Hey Laura, you have some mail. Hang on a minute, where did I put that?" she turned around in the cluttered office space.

I pulled myself up abruptly and my heart leapt into my mouth. "Here it is." She beamed at me across the desk. "Have you had a good day?"

I nodded and grabbed the letter, thanking her absentmindedly as I zoomed in on the writing. It couldn't be hers. It was too quick. The writing looked familiar. I turned the envelope over. It was her address on the back! So quick. Well done Posties. I walked off studying the envelope. My excitement grew realising she must have responded straight away.

I dropped my bag on my bed in the dorm and headed to the privacy of the toilets with my precious letter. I sat down in the cubicle and studied the writing. My guts churned and I bit my lip.

The letter would have a strong influence on the life that lay ahead of me. I took a few slow deep breaths, preparing myself for what it may contain before carefully ripping it open. It was brief, like mine.

> *Dear Laura*
> *How lovely to hear from you. I am sorry things did not go well with Jordi. I sent you a letter for Christmas to his address and wondered what was happening when I did not get anything back from you. Smulan and I are well. We miss you. Work is the same, I still love it. It has been cold of course and we have been staying inside for too long. It's probably almost as cold in Edinburgh. It would be great if you could come over and stay again. Tell me how and when you are arriving so I can come and pick you up. I don't want you to get lost in transit!*
> *I am looking forward to giving you a big hug and hearing all your news.*
> *Lots of love*
> *Olivia*

I read it through three times, slowly and carefully, searching for deeper clues and my heart swelled more and more each time. I looked up, at the back of the stall door, allowing the letter in my hands to drop onto my lap. I had so many thoughts and feelings rushing through me. It was settled, I was going to Sweden! Oh my God. Was I sure? Was I really sure? Yes, I was. Inside I was more confident and grounded about this than I had been about anything for ages. How exciting, how scary! I felt elated, and also sick. I raced down to the local travel office the next morning and booked my journey through to Stockholm for the Saturday, the day after I finished work. I would be taking a bus to Newcastle in the north of England. From there I would catch a ferry to Gothenburg and finally a train from Gothenburg to Stockholm.

I didn't tell anyone, not even Fern what I was doing until a few days before I left. I didn't want to talk about it, I was too emotionally charged already. On my last day on the job my work mates threw me a lovely festive morning tea. Everyone wished me well. They gave me a little Scottish highlander doll with scraggy red hair and a kilt with a large set of hairy genitals underneath. I named him Jock and expressed my appreciation. From that day forward, I said, I would always have a man beside me on my journey through life. They had laughed but really had no idea of the deeper meaning hidden in my joke. I had told them I was crossing to Scandinavia to continue travelling. That's what I told everyone except Fern.

She saw me off from the bus depot, having insisted on carrying my case for me. She gave me a big hug goodbye. "I'm bloody proud of you Lor, you've got guts girl. I'll miss you though."

I hugged her back and thanked her for everything she had done for me. I really believed I wouldn't be standing there, emotionally whole, ready to embrace my future with courage and confidence if it hadn't been for her nudging me to get over my shit. We were both aware we would probably never see each other again, but that was okay. She was an angel who had come into my life right when I needed one. I turned and waved as I hopped on the bus and then watched her as she walked away. I settled into my seat eager to begin my long journey to Olivia and what could just possibly be my happy ever after.

Twenty-four

The train trundled into Stockholm Central Station around lunchtime on Sunday. I recognised some words, scents, and landmarks beneath a slight dusting of snow. I had been too excited, too full of thoughts to sleep much on the journey so I arrived tired, smelly and dishevelled. I still wasn't sure whether I was coming as a friend or a lover, for a few days or forever. I had imagined and analysed all the various possible outcomes. As the train slowly stopped, I saw Olivia standing on the platform. My heart leapt and my focus was simply on how good it felt to see her.

I waited impatiently in the aisle for my turn to step out of the door, my pack on my back and my case beside me. I caught Olivia's eye as I stepped onto the platform and grinned broadly. I took three long steps forward, clearing the exit and dropped my case as Olivia swept into my arms.

"Oh Laura, Laura, it's so good to see you." We held each other tight, cheek against cheek.

She stepped back, holding me at arm's length and studied my face. We were both a bit teary. I was so full of emotion I struggled to speak. I smiled and nodded as I swallowed hard.

She hugged me again, her lips close to my ear. "Let's go home." I nodded again and she took my hand. We caught the subway south to *Mariatorget* station in Sodermalm and walked on to her apartment building.

She opened the door, sweeping her arm out as she had done the first time, allowing me to enter before her. The same wonderful scent I had committed to memory on my first visit immediately engulfed me. I closed my eyes for a moment, letting it wash over me. Opening them again, I quickly scanned the apartment. I thought it might have changed, but it looked the same as when I had left almost six months before.

I stepped out of the bathroom, toasty warm and sweet smelling from my hot shower and was met by the delicious aroma of lunch. What a heady combination for the senses. Olivia, in a bright cherry patterned apron was lifting a casserole dish out of the oven. The coffee table had been covered with a cloth and adorned with cutlery, crockery, wine glasses, a long red candle and a small vase of flowers. It was obvious that she had gone to some effort to get the desired effect. My heart welled up with happiness and appreciation. The lunch was delicious, chicken and bacon casserole with mashed potato and greens. This was followed by chocolate cake and cream, washed down with a generous amount of Rosé. What a delight. The rest of the day we spent eating, drinking, and talking until late. We had a lot to catch up on.

"Is Oscar about?"

"He came back. He stayed for a few weeks. He met a Canadian Filipino woman, Abbie, working at the same place, at AIMS. She came here with him for a visit. They have gone to Canada to live and work."

"Oh really, how did that affect you?"

"That's fine. I love Oscar, but not romantically. He's like ... he's like my brother, really."

"Okay", I nodded, happily striking that possible future off the list. "And have you met anybody else?" I tried to make this question light hearted.

She smiled at me a little sadly and slowly shook her head. "No. But what about you and Jordi, what happened?"

I told her the whole story. It felt so good to be able to share it with her.

"That sounds awful. I am so sorry to hear this." She took my hand in hers, her touch warm and soothing. "I wish I had been there for you, to help you. It must have been so scary for you when you left. I don't know but ... I mean, he sounds like maybe, he can be violent. I'm so glad you got away safely. You could have come back here?"

I nodded. "Yeah, I thought about it, but I really needed time out. You know, carrying way too much baggage. I had to sort my shit out." I paused to get my words right. "I didn't want to come back in little pieces." I shrugged. "I was a mess. It wouldn't have been fair to put that on you. That's why I didn't contact you, I didn't know who I was anymore or what I wanted." My courage stalled. I bought time by reaching down and patting Smulan who had crawled into my lap. Fear reached up into my throat as I headed towards the vulnerability of a confession. "I'd lost touch with myself. I needed to untangle the layers of emotions instead of ... you know, bouncing from one relationship to another. I had no ... no confidence in my decisions while there was so much, you know, inside." I winced on the inside and tried to stop the flush in my cheeks. I had used the "r" word.

"I understand. That was very hard for you, but it sounds like you are ... you seem ... much better now. What did you do?"

I told her about Fern and the wise counsel she had given me. I described how I poured out my emotions into letters to Jordi and my father and my late-night muffled raging in the toilet cubicle. I stopped myself from confessing my new commitment to choose love over fear.

She nodded, admitting to going through a similar process with her own traumatic past. "What did you do with the letters?"

"I ripped them up and I burnt them."

"Okay. And did it make a difference? How did you change, what did you find when you ... you cleared away all of that emotion?"

I looked at her and took a deep breath, summoning my courage, consciously choosing love. "I found that I missed you — terribly." Tears came to my eyes and my voice wavered as I continued. "Until then I had pushed my feelings for you so far down under all the other stuff I had to deal with. I didn't know what was there, but when I opened the box and let those feelings out, they were ... so strong ... overwhelming." My chin wobbled and tears spilled down my face.

I hesitated, trying to get on top of my emotions and was encouraged by Olivia's touch as she gently squeezed my hand in hers.

"I had to try to understand — how can I be so attracted to a woman? I'm sorry, but I wasn't comfortable with that. It's never happened before. I didn't think it possible or ... part of my ... my identity. I didn't know what to do." I stopped, took a breath. "I had to learn to trust myself, you know, to trust my feelings." I shrugged. "I'm sorry if ... perhaps I shouldn't say all this. I don't know ..." I raised my hands in a helpless gesture as words failed me. Smulan, probably sensing the heavy emotional charge, jumped from my lap.

Olivia leant forward, reaching out and brushing a tear from my cheek. "When you left, I was so sad. I really wanted you to have a good life with Jordi. I wanted the best for you and I put on my brave face because you had to go. But, the truth is, I was so lost, I just got up and went to work and didn't want to come home. The place seemed so empty. Everything reminded me of you." She paused, brushed some crumbs off the table cloth. "The week, having you here with me, was so good, so ... comfortable and happy — the way we laughed and played. I enjoyed it so much. You were so easy with Lucas and Issa." She wiped a tear from her own cheek.

I found myself holding my breath as I waited for her to continue speaking. Was there a "but" coming?

"I have, as you know, had a relationship with a woman before so I did not go through what you have. Besides, I think these things are not such a big deal in Sweden. So, ... it was not uncomfortable for me to be with you, to think about a future with you. But I did not dare to think like that because you had a life somewhere else. You had another love, another future." She reached out for the tissue box, handing me a couple before wiping her face. "I was just happy that you had been here, that I had known you, that we had been together. I ... made myself better thinking those things. It gave me strength if not happiness."

I across at her, deep into her eyes as I reached forward and took her hand in mine. "You are such a funny, wonderful, wise person and you have such a good heart." I paused, looking down at her hand in mine. "I want to be with you, to explore life with you, whatever that means and for however long we choose." My words came out in a whisper now as my throat tightened with emotion. "I have worked so hard to reach the point where I can say that with all my heart and all my soul. I love you. I really love you. I just love being with you."

"Oh Laura." She leaned forward and embraced me. "I want you to stay with me. I know that there is a lot to work out. We will have to take each day as it comes. That's okay, I really want to try to build a life with you here, if you will stay with me. I don't have much, my apartment is small for two people possibly but ..." It was her turn to run out of words.

"Yes, please." I beamed at her through my tears. "I really want to stay. I have worked so hard to get to this point, to be ready for this moment." I grinned at her through the tears and she grinned back at me. "I must look a mess. Your face handles being upset so much better than mine."

We broke into laughter and fell on the rug on the floor, rolling around and holding each other like little children. "So many bloody tears!" I said sniffing and reaching for another handful of tissues. I wiped my face, threw the tissues away then pinned her shoulders down and looked down into her face. "No more tears, alright? No more tears, no more snot, we don't need to do that anymore, okay?"

"Yes, yes!" She grinned at me and giggled. "No more tears, no more fucking tears!"

I propped myself on my elbow, drew her close against my body and gently almost timidly caressed her face with my fingers. "I have never felt this way about anybody." I confessed. "The strength of my feelings for you, the love I have, the joy I experience being with you. It's a bit overwhelming, a bit scary." I sighed. "And I want to say thank you, thank you so much, for your patience, your understanding, for your generosity. Thank you so much for ... for waiting, still having your heart open to me. I mean, you could have responded to my letter with 'How sad, too bad, too late, piss off.' When I think about how I threw away my first chance to be with you ... how I was too screwed up to see what ... what I had, here, in front of me ... I might have lost you, what an awful thought."

We made love then, right there on the rug in the sitting room. I let myself go, moving instinctively, no longer feeling like an awkward teenager. Instead it was a wonderful journey of reacquaintance. The shape of her breasts, the softness of her stomach, her scent, the touch of her warm silky skin on mine. Our love-making was tender and sweet and there were just a few more tears as the storm clouds in our hearts finally broke up and moved on.

Twenty-five

I slept heavily but dragged myself out of bed in the morning while I was still groggy. I wanted to have a few minutes with Olivia before she left for work.

"Go back to bed my darling, have a rest." She was ready to leave, hair up, a touch of make-up, very professional.

"Hmm, I might. I just wanted to hold you one more time before you go."

She ran her fingers through my hair. "Have a good day. I won't be late."

"I'm missing you already. Are you sure you are not sick?"

She laughed. "Very tempting ... but I must go."

The sun was shining in through the window as I made my way to the kitchen for breakfast. I noticed the days seemed similar in length to Edinburgh. My attitude towards Stockholm was very different this time. I set about establishing a routine that would support me to acclimatise and find my place in what I saw as my "forever home". I grew excited, day dreaming about my life ahead with Olivia in the beautiful city of Stockholm.

We had talked through the nuts and bolts of me staying the night before. I was only free to stay in the country for three months legally as a tourist. That gave us until the end of May. By that time we would have a better idea how compatible we turned out to be and whether the tiny seedling of our relationship would grow and be fruitful. The idea going forward was for me to apply for a study visa. First, I would study Swedish for a year or two and then hopefully something at university. Most young people in the major cities spoke English well and many people spoke it a little. I wanted to study Swedish though because Sweden was going to be my home. If we were destined to live out our lives together, it would most likely be in Sweden. I didn't want to be the perennial dumb foreigner.

Once a person had been in Sweden for five years they could apply for permanent residency. This would kick in conveniently around the same time that I finished my university studies. That was planning a long way ahead for such a new relationship. We acknowledged that but at least it gave us a sense of security. We knew we could stay together as long as we wanted without fear of me being kicked out of the country.

The other issue was our relationship. Sweden was one of the more progressive countries in the world, having legalised same-sex relationships as early as 1944. The sticky bit was that it had been just over ten years since homosexuality had been declassified as a mental illness. Therefore, same-sex relationships had the dubious value of being legal but not "normal" in many people's eyes. Fortunately, lesbians tended to have an easier time of it than their male counterparts. So, as far as the public were concerned, we were flat mates and that was fine with us. Swedes tend to be a bit reserved with people they don't know anyway, they certainly don't pry or ask awkward questions. Olivia's friends were great, just accepting that we were a *sambo* (couple living together). They seemed less interested in our sex life than they were with the amount of alcohol we could put away on the weekend.

I would come to understand that while the Swedes were reserved, they held pretty relaxed views about sex. That was something I found odd but attractive. Though I wondered whether I could ever replace my own early conditioning. I grew up learning to feel nothing but shame and dishonour about my own adolescent and teenage sexual exploration and expression. Little Swedish girls, I learned, were not raised to harbour guilt about their sexuality. Little boys were not raised to believe they were sexually entitled. What a refreshing change from the double standards of my upbringing in Australia.

I got out and about as much as I could, familiarising myself with my new home city. Stockholm was so beautiful and so safe, the people genuine and friendly once you connected with them. I found it easy to settle into. They value nature, they value peace, order, cleanliness, self-responsibility, self-restraint. I loved it. I ventured out each day walking, sightseeing, learning my way around. I would return in the afternoon to cook dinner, read, meditate and study Swedish, including watching some Swedish TV shows. Just as in Scotland, I focussed in the beginning on the phonology of Swedish speech and began parroting, horribly at first, the sounds made by the people on TV.

Being with Olivia was like having the whole package rolled into one. The click of her key in the door as she arrived home from work became my favourite sound. We would settle down with a glass of wine and talk about our day. We moved effortlessly from serious to funny topics, empathising, encouraging and supporting each other with warmth and an easy intimacy.

Olivia talked passionately about her work in fertility research. She lit up as she explained the breakthroughs and the stories of couples she had helped — both those who had been successful and those who hadn't.

"Do you ever think about having your own kids one day? I mean, is that something you would like?"

She shrugged, sniffed. "Not really. Oscar and I had this crazy idea once that we could co-parent a child. We even went so far as to harvest his sperm. In fact, I still have it frozen at the lab." She laughed when she told me this. "Oscar happily provided as many samples as I wanted, as long as I helped him produce them."

"But no, I don't really think about it. I ... I ...I don't. I think it is better to have a cat."

"But family is so important to you."

"Ja, I have a family, and now I have you, what more do I need?" She leaned over, fluffed up my hair and pushed me playfully in the ribs.

With each day that passed our relationship became more stable and our feelings more sure. We just got along so well, and this confirmed to us our decision to be together. Olivia became my best friend, my confidant and my lover. She was very encouraging and supportive of my efforts to learn about the language and culture but never pushy. It was so different to the blind patriotism and mind control I had experienced with Jordi. I didn't spend much time comparing but still — it was a much better space to be in.

Meanwhile, I worked hard to stay independent. I made a few of my own friends that Olivia welcomed and did some volunteer work at Stockholm's *Stadsmission* (Stockholm City Mission). I found volunteering difficult as it was nearly all in Swedish. I had to dig deep, find enough resilience to get by. It was worth it, I enjoyed the social challenge and mental stimulation. It wasn't as if I contributed directly to helping people anyway, I simply chopped vegetables, washed dishes and sorted donations. Still, I had a purpose and I loved the warm relaxed atmosphere. As the coordinator and the other volunteers became more familiar with me they included me into their circle, involving me in their jokes. They helped me learn a lot and in return I answered all of their questions about Australia.

Between our busy, fulfilling lives and our growing relationship, time flew by and soon May arrived. I applied and received a student visa to study Swedish for the next academic year, starting with a summer semester that would keep me busy. I was excited to be returning to the books and eager to develop my language skills.

On the weekends we would go exploring. We would either take backpacks and a picnic out into the beautiful parks and forests surrounding Stockholm or get lost in the city. We loved finding new and interesting places to have coffee and cake. When it was too wet, or we had had enough adventuring we curled up on the couch and watched videos or had cook ups that would feed us through the next week.

I also experienced my very first Midsommar festival which aligns with the summer solstice in June each year. For many Swedes the festival is more important than Christmas. It is a time when Swedes leave the city in huge numbers to join friends and family at local festivities throughout the land. There is always a bank holiday the following day which works well as many Swedes would be far too hung over to work, anyway. I loved Midsommar. So much food and drink and to top it all off, drunken dancing around a giant penis. Apparently, it goes back to the ancient Scandinavian god Freyr, a phallic deity representing fertility and love. It is also associated with prosperity, abundance, masculinity and ... sex. In preparation Liv showed me how to make our own flower garlands and we took them with us when we joined our friends in their car to head off for the festival.

We arrived at the party in time for a large community lunch of pickled herring and new potatoes. I must admit I found it hard to embrace the Swedish enthusiasm for pickled fish. I would get queasy just getting a whiff of some pungent fish or crustacean but when you pickle it, the smell seems to go into overdrive. The potatoes, flavoured with dill were quite delicious and enough for me. Of course, we washed it all down with copious amounts of beer and *nubbe*, Swedish vodka served icy cold in a shot glass. The general rule stated that you had to drink two beers for every shot of vodka. There was also a special song we had to sing while we raised our shots prior to downing them. It was a recipe for a lot of fun and much drunkenness. Liv and I both pulled out after our second round, neither of us wanted to wipe ourselves out and miss the afternoon's festivities.

After lunch we wandered over to where they were erecting the Maypole. I laughed when I saw it. It was modelled to resemble a giant wooden penis that came up out of the ground. It was hilarious. Some feminists and intellectuals insist the whole penile focus is sexist. They say it is not in keeping with the abundance that comes from Mother Earth, advocating instead a vagina shaped "Mayhole". We didn't care. In fact, given that it was the only penis we played with all year, and we were somewhat inebriated, we danced around it with unrestrained enthusiasm.

We had a great day. We took part in the music and dancing, tug-of-war games, egg and spoon races and had lots of good old-fashioned fun. We rented a cabin for the night. It was just as well as nobody appeared sober enough to drive back. Late in the evening after stuffing ourselves with more food and drink we joined a mixed group for a skinny dip in the local lake. My body had grown used to the freezing cold water by then. Afterwards we dressed and stood around the bonfires for a while, singing, dancing and, yes, a bit more drinking. What an amazing day. The hangover the next day was well and truly worth it as we made our way slowly back to Stockholm. No more singing, no more dancing, just coffee, buns and paracetamol.

Alcohol is not cheap in Sweden, but this doesn't seem to slow their enthusiasm for it much. We had to be a bit more careful with Olivia being the only breadwinner. I could contribute very little financially. This didn't appear to bother her, but it did me a bit. Olivia dealt with it with a simple practicality as she did with most things. She would say I was only there because of her, if not I could be somewhere else, in another country in a good job. Therefore, she accepted some responsibility to support me. Besides, she would explain, who pays the rent is hardly important compared to whether we can be together or not. I had a bit of money invested back home but we both agreed that I shouldn't touch that unless I had an emergency.

After a few months of learning Swedish, I got a casual job at the Tudor Arms. It was Stockholm's original English-style pub. My job gave me a little financial independence as my travel account had drained away to almost nothing. I had never worked in a pub before but Arthur, the manager, was very welcoming and encouraging as were the rest of the staff. They were mostly a young fun group, from all parts of the world, and a lot of us hung out together socially. I took orders, delivered meals and drinks, cleaned up and loved all of it. The place had such a great atmosphere, really fun and high energy. Even when I finished late, after a long shift, I still felt buoyed by the experience. The service standard was high, they played great music, had games nights and themed parties, and the food consisted of some of the best genuine English pub food you will find anywhere.

Most places I have worked I was happy to get away from but there was just something special about the Tudor Arms. The staff looked out for each other, like a real work family and Liv and I would go for dinner or drinks there at times when I wasn't working.

Over the summer we got seriously into skinny dipping. There were so many beautiful waterways in Sweden. I was a bit nervous and self-conscious at first. It was definitely not a socially acceptable pastime in Australia. It was seen as something a bit immoral, more akin to sexual deviancy than naturalism. The freedom and sensuality of swimming naked in a pristine body of water however, was a joy and not to be missed. After the first time my reluctance was already more about diving into the chilly water than about getting my gear off. The combination of the cold water with the release of inhibition that nudity brings was exhilarating. It was one of the two situations that you would see Swedes break out of their natural reserve. They could be seen frolicking around, giggling and just letting it all hang out. The other time they let loose of course was during that great Swedish pastime of getting pissed.

Most Friday nights when we were home, we joined a group of friends for a dinner party either in-house or at a restaurant. Fortunately, like myself, Olivia was generally not a big drinker. We had a drink most days but were both able to have loads of fun and get quite silly without the need to get totally drunk.

Olivia's friends were mostly socially progressive, well-balanced and interesting. They would often speak in English quite naturally. Though at times, especially in the early months I would get left behind during an exciting conversation as they began to talk faster and switch back into Swedish. I didn't mind. Even though I found learning Swedish to be quite difficult, I was studying hard and improving. Also, I added my own friends to the mix. In particular, an English couple, James and Brenda, living and working in Stockholm. There was also a series of English-speaking tourists from Australia, the States, Canada and Britain that I managed to pick up in the street on an almost weekly basis.

To celebrate our first year together in a committed relationship, Olivia took me on a special holiday. We travelled more than 1200 kilometres north of Stockholm to the Ice Hotel in the Lapland province. The area was home to the Sami people or Laplanders as they used to be called. The Ice Hotel sits just over 200 kilometres north of the Arctic Circle. The hotel melts over summer and is rebuilt every November from snow and ice, complete with guest rooms, a large reception hall, ice chandeliers and ice furniture. Meanwhile, away from the well-maintained paths, many people moved around on skis. There were even shopping trolleys in the local village of Jokkmokk that were mounted on skis. We only actually stayed in the hotel for one night as the ambient temperature hovers at a bit below zero which is an unforgettable experience but rather chilly.

During the few hours of sunlight each day we went on a reindeer safari, a dog sled ride and did heaps of cross-country skiing. The other amazing experience we had on that trip was seeing the Aurora Borealis or Northern Lights. Nothing I had ever seen before prepared me for the breathtaking experience of watching the colours dance across the dark sky. It was absolutely spectacular.

Twenty-six

One day Liv received a letter from Oscar, letting her know he and Abbie would be coming to Sweden for a visit in June. I had to confess that I had mixed feelings about their visit, Oscar being Olivia's former lover and all.

"Where will they stay?"

"In Oscar's flat, where Lucas lives. That's where they stayed last time."

"How long are they coming for?"

"He says a few weeks." Liv picked up on my concern. "It's okay my darling, you have nothing to fear." She came forward and took my hands in hers. "Oscar is aware of our relationship. He is like a brother to me. He will realise how happy we are together and that will be all he needs."

"What about Abbie, did you meet her when she was here with him last time?"

"Yes, when they visited on their way to settle in Canada. She was ... nice, a little fussy ... I don't know. I suppose it was not easy for her, knowing my history with Oscar. The important word here is 'history'." She shrugged. "That's all it is." She smiled a seductive smile and ran her hand slowly, tantalisingly down the side of my face. She continued down my neck, over my right breast causing my nipple to become erect. Her hand slid over my stomach and around my waist until she was cupping the inner warmth between my thighs. "Now you and I are making our own history."

She pulled me close, encircling me with her arms and kissed me deeply.

"Oscar who?" I thought, as my desire overtook me, and I began pulling off her shirt.

We had a dinner party for Oscar and Abbie the day after their arrival. Lucas and Issa were coming too. Issa brought her new boyfriend Erik, a slightly dorky young engineer. Lucas rarely seemed to hang onto a girlfriend for long enough for us to meet her. With his ongoing travels across Europe in the truck, Liv and I thought he probably lived like a sailor with a "girl in every port".

Issa and Erik arrived early to help us get set up. Liv and Issa entertained us by telling stories about Oscar and discussing his relationship with Abbie. There was also conjecture whether this trip may bring news that they were getting married and starting a family. There was a lively discussion on this point just as the doorbell sounded at the same time a key turned in the lock.

In walked Lucas with Oscar and Abbie. I had seen pictures of Oscar and Abbie, Oscar and Olivia, but I was still a bit shocked by his dominating physical presence as he ducked to come through the door. He was huge. He was probably six foot five or more. He was broad across the shoulders, had enormous hands, and a large, slightly balding head. One glance at his features was enough to clear any doubt about his Viking heritage. He had a big grin on his face and immediately came forward seeming to swallow Olivia whole as he took her into his arms in an enthusiastic bear hug. I stood, mesmerised for a moment, smiling at their obvious joy in seeing each other. At the same time, I couldn't help but note the look of discomfort on Abbie's face. I quickly snapped back to my senses and moved forward to greet Lucas.

"G'day Lucas." I gave him a warm hug.

"Hi Laura, good to see you, how's everything?"

I loved Lucas. We saw him regularly. He was warm and funny, but with a certain sense of melancholy that seemed to follow him through life like a second shadow. Liv and I both wanted to help him but Lucas wasn't into the idea of digging up old bones as he put it. He closed down any attempt made to talk about his feelings or his past traumas.

Liv, still with Oscar's arm around her, brought him over to meet me. "Hello Laura, I've heard so much about you." I moved to extend my hand, but he slipped past it and wrapped me in a full body hug.

"Hello Oscar." My words were muffled, my face buried in his chest. Eventually I was able to step back, a little breathless and flustered after being surrounded by such a mountain of masculinity. "It's so nice to finally meet you."

Olivia joined me, slipping her arm about my waist as Oscar twirled around and motioned to Abbie to join us. Taking her hand, he announced, "And this is Abbie, my wife. We got married two weeks ago, just a quiet little wedding. It was so much easier than trying to coordinate all the people from here and The Philippines and everywhere else. So, we are actually on our honeymoon."

Exclamations of surprise and delight rose around the room.

Petite, pretty, coffee-skinned Abbie stepped forward and smiled a little uncomfortably at us. Olivia motioned Issa and Erik forward to complete the greetings, introductions and felicitations. Issa was swallowed up in her own big bear hug.

We had added an adjustable dining table and chairs that we could set up in the small sitting room but a party of seven still overflowed it. Nobody seemed to care as we juggled food and drinks amid much laughter and storytelling. I wanted to find out about Oscar and Abbie's adventures in Australia and Oscar appeared more than happy to share his experience. He seemed keen to get to know me, to satisfy himself that Olivia was in good hands. I was equally eager to learn about the man who had been so important in her life. Fortunately, we hit it off well, he had so much energy and life about him, like an oversized puppy.

I am not sure whether it was because he was larger than life that Abbie seemed so small. I don't mean in stature, which she was, but in personality. Liv tried to engage her in conversation a few times as did the rest of us. Her answers though tended to be short, shy, with no return questions or comments that would keep the discussion going. She drank little and picked at her food. It didn't help, of course, that she had no Swedish. Most of the discussion was in English but, as usual, when they got excited, they reverted to Swedish.

I could pretty much understand most things they were saying. The three siblings and Oscar however, had known each other for so many years. They had an intimacy and a rich history of common references that no command of language could overcome. That point didn't bother me, in fact at times I just sat back and relished being witness to the spirited laughter and quick-witted banter going on around the table. Erik and I rolled our eyes at each other and grinned as they dived into yet another "remember when ..." story.

It was late when we called taxis to take them all home. They had insisted on helping to clean up. As a result, when we finally closed the door behind them, we only had to put the coffee cups in the sink and then head for bed.

"Oh, what a night, did you enjoy it?"

"Oh, Liv, that was great. Oscar is amazing. I don't understand why you two are not together. You love each other, you are great together. I'm not saying I am threatened by it, I'm just curious."

"I do love him, very much and, as I said, we tried to make it work as a couple but ... we are like family. It felt almost like having sex with my brother."

"Like having sex with your very big brother, I imagine."

Liv snorted with laughter and nodded as her eyes widened. "Yes, that is true, he is a big boy — all over."

"My God, what about Abbie then, she's so little compared to him?"

"Ja, I have thought this before." She winced as she thought about it again before moving on. "I don't know about Abbie, she didn't seem happy, or relaxed. I am not sure that it is a good match. Oscar has so much energy it is easy to be squeezed out, to be smothered by it." She put her arm over me as we lay in bed and kissed me on the cheek. "I was so happy to share the night with you, to watch you talking and laughing with everyone. Thank you for being so warm and friendly. I could tell that Oscar liked you very much, everyone likes you."

"Ah, but I only have eyes for you. When everyone goes home, I get to stay. I'm the one who gets to curl up in bed with you. It was a fun night and it was great to see you so animated and to listen to the old stories."

"Hmm, one day we will have dinner with your family and I will find out some of your old stories. Maybe even meet an old boyfriend or two?"

"I doubt it. My old boyfriends are not nearly so charming or delightful as Oscar, but yeah, some day we will make a trip to Australia to visit the family. I think my family stories are a lot more embarrassing than yours."

We saw a lot of Oscar and Abbie over the next few weeks and each encounter reinforced my early impressions. Oscar was lovely, Abbie was somewhat constrained. I noticed how she would quietly complain to Oscar, encourage him to leave early. She often seemed to have a headache or be slightly unwell. He would be crestfallen, give their apologies and they would leave.

Towards the end of the visit the four of us were out for dinner one night. She pulled the "I've got a headache, it's time to go home," while we were still enjoying our main meals. It was the first time I had seen Oscar's easy-going nature fray at the edges.

"Come on Abbie, we are in the middle of dinner."

Her mouth was sulky, pouty, her eyes downcast and she gave just a faint shake of her head as she fiddled with her napkin in her lap.

"Abbie, take some tablets if you need to, please. This is our last meal together."

Her mouth turned down even further and she sat there, staring at her lap. We all tried to re-engage her, bring her back into the conversation but the harder we tried the smaller and sadder she seemed to become. They left the restaurant early, again. Oscar was obviously disappointed, but trying to act as if it was no big deal.

A couple of days later we said our goodbyes to them both, promising to come visit them in Canada as soon as we could. Oscar gave me one of his big bear hugs, adding quietly "It has been good to meet you Laura. I am so pleased to see Olivia so well and happy. Please take care of her and call me anytime if there is anything I can do to help you."

Then it was Olivia's turn. I couldn't pick up everything that he said, but I heard him whisper in Swedish, "I love you Liv."

We gave Abbie a hug and helped them into the taxi that would take them to the airport.

We were both sad to see Oscar leave and worried about their relationship. We had witnessed Abbie sucking so much joy out of him. Once more I counted my blessings that I had found someone I could have such a great relationship with.

Life without Oscar seemed quiet and small for a while. I would catch Liv deep in thought, staring out the window or off into the distance as her coffee grew cold. I knew she had things she had to process and that it wasn't about us. I tried hard to give her the space she needed and yet be there for her when she needed me.

I came up to her one day as she stood by the window and noticed tear tracks on her face. "Oh Livvy, what's the matter, sweetheart?"

She turned to me, tears filling those beautiful dark eyes. "I miss him." Her voice was husky with emotion. "And he is not happy but there is nothing I can do." The tears fell down her face and she turned and buried her head in my shoulder.

I held her gently and stroked her hair. There was no need to explain who "he" was. "Oh sweetie, it's true, there's nothing you can do. You know, we each have our own story to live. He is a grown man and he is where he needs to be. Okay? You just have to let him live with the choices he has made. He'll be alright. Who knows what will happen in the future? Maybe they will grow together, maybe not ... he wouldn't want you to be sad for him. You have your own life to lead."

"Ja, this is true. And I am so sorry, I have not been much fun lately. He has been on my mind, I have been worrying about him. I feel responsible somehow."

"You are not responsible for his choices. There is nothing for you to be guilty about. You are not children anymore. You understand?"

She nodded.

"He has lessons he needs to learn, just like I did in my bad relationships in the past." I smiled at her and smoothed the frown line that was forming between her brows. "It wouldn't have helped me if someone had taken me out of a shitty relationship before I was ready. I had to stay and wallow in it until I had learnt all that I needed to learn. And I did. Look at me. I am proof that we can learn and grow out of our bad choices. Oh, how wonderful I am now." I smiled and did a silly little dance before her, trying to make her smile.

"Hmm, you are."

"Oscar is no different. He will stay until he has learnt what he needs to with Abbie. Perhaps they will learn, make it work somehow, perhaps not, but for now they are where they need to be. You'll grow old quickly if you try to be responsible for other people's lives, my dear. I will still love you when you are old and grey but I don't want it to happen too quickly, please."

She smiled at me. "Thank you. What you say makes sense. I have been carrying a burden that is not mine to carry. You are right, he is where he should be."

"And we are where we need to be, except right now I need to feel your beautiful body, pressed against mine." I took her into my arms in a tango position, raising her knee high and bending her backwards as I kissed her. Together we laughed and danced badly around the kitchen bench.

The summer flew by and it was soon time for me to return to study. I had elected to learn Swedish for a second year to prepare myself for university. I was hoping to get into Psychology and would therefore need to be able to be fluent enough to read academic papers and write essays.

Later that year we attended Olivia's graduation where she received her doctorate. She was so dedicated and the research she was undertaking in fertility and reproduction was getting attention. She had attended a few international conferences across Europe but now she was being asked to present her own research papers. I was so proud of her. She got an invitation shortly after graduation to talk about her doctoral studies at an international conference in Kingston Jamaica, in the Caribbean. We were so excited, jumping up and down and squealing like excited school kids when Liv opened the envelope.

Olivia's flights and accommodation were fully paid for, so it cost us little for me to tag along. The conference went for four days and we took another week to have a look around, soak up some sun and max out on everything reggae. Each night we went out to the bars and cafes. We danced, drank and revelled in the rich colourful street culture, colonial architecture, and warm relaxed company of the locals. We took a day trip out to the magnificent national park and had a hot sweaty hike through the pristine rainforest.

Another day we visited the Bob Marley Museum. Bob Marley had died of cancer in 1980 on a stopover in Miami, on his way home. His final words to his son, Ziggy, who accompanied him, being "Money can't buy life". That impressed us both so much that later that night after a few drinks and a little weed we determined to go and get it tattooed on our forearms. Matching tattoos, right then and there. Neither of us had a tattoo and we had never really talked about getting a tattoo before but to our slightly addled brains it seemed like a great idea. Fortunately, the finished product was very professional, very well crafted even if we both woke up a little remorseful and embarrassed about it in the morning. We arrived home with a bag full of reggae albums, Rastafari posters and with skin as brown as berries.

A while later we celebrated the end of my Swedish language studies and my acceptance into Stockholm University to study Psychology, starting in the Autumn. I was pretty nervous about my standard of Swedish. I didn't know how well it would serve me in a tertiary environment but I wasn't going to let that stop me from trying.

Twenty-seven

I had been in Stockholm for nearly three years when I received a call from home as I came out from the shower one morning. It was my brother Jack. We had exchanged letters back and forth during the four years or so since I had left Australia. I had posted photos of my adventures and presence at major tourist attractions. Occasionally I picked up the phone and called my parents or Jack, usually for Christmas and birthdays and we even sent audio-letters on cassette tapes.

Despite this, for some time, a little voice had been telling me it was time to go home, time to visit my family. My life was full though and I had continued to push the idea away. They were aware I was living in Stockholm. "Why Stockholm?" my mother asked at first and repeated in one form or another almost every time we spoke. "What are you doing in Sweden that's so important you can't come home?" There was always a strong undertow with Mum. Every time she managed to make me feel guilty for being away so long, always attempted to sway me to return home. It was as if she believed my life were in limbo, like I had gone on a holiday and not come back. I suppose in a way that was true. The real issue was she never accepted that I actually was getting on with my life.

Jack was a lot more philosophical. He really didn't give a rat's arse (his words) where I lived as long as I was happy and safe. He was busy in his own life, still travelling the length and breadth of Australia with a shearing team. His body was now starting to show signs of wear though and he was looking for a way out. He also had a long-term partner now, Nancy. I hadn't met her yet.

"Halla?" I heard the long distance click and waited.

"Lozzie, is that you?"

"Grub? G'day, what's happening?" I had to speak up, there was noise, voices in the background.

"Umm ... ah ... it's about Dad."

"Dad? What's going on?"

"Er, umm ... he had a heart attack, died ... he's dead Lozzie."

"What? When? How?"

"He's been a bit crook lately, nothing specific ... a bit fluey or something. Anyway, he was driving to the Doctor's this morning ... they reckon he had a massive heart attack while he was driving."

"Bloody hell. Where was he?"

"He was going up Skipton St, you know, near the shopping centre. He veered off the road, pranged into a parked truck."

"Shit!"

"Yeah, a guy in a car behind him reckons he was all over the place before he crashed."

"Bloody hell. Did anyone else get hurt?"

"Na, no one else, he wasn't travelling very fast. They reckon he musta fell forward and hit the horn so there were people on the scene pretty quick."

"Okay?"

"Yeah, they couldn't get him out of the car though, the front got smashed, but a nurse climbed in the back, checked him out ... he was gone."

"Did someone call the ambulance?"

"Yeah, the ambos arrived, pronounced him dead, then the rescue guys showed up and cut him out."

"Wow." That was all I found to say as I mulled over the story in my mind. I looked about me, noticing the dishes I needed to do, the half full bottle of Rosé on the side bench, the shopping list on the fridge. These tiny unimportant details made up my normal reality, but suddenly reality had shifted.

"So, where are you?"

"Well, I was up at Hay but I've left the team and come back to Mum."

"And, how is she? How did she find out?"

"She's pretty shook up ... Someone, I don't know, maybe the nurse, I'm not sure, grabbed his wallet, found his address."

"Okay."

"The cops went around to tell Mum." He paused and I heard him speaking to someone else. "What? Yeah, hang on, just a minute. Um, anyway I've called the family and, you know, everyone I can think of. There's a few people here at Mum's. We waited to call till we reckoned you'd be up. Couldn't see any reason to get you outa bed. There's nothing you can do."

"Ohhh shit, I suppose I'll have to come home for the funeral and all. Any idea when that might be?"

"Well, apparently they have to do an autopsy, you know, to prove it wasn't foul play or anything. So ... the funeral probably won't be for ... for a week or so they reckon. The body's at the funeral home. It has to go off wherever then come back."

"Ok, well, umm, thanks Grub. Are you staying at Mum's? Is she there?"

"Yeah, Nancy's here too. We'll stay with her tonight and see how it goes. Here's Mum now."

"Ok, thanks. I'll call tomorrow and tell you what I'm doing. See ya."

"See ya, Lozzie." Then I heard the phone being handed over.

"Hello love."

"Hi Ma. What a terrible thing to happen. How are you?"

"Yes, it's bloody awful, it is. I just don't know what to ..." Her voice trailed off. "I was here, doing some washing, making an apple pie for dinner when the doorbell rang. I rinsed my hands and went to open the front door. I thought it was just old Bill or Lorraine from next door, and there was the police." Her voice sounded thin and tired. I had to strain to hear her. "Jeez Laura, it gave me a fright. I don't reckon there's ever a good time to open the door and find the police there."

"What did they say, Mum?"

"They asked who I was and when I told them they asked if they could come in. They were very good, it's a shitty job. When they left, I shut the door and just stood there looking at the t-towel in me hands ... like it was gonna to talk to me. I just can't seem to make sense of it at all."

"It's okay Mum, you don't have to process it all now. You only need to get by, make it through one moment at a time. Have Grub and Nancy been good?"

"Yeah, Nancy's alright, she's been helping in the kitchen, making tea. She even made a batch of scones for everyone, not quite as good as our scones but they came out alright. There've been quite a few people coming and going through the day. I suppose they want to show they care but I wish they would all piss off and let me have some peace. When are you coming home love, you are coming now aren't you?"

"I don't know what I'm doing yet Mum. Shit, I need some time to get my head around it all. I said to Grub I would call you tomorrow after I sort out what I'm doing, call the airlines, etc."

"That's good, it's time you came home, you've been away too long, Laura."

I avoided responding to her attempt to influence me. "I'll talk to you tomorrow Ma. I love you."

"Thanks love, I know, I love you too. I just wanna see you, I miss you." Her voice filled with emotion, I could tell she was starting to cry.

My own emotions responded, my voice threatening to crack. "Yep, I miss you too Ma. Talk to you tomorrow."

"Ok, night love, or morning or whatever it is."

"Goodnight, I hope you get some sleep."

I hung the phone up and looked about me. "So ... so, the bastard's dead." Olivia was at work. I would need to call her but first I needed time to go over it in my own head.

I made coffee, picked up Smulan from where she lay on our bed and settled down on the couch.

"My father died, puss. Apparently, he had a heart attack when he was driving the car. He's dead. The bastard's dead." Smulan purred and rubbed her face on me. I stared vacantly across the room as I reflected on the news and what it meant to me. My world had changed, but how? I felt numb and disorientated, in shock, yet experienced no surge of grief, no tears, only a deep sadness. I had always hoped that, as my father aged, he would mellow. I imagined we would eventually have a good relationship, that he would one day be my Dad.

Tears came to my eyes as I acknowledged the secret wishes I had held for our future, where we talked easily, honestly, loved, supported and respected each other. I had seen a time when he would be filled with remorse for all the awful things that he had done. For many years I wanted that so badly. I thought I needed it to help me heal. But none of that would ever happen now. He was gone. What a waste. I hadn't realised how much I craved that closeness with him. I had tried so many times. I had looked past his intimidation, ready anger and lies, shrugged off the hurt, shoved down the fear. I had always opened my door to him, hoping, one day that our meaningless superficial chit chat would get real and we would heal our relationship. I allowed myself to cry quietly, soft sad tears.

I rang Olivia mid-morning when I figured she might be having a break. I didn't normally call her at work, she was usually engrossed in whatever she was doing.

"Hey Livvy, how's your day?"

"Laura, hello darling, my day is good, what about you? Is everything okay?"

"Umm, not really. Grub rang. My father had a heart attack and died early today."

"Oh, no, I'm so sorry, are you okay? Do you want me to come home?"

"No, no thanks, there's no need to come home, I'm really okay. It's ... well, the funeral will be in about a week. I want to be there. So, we need to work out whether I go or we go and all that stuff. I just rang, you know, wanted to tell you so you can have a think about it."

"I will fit in with whatever you want. There is nothing happening here that is urgent or that I can't hand over or postpone for a week or two. Just think what is best for you. I love you, I'll give you a big hug when I get home, I won't be late. Will you be okay?"

"Yep, I'm alright. Thanks, I'll see you when you get here."

I put the phone down, sat back in the couch and realised that this would be bigger than I imagined. It wasn't as simple as Olivia and I just rocking up to my folks' house, to my father's funeral. The truth was, as comfortable as I was in my relationship and life with Olivia, I hadn't gone into any detail about it all with my family.

They were aware we shared a flat. They saw us in photos together but while they may have wondered what was going on, I never discussed our relationship. It hadn't seemed important. It was much easier to put it on the shelf and forget about it. So, it appeared the biggest question was not whether Olivia would come with me but, if she did, what would we tell people?

We talked it over that night and agreed we would both go. It was a good opportunity to introduce Olivia into the family. I would explain our relationship to my mother and Jack and everybody else could think what they liked. I rang my parents' house, or should I say, my mother's house, after booking airfares the next morning. Jack answered the phone.

"Hello."

"Hi Grub."

"Lozzie, how are ya doin?"

"Yeah, pretty good. How's everything there?"

"Yeah, not bad. We've got rough dates. Funeral will probably be next Tuesday. Are you going to make it?"

"Yeah, Liv and I are both coming. We fly out on Friday night, arriving mid-morning Sunday, Malaysia Airlines via KL. Would you be able to organise a pick up for us please?"

"Yeah, she'll be right, I'll come and pick you up meself."

"Thanks, umm ... I ... I wanted to let you know, we haven't really talked about this before. Liv and I, you know ... we're a couple, not just friends ... you get what I mean?" I flushed as I said it but felt relieved to have put the news out there finally.

"Yeah, we sorta guessed that Lozzie. Even Mum. She can't quite work out what to make of it but at the end of the day, it's your life. As long as you're happy and healthy, who gives a shit, right?"

I smiled to myself and thought, that's the brother I know and love.

"Thanks Grub, your support always means a lot to me and it's nice to have it out in the open. I'm sure you'll like Liv, Mum will too if she gives her a chance."

"I'm sure we will, but don't underestimate your mother, it's been a bit of a stretch but she's getting there."

I gave him our flight details and we said our goodbyes.

By the time we reached the departure lounge at the airport on Friday night I felt excited about having a trip home. I was really looking forward to introducing Olivia into the family. I was also keen to meet Nancy, to catch up on some local gossip, and generally soak up all things Aussie.

Twenty-eight

The first introduction I made to Liv was from the sky. I was standing near the toilet at the rear of the plane looking out of a window at the arid Australian outback. I loved the contours, colours, textures and patterns the red centre presented from above. It was made even more splendid by the early morning sunshine. As I looked further ahead, I spied one of Australia's greatest icons, Uluru (Ayres Rock) sitting among the red desert landscape way below. I raced back to my seat and tapped Liv on the shoulder as she sat dozing.

"Livvy, Livvy, quick, you gotta come see this, Uluru, out the window!"

"What? What, okay." She excavated herself from under the pile of rugs, books and headphones and joined me in the narrow passage. I held her hand and pulled her along to the window.

"Look, there it is. Just one big red rock."

"Oh wow. It must be huge."

"Yep. We did a project on it in Geography at school. I still remember. It's nearly 350 metres high, above ground but it's like an iceberg, there's something like two kilometres of rock underneath, apparently. We both stood and watched as it moved from the front of the window to the back and then out of sight.

It was great to spot Jack's face among the crowd as we came out into the arrivals hall. Jack and I came together in a big hug amid laughter, some head rubbing and happy sibling banter. I stepped back and we studied each other a moment.

"You're looking good Lozzie."

"You too Grub." I grinned at him but inside I was a bit shocked to observe how he had aged. "And this, of course, is Olivia. Olivia, Jack, Jack, Olivia."

Olivia stepped forward and smiled at Jack, a little unsure how to greet him. Jack grinned at her, reached out and drew her in, giving her a big hug. "Let's not be formal. If you're gonna be a part of the family, you're gonna get a hug and a head rub like everyone else." He returned her to her own space. "Nice to finally meet you 'Livia."

"And you too Jack." She grinned from Jack to me in a teasing manner. "Now I know what you would look like as a man."

We all laughed and headed for the car.

Nancy stayed with Mum to help her while Jack picked us up and they kept Sunday lunch on hold for us. After hugs and introductions on arrival we sat down to a table laden with roast lamb and all the trimmings. It was delicious, but we all made room for homemade apricot pie with cream and ice-cream afterwards. We washed it all down with a couple of bottles of Mum's favourite Lambrusco. All up it was a combination almost guaranteed to lead to a long siesta. I fought the urge, deciding to soldier on through the jetlag, stay up through the afternoon and fall into bed after dinner.

Jack and Nancy left to go to their place, about half an hour away and Olivia and I took over the guest room. Liv had been working long hours to get ahead the last few days before leaving. As a result, she was almost dizzy with fatigue so she gave in to the need for a nap, allowing me to have some time with Mum. The house became still and quiet and Mum and I took our cups of tea out onto the back verandah. I was anxious to get to the bottom of how she was really doing. My parents had a rather rocky relationship but stayed together through it all. Mum had a pretty hard and isolated life on the farm. She was more akin to a labourer than a housewife. Through it all she put up with intermittent rages and emotional abuse due to my father's mental illness. They only recently sold the farm and retired into town. Mum's life improved in many ways as a result of the move, she made friends with the neighbours, took up golf and started volunteering one day a week at St Vinnies charity shop.

"How are you doing Mum?"

"Oh love, I don't know." She sipped her tea and gathered her thoughts. "After everything we have been through, all the shit in our life. How can he just keel over at this point when all the hard work is done? I don't understand, I just don't. How he could do that to me, not now, after all we've been through. The bastard." There was real venom in her voice as she spat these last words out.

"You know we have a new caravan in the shed. I've been busy stocking it up with everything we need so we can finally take that long trip up north. We were going in May ... not coming back for at least six months, just cruise on up the road, stopping wherever we wanted. No stress, no drama. What am I supposed to do now?" Her chin trembled, and tears came. Mum was never any good at showing her feelings, having learnt early to regard tears as a sign of weakness. I think she had been bottling them up for so long she was afraid of what might come out if she really took the lid off. I was aware that hiding below the surface was a dark oily pond of bitterness, anger, and frustration at the way her life had gone.

I put my arm around her shoulders. "Oh Mum, it'll work out. There will be good times ahead, you'll see."

"Oh Laura, I don't know. What did I go through all those years for? This is supposed to be the start of ... of the good times, our retirement. I worked bloody long and hard ... put up with so much crap for so many years. All so we could have a better life at the end. It's supposed to be the reward for all those years ... all that shit." She stopped and blew her nose.

I had heard the story before. I rubbed her back and stayed quiet, listening.

"We didn't enjoy life, not really. We didn't ... buy nice things, splurge on anything, did all the hard work ourselves so we didn't have to pay anybody. You know, you and Jack were there. You kids did more work on that bloody farm than any kid your age should. We worked hard, didn't we?

"Yep, we did."

"We saved every bloody penny for the day we deserved to stop work and start enjoying life. Why? It's all gone now. Everything we dreamed of, everything we planned." She looked down at the crumpled handkerchief she was wringing in her worn arthritic hands. "We had plans to go overseas, to New Zealand, to England, come and visit you, maybe take a cruise. The bastard! How could he do this to me now? It's cruel, just bloody cruel." Her face flushed and her body trembled from top to bottom in her effort to contain her emotions. Her shoulders started to shake and tears rolled down her face but she didn't make a sound. There would be no gut-wrenching sobs, no screaming rage, no broken-hearted moans, just tears, silent tears.

"Oh Mum, you can still do those things, in the future, when you get passed this a bit ... and you will. You can still go places. You don't have to do it on your own, there's lots of ways —"

"No, I can't." Her voice was muffled in her handkerchief but anger made it strong. "I'm not going with a bunch of strangers. It's not the same."

Tears ran down my own face as I held her trembling body, noticed how tight, how tense she was, how frail she had suddenly grown. I had no more words of encouragement. My mother was filled to the brim with pain, the pain of a lifetime. I started to become afraid for her, for the longer-term effects of this powerful build-up of grief and trauma that she kept locked within. There was nothing I could say or do that would reduce her pain, that would make a difference.

Liv seemed only half conscious as we sat down to cold meat and salad for dinner then excused herself and headed back to bed. I think Mum was a bit disappointed, she was eager to get to know her.

"Sorry about Liv. She's been working crazy hours, so she could get ahead. She really wanted to come."

"Does she normally talk?"

"Yeah Ma, she does. Just give her a chance to catch up, you'll see."

We made another cup of tea and took it out onto the verandah. We talked through the funeral arrangements and other details, and then I dared raise a delicate matter.

"Mum, I want to see him. I want to see the body."

"You what?" She turned to me with a quizzical expression.

"I wasn't there when he died and I didn't see him for nearly four years, I need to see the body."

"Okay." I watched as she thought it through. "I'll come with you, not sure about Jack, we'll have to ask him."

"Yep, that's okay. I won't bother him again today. I'll call him in the morning and have a chat, work out if we can organise a time to go together if he wants to."

I rinsed the cups, said goodnight and gave Mum another hug before tiptoeing into our room, undressing and sliding into bed. Liv was fast asleep. As my body settled I reflected on what Mum had told me. It was interesting to witness her grief, to hear what she grieved for. I found it ironic, her grieving for her lost future, a better life with her husband, as if, sailing off in the caravan in the sunset was the reward for past suffering, the happily ever after at the end of a long painful journey. The overarching paradigm of their existence had been that everything should be sacrificed for the farm. Pleasure and leisure were earned by enduring all the shit life threw at you and lots of hard work. Happiness was something you *may* eventually get *if* you deserved it. Retirement was that wonderful place you inhabited between the long years of hell at work and the nothingness of death. How depressing. I felt so relieved and happy that I had managed to extract myself from that way of thinking.

As I glanced sideways at Liv, I experienced an overwhelming gratitude at the wonderful life I had. I became so aware in that moment that if I had chosen to ignore my feelings or postpone my happiness I would not have that precious woman beside me. I was so proud to be with her, so proud of the quality of our relationship. My heart swelled, tears filled my eyes. I stared up at the ceiling wondering what I had done to deserve such goodness in my life, such blessings. I thanked my inner self for having the courage to plunge forward into the unknown that had become my whole life.

Mum and Jack and I drove together the following afternoon to view the body. A woman led us into a small room at the funeral parlour. The casket sat at the other end of the room on a stand and we walked up to it as one. There, in the coffin lay my father's body, dressed in his best suit. For a moment I allowed myself to think about the massive wound where they had sawn through his chest as part of the autopsy, now conveniently hidden from sight by the crisp, white, dress-shirt and tie. Nice thought. I peered into his face for the first time in years. Visions of the wild angry eyes, the mouth spitting angry words passed through my mind. My stomach tightened. Yet there was no tension between his brows as I looked down on him in that moment. Instead, he appeared strangely peaceful, eyes closed, hands resting one on the other on his chest. I felt oddly calm, but not detached as we stood looking down on him for a few minutes in silence. I reached out and put my hand on top of his. I heard Mum gasp, saw in the corner of my eye how she grabbed Jack's arm and together they quickly stepped backwards. His skin felt cold, tight and unyielding. I withdrew my hand quietly and took a small slow step backwards, my eyes still on the body.

"Well, wherever he is, he's not here. I'm done. How about you guys?"

They both nodded mutely and we turned and walked out. I'm not sure what I had been expecting, I just knew I had to see him. Somehow it made a difference, it allowed me to understand at a deep level that he was gone.

I had a few discussions with Mum about what I was doing and where my life was heading. She appeared to understand my choices better each time. Mum and Olivia had a few chats of their own and I loved watching them get to know each other better with each day. They gained a genuine respect and fondness for each other. Mum seemed to delight in Olivia's sense of humour and warmth. From Olivia's side, she enjoyed being among family and having a Mum around. She had been so young when she had lost her own mother, something that encouraged my Mum to draw her nearer.

The two points of sadness that darkened Mum's brow were that I was living so far away and my relationship would be childless. Jack and Nancy would surely have kids sooner or later but that wasn't quite the same. There seems to be often a special bond between mothers and daughters that bring them closer together in the business of child rearing. I pretended like it was no big deal but inside I was also carrying sadness that I would never be able to have children.

I confess, I really enjoyed the funeral. It was a big turnout. The church packed out and there were people standing outside. I greeted so many people I hadn't seen in years. Uncles, aunts, cousins, friends, neighbours, some former golfing and tennis team members of my father's. After the service we followed the hearse out to the cemetery. A hot northerly dominated the atmosphere leaving us all red-faced and sweaty. By the end of the graveside service we were blinking at each other through squinting eyes to avoid the grit flying through the air.

After that it was time for the highlight of the day — afternoon tea put on by the Country Women's Association. Those women are legends. The trestle tables in the church hall sagged under the weight of their efforts. There were towering cream-filled sponges, with passionfruit icing and strawberries, delicate cream kisses, chocolate eclairs, sausage rolls and of course lovely soft white scones buried under loads of strawberry jam and whipped cream. I think I had at least one of everything, discretely, while unwinding with a few glasses of wine. I caught up with so many old faces, chatting and laughing my way around the room. Olivia spent most of the time with Nancy, they both seemed a bit reluctant to get out there and mix with my weird rellies. Occasionally I grabbed her to introduce her to people.

A few people asked me about her, who is she? I introduced her as my friend, or my girlfriend, from Sweden, depending who I was talking to. We didn't sensor ourselves, we were still holding hands and whispering together intimately. It seemed, on the day that the whole relationship issue was really unimportant. Maybe funerals encourage us all to get our priorities right and just accept the good in humanity, whatever form it takes.

There really weren't a lot of tears on the day. Mum shed a few here and there, she struggled, but everyone took good care of her. I smiled as I spied her talking to Ralph, our old neighbour. Ralph was a widower and I think at one-point in the past Mum might have had a bit of a soft spot for him. It was an innocent thing that would have both lightened her experience of living for a while and also caused her increased suffering. I wondered what might have happened if Ralph had been a more passionate man.

The rest of our stay in Australia flew by very quickly. We borrowed Jack's wagon and drove to Melbourne and along the Great Ocean Road for a few days before coming back to Mum's.

There were bear hugs and tear smudged faces all round when it came to say goodbye. I felt pretty awful and guilty about leaving Mum. As I held her tight, I told her I would ring more often, send more letters and photos and I would be thinking of her every day. We promised to visit again soon. We made Mum promise to think about visiting us.

As we settled onto the plane that would take us home to Sweden I turned to Olivia, brought her hand to my lips and kissed it. "Thank you. This hasn't been an easy time for any of us but you were wonderful, just there, in the background. I really appreciated having you with me. And because you are so amazing Mum is much more comfortable with our relationship than she might otherwise have been. I sorta hope she does come and stay with us though I'm not sure where she would sleep."

"That's fine. I just wanted to be there for you. Your Mum is very sweet. She has so much sadness. She misses you so much, even more now. I hope she comes to stay too." She grinned cheekily. "I'd be happy to have her cook for us for a while."

We both laughed, then I closed my eyes and gave myself time to reflect on everything that had happened. I was pleased we had made the trip, glad that Olivia had finally met my family, happy I was there to see my father's body go into the ground. My eyes filled with tears as I replayed our farewell, Mum trying to be brave as she waved us goodbye. Despite our invite to come stay and our promise to return soon I could tell that from where she stood life looked bleak at that point. That bothered me. For her sake I hoped Jack and Nancy would have kids soon. I desperately wanted, in that moment to give her grandkids.

We arrived home from the airport on a beautiful clear Wintery morning. As we paid the taxi and lugged our bags up to the apartment, we were both looking forward to getting back to our day-to-day lives. The winter was about over and we wanted to make the most of the months of good weather that would soon be upon us. Our neighbour across the hall had been baby-sitting Smulan and I started unpacking as Liv went next door to collect the cat and our mail. Coming back inside Liv put Smulan down and began sorting through the mail. Suddenly she let out an excited shriek.

"Laura, Laura, quick, quick, look at this!"

I dropped the toilet bag down on the bed and raced out to the kitchen. Liv was holding up a letter, reading intently. "What is it?"

"I've been asked to submit my research for a conference in Japan in July next year!"

"Oh my God, *konichiwa*! That's so exciting! Let me see." I read through the letter quickly. "They are certainly getting organised well in advance. That's the Japanese for you. I'm definitely coming too!"

"Of course, you are. I've always wanted to go to Japan. I have a few months to get my work organised and confirm. We will have to do some research, plan our trip."

"Yeah, break out the green tea. We've got heaps of time. Maybe we can learn a little Japanese."

"It's in a place called Sapporo, Hokkaido, I have no idea where that is but I'm sure we can get there."

I put my hand on her shoulder. "Well, I'm sure you can find your way and I'll just hang on tight to your shirt tail."

Twenty-nine

Our trip to Australia had brought us even closer together but there remained one large issue that we disagreed on, sometimes arguing heatedly. I wanted children, Olivia didn't. Before going to Australia, I had attempted to talk it through with her a number of times. For some reason she always stonewalled me or turned it into an argument about something else. I was sure there were ways we could make it happen and Liv loved family. It baffled me why she would become so defensive when I raised the topic. I didn't get it; I didn't understand. I needed to try again to discuss it with her.

I chose an evening, a week or so after we had settled back into our old routine. The dishes were done and we were sitting, watching some corny TV show with a cuppa.

"Liv, there's something I need to talk to you about."

"Hmm, what is it?"

"I need to talk about having a family, I want to have kids, I —"

"But we've talked about this. It's not possible, it's not happening. Don't we have a good life?"

"Yeah, of course we do. I love our life, it's just —"

"It's enough Laura, let it be enough, please."

"But I don't understand. You love family, why not raise our own?"

"No, Laura, stop pushing me. I've told you —"

"You haven't really told me anything! That's the problem. You just keep saying no. I don't understand." I was on my feet now, my emotions rising. "I've seen you, when we've been around kids, you watch them, you smile, you appear sad, but you never seem disinterested. You love kids, I can tell, so why not?"

"Just no, Laura, just leave it, please." She folded her arms and wouldn't look at me.

"No Liv, I can't just keep leaving it, not any more. Your attitude doesn't make sense. What the hell are you not telling me? I deserve to know."

Her face grew dark and broody and she shook her head as she stared at the floor.

We undressed and got into bed that night not talking to each other. As I lay there staring at the ceiling, I felt so torn between my love for Olivia and my growing desire to have children. I really wanted a child, but did I want it so much that I would destroy our relationship to get it?

I looked ahead at our lives together. I imagined us with a baby, Liv making faces, laughing, spooning food into a cheeky little face. I delighted to see our toddler running in the park, playing in the fallen leaves. Saw all three of us cosied up in bed reading story books. Dancing in the living room, picnics in the forest, mending scraped knees, exploring the world through new eyes. Little boots, little socks, little overalls. I wanted it so badly.

I got up the next day after Liv had gone to work. I travelled out to Uni, did my classes, chatted with friends, worked my shift at the Tudor Arms but my heart wasn't in any of it. I was overflowing with a deep sadness. I arrived home late. Olivia was already asleep. Lying in bed beside her I felt alone for the first time in ages.

She was already up when I awoke the next morning. I yawned and stretched and she came in to me.

"Good morning sweetheart, how are you?" She was chirpy. It was her way of gliding past difficulties, but this time, I didn't want to play that game.

"I'm fine, how are you?" My tone was flat.

"Well, the sun is shining, the birds are singing, and I thought it might be fun to wander down to the market. What do you think?"

I shrugged. "You can go, I'm not really in the mood." I got up went to the bathroom, shut the door.

When I came out she had my coffee ready.

"Thanks."

"Laura? What's the matter?"

"Nothing ... nothing new. Nothing I want to talk about."

She stared at me with a sad puzzled expression.

"Come on Laura." She moved closer. "What's upsetting you? Please share it with me."

"Share it with you? Bloody hell Liv, I share everything with you. There's nothing you don't know about me." I spread my hands wide. "But what about you? Practise what you preach Liv."

I stomped into the bedroom, threw on some clothes and headed for the door.

"I'm going out. I need some space."

She stood silently and watched me leave.

I walked out onto the street, not knowing where to go or what to do. I wandered aimlessly along the familiar route towards the *Tantolunden* gardens. I sat on the hillside staring out at the water, my insides a mess of thoughts and emotions.

I felt frustrated and powerless. I had no idea which direction to turn, how to make it through this dilemma without long term suffering for one or both of us. I thought about packing my bags and heading back to Aus. A fresh start in Melbourne, maybe look up some of the old crew. I wouldn't have Liv but I would hold the chance to have a family someday. I would know I had that choice. But fuck, what a choice.

After a couple of hours, I returned home. I hated leaving issues unresolved. In that way Liv and I were sort of opposites. She liked to sweep stuff under the rug and smile bravely while I was like the Princess and the Pea. If there was something uncomfortable in the air, some tension, it magnified inside me so that all I could focus on was finding a solution.

Liv had her work spread over the dining table but looked up as soon as I walked in.

Her eyes appeared larger, rounder and questioning but she said nothing.

I sat on the couch and looked across at her. I really needed to get to the bottom of it all.

For a few moments we just sat and stared at each other until my eyes filled with tears and I looked away.

"You look so sad."

I sniffed, shrugged. I didn't know what to say.

She came to me, knelt in front of me, wiped the tears from my face. "What's going on?"

My lip trembled, and my voice came out all husky. "I want a baby. I can't just turn that off. I want to have a baby, but you don't, and I have no idea why. I feel ... I feel like I'm going to be forced to choose between you and children, and I don't ... can't work out what to do." I buried my face in my hands and sobbed.

Olivia sat on the couch beside me and rubbed my back.

"I've tried to turn it off, to stop the feelings but I can't. I don't understand why you don't want one. I don't understand, and you won't tell me, and I hate what this is doing to us."

She let out a deep sigh. "Oh Laura, oh my darling. I am so sorry. I am so sorry. This is all my fault. Oh, how did I let this happen? This is hurting you so much."

She put her hand under my chin and turned my face towards her. Her face was full of emotion. She nodded at me. "I need to tell you. You are right, there is something I must tell you. I didn't want to, but I must." She looked around the room. "I need a drink."

"It's not even lunchtime."

"It is somewhere." She stood up, walked into the kitchen, got the wine, and some crackers.

She poured both of us a generous amount of wine, sat back facing me from the corner of the couch and took a long swig from her glass.

"I'm so sorry Laura. I should have told you a long time ago, but ... I don't even like to think about it."

"Whatever it is, it's okay. I love you, I'm here for you. Just tell me, Liv, please."

"Thank you, *ja*." She closed her eyes for a few moments before she began. "I told you how my mother died when we came to Sweden, yeah?"

"Yeah."

"My father ... he struggled. It was not easy for him. He started drinking. Well, he always drank, but it got worse." The words came out hesitantly. "He found it very hard to adjust to his new country, especially without my mother. She always calmed him down. He worried himself over the political situation in Chile. People disappeared, a lot of people. There was so much suffering. He would call himself a coward for leaving. Sometimes he became very angry and abusive, other times he was so needy, sobbing and clinging."

She stopped for a moment, the only noise being the cars down in the street. She picked up a cracker and munched it distractedly. "Lucas left home not long after our mother died. Papa, in his drunkenness beat him up, more than once. He called him a coward for running away from the fight. He was ... unwell, mentally ill, delusional."

She finished her wine, put her glass down, stood up and walked slowly over to the palm. Still facing the other way, she continued in a voice trembling with emotion. "At this same time my father started to ... to ... to molest me ... sexually. I was trying to do my best to raise little Isabella, to keep her safe, then I realised I was pregnant. I was 13."

She turned and looked at me, tears streaming down her face. "I was only 13. I didn't know how to stop him."

I held her gaze. "Oh Liv."

"I tried to hide it for a few months. I had no help, no other women to help me understand what was happening to me. I just knew ... that I missed my periods, and this meant pregnancy. My breasts ... were ... became tender and swollen." She took a deep breath and settled a little. "I was determined to get Isabella and myself out of there before he started to ..."

She came back to the couch, poured herself another wine and sculled it. "My father came home one night. He was drunk and upset and he shoved me against the kitchen bench ... touching me." Her face screwed up with disgust. "I tried to ... I pushed him with all my strength. I didn't care anymore if I hurt him or even killed him. He backed off for a moment. He was swearing, cursing at me. Then I grabbed the kettle off the bench, I swung it in the air, and I rushed at him. I wanted to ... wanted to hit him on the head but he saw me and he kicked me in the stomach, he kicked me so hard." She sobbed as she stepped backwards away from the couch. "It threw me back, across the room. I crashed into the ... the corner ... the couch. I fell or collapsed, I don't know. It took my breath out of me. I was dizzy, confused." She stared into space, lost in the terrible memory. "The pain ... so intense." She put her hands on her stomach as she relived the terrible experience in her mind. "I couldn't breathe. I must have passed out. When I woke up, hours later, there was ... th ... there was blood on my pants, on the floor ... between my legs."

"Oh fuck, Liv. How long have we been together? And you've never told me? After all the deep and meaningfuls we've had, as close as we are. I just don't get it." I struggled to suppress my frustration.

She looked me full in the face. Here chin was wobbling and her eyes were wild with pain and anger. "I hate talking about it. You don't want to hear this! Why would I want to tell you, to upset you with this?"

"Yes, I do, I do want to hear it. It's part of you, and I love all of you. I need to understand. Liv, I need to understand. What ... what happened to you, what did you do?"

"Well, when I could stand, I moved, very quietly, through to the bathroom. I saw my father passed out on his own bed. I was so relieved. I cleaned myself up ... as best I could, changed my things quickly, then I woke up Isabella." Her voice was a little calmer now. "I took the grocery money from on the top of the fridge and we left."

She fell silent for a few minutes, her emotions settling. "It was early in the morning, they were collecting the rubbish, it was crazy. We walked, it was very painful, Issa was upset, eventually we managed to get a taxi to the hospital."

"Oh my God."

"I lost the baby ..." She shrugged. "That wasn't so bad for me but then they told me I would never be able to have children because of the damage." She looked at me sadly, tears filling her eyes.

"Oh, Liv, oh, you poor thing, that's so awful. What did you do, where did you live?"

"They put us into state care. It wasn't so bad. Lucas joined us, he had been living on the streets."

"Oh, dear. Did your father find out where you were?"

"No. When I went to hospital, I told them what happened. They arrested him. There was a trial, it was awful ... tests ... so many questions ... talking about it so much in front of ... people."

"Bloody hell. Was he found guilty?"

"*Ja*. He got sentenced and put in jail. He died in there some years later. Cancer. None of us ever visited him in prison, but we did go to his funeral. Like you, I wanted to see his body. I needed to be certain he was really dead."

"Bloody hell."

"So, I didn't say, but yeah, the trip to Australia ... the whole funeral, and your relationship with your father ... I understand. When I went to see him, I stood looking down at his body, he looked so peaceful. All I thought was, why did he do that to me, to us, to his children, how could he get so screwed up?"

I shook my head, trying to process everything she had said. "Wow, that's awful, bloody awful." I got up and walked over to her, taking her hands in mine. "I can only try to imagine how hard that must have been for you to talk about. I'm sorry I didn't just let it be, sorry to put you through that, but I'm glad I am aware of it now. Thank you, thank you for sharing it with me."

I hugged her then and as I did, her strength dissolved and she sobbed on my shoulder.

"I wanted ... I ... you to understand. I didn't know how to tell you ... and I was ... frightened, frightened by what you ..."

"Oh Livvy, I love you so much, sweetheart. There's nothing you could tell me that would change that."

She started sobbing again, huge gut-wrenching sobs. "I'm so sorry I didn't tell you. You have a right to know. I'm so sorry."

All I could do was hold her while she let it all out. "Shhh, it's okay, everything is fine." I stroked her hair, kissed her brow.

"But I don't want people to hear this about me. I don't want pity, I don't want that part of my life to be part of who I am." She extricated herself from my arms, defensive once more. "I don't want people to think about that when they look at me. I have had lots of counselling. I have dealt with it as much as I can for now. I just don't want to go to that place anymore."

"It's okay, it's okay. We don't have to talk about it anymore unless you want to."

She sniffed. "Thank you."

"Does Oscar know?" My tone was soothing and I opened my arms to her again.

She nodded and stepped closer, taking my hand. "Yes, he was a friend of Lucas's when they were on the streets."

"Okay, so he has his own story."

"Yes, he does."

"And so, all this is why you are so passionate about your research and your work."

"*Ja.*"

We went and lay on the bed for a long time holding each other, letting our emotions and the whole story settle.

I was surprised when the next morning over breakfast Olivia raised it again.

"Thank you so much for everything, everything you did to help me, support me, yesterday. It is a relief to finally tell you. I didn't like keeping that a secret from you. I ... I didn't realise how hard it was to carry around."

"That's fine, Livvy, that's part of being together. I am here for you, no matter what. Okay?

She nodded at me. "There is something more I must tell you."

"Okay ...?" God, I thought, what else could there be.

"Before I met you, when Oscar and I were on and off again, I wanted to have a baby. I wanted to try. Oscar and I decided to try to have a baby together, as friends, co-parents." She looked off into the distance. "Maybe it was a way for us to try to stay together, I'm not sure." Turning back to me she continued. "We even tried an embryo implant, IVF, through the clinic. In fact, I still have some in storage. You see, I am fertile but my womb is damaged. We failed, I failed, and that told me what I already knew, I would never be a mother."

I reached over, picked up her hand and held it against my cheek. "I'm so sorry sweetheart."

Finally, I was confident we had got to the bottom of things.

Thirty

I let the whole baby thing drop then and just focussed on getting our relationship back on track. We both needed time to settle and process how these new pieces of the jigsaw fit together in our lives. We had a good life together, I now felt closer to Liv than ever before and I considered, maybe that was enough.

Olivia, however, was going through her own process and about ten days after our last discussion she raised the topic herself.

"I want to talk to you about something."

"Okay?"

"Well, I have one more secret to share with you."

"Hmm...?"

"I ... I don't know how to say this best, but ... I ..."

I gave her an encouraging smile. "I'm listening, just say it."

"I said I didn't want children, but the truth is, I do want to have children. I do want us to have a family. You see ... I just ... well, I know I can't and that's been really hard to accept. I just couldn't separate these things in my mind."

"Oh, sweetheart." I reached out and took her hand.

"I always wanted a family and when I found it wasn't possible ... I ... I was heartbroken, so, so sad, lost, so angry. To realise that man had taken away not just my innocence but my future family ..." Her face was distorted with pain. She shook her head. "I couldn't face that, it was too much. I wanted to kill myself, it hurt so bad. Oscar stayed with me and helped me through but I didn't ever want to go to that place again."

"And you were fine until I pushed you."

She shrugged. "Was I really fine? I'm sure I had to face it one day. I'm sorry I hurt you."

I smiled at her. "None of us are perfect, never will be. I just needed to understand."

We were suddenly on the same page. We both wanted to start a family, our own family. It would probably be fair to say that now Olivia had opened up her own feelings, she probably felt a greater biological need than I did. I am not sure why. It may have been because she was a couple of years older or because fertility was the centre of her career. Then again, it could just be a reaction to the fact that she would never have her own children. She spoke with passion and emotion of the couples she had assisted to achieve live births through her research and treatment at the clinic. We talked about the subject more and more. We both looked with longing, out in the street or down in the park at other parents with their young children.

We were confident in our ability to stay together and raise a couple of children, and over time, it became more and more the centre of our focus. We explored the options a number of times. We weren't able to register as a same-sex couple so we were not allowed to legally adopt together. If someone was going to bear a child naturally it had to be me. I was quite happy about that except that I sensed Olivia would be left somewhat unfulfilled, placed in the role of unofficial step parent. Also, if I were to get pregnant, and have a child then obviously there had to be a man involved. As much as I may have questioned a life without a penis at the beginning of our relationship, I had no desire to go out and find one. Not anymore, even if it were for the best cause of all — and how would we choose one, anyway? We joked about posting an ad, calling for resumes, and holding interviews.

After yet another fruitless discussion on the point, I decided it was time to get my note pad out. I needed to work out the pros and cons of the various choices in front of us.

Baby facts
1. *We both want a baby*
2. *Olivia has eggs but cannot carry a pregnancy*

3.   *I don't know my fertility but with an early miscarriage ...???*
4.   *If possible, we want the baby to be genetically hers or mine*
5.   *Adoption is therefore a last resort*
6.   *Therefore, I have to carry the baby, if I can*
7.   *This makes Olivia a step parent*
8.   *We need sperm!*

I ruminated on the list and pondered on the more casual Swedish attitude towards sex. I was reminded of what Olivia had said about having 'the ingredients' frozen at the lab. I was curious whether they would be still okay. Also, how Oliva might respond if I raised the idea of using them. I also wondered how Oscar would feel, or (and I felt guilty at the very thought) if he needed to know. He was still in Canada with Abbie.

I went for a walk out into the late-afternoon twilight as I continued to go over it all. As I allowed myself to relax and my attention to be taken over by the surrounding beauty a new idea popped into my mind. What if we used Olivia's egg, Oscar's sperm and implanted the fertilised egg into my uterus? In other words, donor egg and donor sperm, or, sort of like a surrogate. That would give both Olivia and I the direct connection with the baby that we both wanted. I was excited about the idea but also anxious. There were so many unknowns — could I carry a baby to term? What would Oscar's involvement be? Would we be able to do this legally? Whose baby would it be?

I waited until we were kicking back comfortably on the couch after work with a wine in our hands before I raised the subject. "I have an idea I want to go over with you."

"I can see." She grinned at me, her eyes twinkling in amusement. "I've been waiting for you to bring it up. Tell me. What's going on?"

"It's about having children," I ventured. "I did my thing today. You know, writing down all the facts, working through the issue logically? So, anyway, I came up with a possible way forward, although I am really not sure just how feasible it is."

"Okay," Olivia replied, her face becoming more studious. "Let me hear it."

"Well, if we are going to have a baby, it has to be me carrying it right?"

"Yes. That is the only option."

"Right. Even though I had an early miscarriage, years ago, it's still possible, we reckon, yeah?"

"Yes, we would need to get you a thorough check up, to be certain, but we hope it is possible."

"Yep." I nodded. "But you have eggs, right? You are technically fertile, even if you can't carry a child, right?"

She frowned. "Yes... but you are confusing me now, and sorry Laura but so far there is nothing new in what you are saying."

"Ok," I took a deep breath. "Do you still hold Oscar's sperm at the clinic?"

"Yes. It is there." She looked somewhat disenchanted.

"Well, what if we use your egg and Oscar's sperm and we implant that in me so that I carry the baby? That way the baby will be yours and mine, and Oscar's if we want, and he knows."

Olivia put her wine down on the coffee table and sat back, her face becoming serious and her gaze fixed as she processed this possibility.

"So, well, I still have fertilised embryos frozen at the lab. The first step is complete. I suppose I could implant them into you as a normal IVF process. It's possible, but don't you want your own children, you are not infertile?"

"I want a child with you. How much more 'our child' could it be than using your egg and me giving birth."

She grinned, and the light came back into her face. "That is very true. It is like having three parents." Then she became pensive once more. "There are many questions, many difficulties. I do not believe we can do this legally. You are not yet a permanent resident so you do not qualify for IVF even if you had a male partner." She sipped her wine, deep in thought. "It is like surrogacy almost and this is not legal in Sweden. Then there is the question of Oscar. How would he react to the news of us having his baby when he has his own partner and they may want children?" She fell silent as she worked through the idea further. "If we did this, it would not be legal even if we did tell Oscar. I would have to do this outside of the clinic, in secrecy. No one else could know. Hmm ... If we told Oscar then of course he would want to tell Abbie, and Abbie would want to tell ... who knows?"

"Yeah, I don't imagine Abbie would handle it well."

"Somewhere there has to be a wall of silence, an impenetrable wall. We would need to be very careful or I could lose my job and my reputation. Already, they will wonder when they see we are having a child. We would have to say that you, or we, had made an agreement with a man somehow."

I saw the anxiety mix with a glimmer of excitement in her face.

"It's up to you." I assured her. "I won't pressure you if you think it's not right — you are the expert after all. You need to be comfortable with the whole idea and I don't expect you to make a decision tonight or tomorrow. Okay?"

"Okay."

"Think about it. Also, think of Oscar and whether it may be better to find another sperm donor."

"Yes, we would have to find a story to tell. Maybe it could be like the opposite of one of those old situations where the unmarried mother is sent away to give birth to the child. Possibly you need to go away for a holiday in Santorini or Tenerife and 'come back pregnant'!"

"Oh, how terrible! Please don't make me do that! I'll do anything but please don't send me to Santorini!" I brought my hands together in a pleading manner and dropped to my knees in front of her. We both laughed as she pulled me up into her arms.

We agreed to park the subject and move on, allowing both of us time to think it through further.

It was a whole week until we talked about it again. It was Saturday morning and we were having scrambled eggs on toast for breakfast. "Are you ready to talk about having a family?" she asked in her typical straight forward manner.

"Yes, I am. I've tried to be patient, waiting for you to raise it. I didn't want to rush you. There is so much for you to think about."

"Hmm. Yes. It has been sitting on me very heavily. I have been considering it from every direction, the options, the risks, the process." She stopped short of sharing her thoughts.

"And ...?" I encouraged her.

"I would like to use one of my embryos. And, to include Oscar as the father. I have worked out a way to try the IVF process. That is, if you are willing to carry our baby, a baby that is not genetically yours. How do you feel about that? Are you really sure?"

I grinned with excitement. "Yes, I will be very happy to carry our baby. I just hope I can! Will you tell Oscar?"

"It is not a decision we need to make until we are successful. I don't want to bring this up with him if there is no chance that it will work out. First of all, we need to get you thoroughly checked out. I will call Tina and book you in with her if that is okay with you."

"Sure, but what will we tell her?"

"We can tell her most of the truth. We are thinking about starting a family, but it would have to be you who carries it. So, we need to find out if that is possible before we look at how to do it. Simple."

It was a typical frosty morning in early Spring when I had my appointment with Tina. Fortunately, I had been sitting in the waiting room long enough to warm up before I was required to strip and put the horrid gown on. I was really nervous. I had met Tina socially. We had had her and her partner Ken over for dinner parties. We had also been to their beautiful apartment in the centre of Stockholm. But seeing her professionally was another story. I was also curious and anxious about the results and a bit concerned that she might ask some probing questions. I needn't have worried. Tina behaved like a true Swede. She was warm and professional and put me at ease. Fortunately, this also meant there was minimal small talk and no hard-hitting questions. She stuck to the Swedish culture of setting a firm boundary between work and private life.

We waited impatiently for the test results. If I didn't stand a good chance of carrying a pregnancy to term, there was no point trying IVF.

I returned to Tina's office for the results. "Congratulations," she gave me a professional smile. "You are perfectly fit and healthy and capable of having a baby whenever you choose to."

I breathed a sigh of relief, detecting a slight curiosity in her eyes and how she studied me carefully as she informed me of the news. I pretended not to notice. "Oh, thank you! That's great. Good to know I have that option." I thanked her, took my report and headed home.

I wanted to call Olivia at work as soon as I arrived home. I hesitated. That boundary between work and home life made it better to wait until she reached home in the evening.

She burst through the door with a look of anticipation. "Hello, what happened today?"

I gave her the good news and we danced around the sitting room and laughed and hugged in our happiness and relief. That was another stage completed in our journey to starting a family. The next step was in Olivia's hands. She had the job of impregnating me in the most unsexy way.

Thirty-one

Months later, after a number of setbacks, including three fails and a miscarriage at 5 weeks we were still no closer to having a baby.

It was a weird time for both of us. Liv buried herself in work. I did the same with my Psychology course. It had turned out to be really demanding with the sheer amount of material I had to read and the essays to write. I read English versions of texts when I found them, and my Swedish was improving but there was so much study involved.

"If you are pregnant, I won't go to Japan."

"What do you mean? No way. This is your thing! If I'm not pregnant, I'll definitely be going with you! If I am pregnant I still might go, but we can work that one out later."

Olivia appeared both excited and reluctant about the conference in Japan. I kept reassuring her I would either be with her or I would be fine. She kept changing her mind, not finding peace with either decision. Just before the deadline she accepted the invitation with some reluctance.

We paid little attention to Christmas and New Year as they came and went around us. Stockholm has amazing Christmas decorations in the streets and public buildings but they brought me no joy that year. Every time I ventured out into the street it seemed to be full of parents with young children. They were all rugged up in cute little hats, thick coats and coloured mittens. I found myself watching them stare into shop windows, seeing little faces filled with awe and delight, adults looking on, with love and tenderness. I noticed the intimacy between the parents as they smiled indulgently at the antics of their small child and caught each other's eye. It was hard, it was really hard.

I ached with the desire for my own child, longed to hold the warmth and softness of that little body against my chest. I lingered in the baby wear departments, picking up little socks with tiny trucks on them, little dresses embroidered with flowers, coloured tights, shiny shoes. We had agreed on a strict rule that we would not buy anything, not a single pair of booties until we had reached the twelve-week mark. I had secretly broken that pact a number of times. I had a stash of cute little bibs, a soft lemon blanket covered in rabbits, a maraca styled rattle and a few books all hidden away in my backpack.

As time ticked by, we talked about it less. We both put on a show of being okay but underneath we were struggling. I was hormonal, Olivia was carrying the technical load. The emotional burden lay between us like a rushing gurgling river, creating distance, making us a bit short tempered, a bit impatient. Neither of us blamed the other for our failures but we focussed with such intensity on the outcome that we lost track of what mattered most, our relationship.

We started arguing which we hardly ever did. One weekend something trivial happened and we both started raising our voices. I don't even remember what it was about but we were both losing control. Our cosy little apartment became unbearably small when we had a disagreement.

I had a sudden realisation, stopped mid-sentence and put my hands up in surrender. I turned aside, wrestling with my emotions. I breathed deeply, focussing my attention on the lush green parlour palm, still growing and looking impressive in the corner. I turned back to Olivia who stood frozen in the kitchen watching me. I walked across the kitchen to her, took both her hands in mine as she stared at me stony faced.

"I'm sorry. This whole pregnancy process is harder, more stressful than I thought it would be. I don't want to do this anymore, this arguing, being stressed. I do not want this possible pregnancy to come between us like this. We are both so tense and anxious, there's no joy in life for us anymore. We have lost the peace, the contentment, the playfulness."

Olivia's face softened as I spoke.

"This child we want is not more important than our relationship. Our relationship is very sound, we enjoy a great life together. We need to remember that, focus on that and stop obsessing about whether we are going to be parents or not." I let out a sigh as my energy started to settle. "Apart from anything else, I am sure the stress is not helping me. I love you, I'm sorry, I don't want to fight with you."

Olivia nodded. "Thank you. I'm sorry too, you are right. I just ... I am carrying so much pressure to get this right."

"So am I and it's not healthy. Let's change that. Let's focus on us, on what is in our life right now. We need to get back to living a happy balanced life. Each day is important just as we are. We gotta stop pinning our happiness on ... on ... something we possess little control over. After all, you are doing everything you can, the best you can and me too. That needs to be enough. Okay?"

"Yes, okay."

"The rest is up to God, the Universe or whoever else may be in charge." I ran my hand over her hair. "The pressure and tension do not improve our chances. If this doesn't work, I will still love you, you will still be enough for me. It will not be your fault."

"And I will still love you. I understand you are doing everything you can, you are taking this really well. If we fail, it will not be your fault either. I'm so sorry my darling." She stroked my cheek. "You are right. We have allowed ourselves to develop an unhealthy attachment to the outcome when we have only limited control."

"Okay," I breathed as I drew her close, breathing in her scent that still drove me wild. "You know what, I am aware we are in for another attempt next week but stuff it, I'm going to allow myself a glass of wine, how about you?" I had barely had a drink since we had made the decision to try for a baby.

Olivia's eyes were twinkling. "Yes, I'll open the bottle. Let's celebrate everything we already have."

Over wine and cheese followed by more wine and dinner we decided to go away for the weekend. We needed some time in nature. We would do some skiing, breathe fresh country air and sip a little mulled wine. It was the perfect time for skiing, with good snow coverage and temperatures that had started to rise a little.

We chose to go to Flottsbro, about 25 kilometres south of the city. It was more laid back than most ski runs which suited my mediocre skill level. We had been skiing there a few times before and also camping and walking in the summers. We were able to hire gear instead of lugging it with us and they had great cabins to stay in.

The weather was cold but clear for our trip, with a light snowfall over night. Best of all, I managed to stay upright most of the time, ending the day with surprisingly few bruises. After a hot shower and a warm dinner, it was absolutely heavenly to relax in the comfy armchairs by the fire. Even better with some warm fragrant red wine that Olivia had prepared. We were soon rosy cheeked and nodding off and not long after dragged ourselves off to bed. It was the perfect recipe for a long deep sleep. Sunday morning was cuddle time followed by a late breakfast and a bit of light cross-country skiing.

When we arrived back to our little home on Sunday evening I was filled with a deep sense of contentment. My life was so good. I reflected on our recent angst around having a baby and made a firm commitment, not to lose my perspective again. Later that evening, I stopped chopping the veggies for dinner and looked at Olivia as she loaded up the washing machine. She straightened up and turned, catching my eye as I watched her. I put the knife down, walked over, and embraced her, burying my head in the scent of her hair, her skin. "Oh Livvy, I love you so much. Baby or no baby, I love our life together." I cupped her face and kissed her gently. "Finding you, building a relationship and a home with you has been such a blessing. I had no idea I was capable of being so happy or living so contentedly with anyone. You are my life, my whole life, and I appreciate you so much. I love your sense of humour, your kind heart, your wisdom, and you still turn me on."

She smiled at me, a tired but happy smile. "Thank you. I love you too. You are also enough for me. We don't have to keep trying for a baby, you understand, we can let the idea go."

"Is that what you want?"

"I'm not sure. I only know that I don't want to hurt us anymore."

"I think we should give it another go this week, as we've planned, and see what happens. I think we can handle it better now, we have a better perspective, we understand we will be fine whether we have the baby or not. If we make a baby life will be great, if we don't, life will be great."

She hugged me tight. "Thank you, my darling. Yes, we can make a baby or not make a baby as long as we are still together and not pulling each other's hair out."

Some weeks later, I peed on a stick and was rewarded with a plus sign. We had reached this point before. It was exciting but also nerve wracking. I wasn't having the full IVF support with blood tests, ultrasounds and so on as we did not want to draw attention to ourselves. We had to do everything in a low-key natural way and wait to see if the pregnancy progressed.

Perhaps it was because of the therapeutic effect of nature. Maybe it was due to less stress around home or who knows but this time I reached the six-week mark and I was still holding the baby. We were handling it all much better than we had in the past. We were excited but also trying not to become too attached to a positive outcome as we made our way through one day at a time.

I reminded Olivia that she was due to go to Japan in July. It was an important conference. I didn't want her to miss it. It was a big deal to be presenting her latest research paper to her international colleagues at such a prestigious event. Also, mixing with other international researchers would assist her in so many ways. She would improve her international profile, and opportunities for collaboration. It may even bring her to the attention of private philanthropists. We had decided it was best if I didn't accompany her but Olivia's ticket and accommodation had been booked for some time. We agreed to take a wait and see approach although the longer we left it the more it would hurt her to pull out of the conference.

We marked off seven weeks, then eight weeks and it became increasingly difficult not to get too excited so as not to fan the flame of expectancy. We talked yet again about the whole boy versus girl thing. We would be happy with either as long as she/he was healthy it didn't matter.

"What if the baby is born with your dark hair and beautiful big brown eyes?" I asked. "People may be suspicious."

"Then we will tell everybody you had yourself a lovely Greek boy." She laughed at me, unperturbed. 'Or would you rather he be Italian?"

We had both had to embrace the secrecy, creating many small untruths or half-truths to cover our tracks. We were aware that we would reach a moment in the future where those details would be unimportant. We looked forward to that but for the moment it was a closely guarded secret, kept between the two of us.

I also asked Olivia once more about telling Oscar. She was uneasy about it, not knowing how Abbie would take it. She didn't want to say anything to him if he felt he couldn't tell her. She decided to put off letting him know until sometime after the baby was born (we had started dropping the "if"). She would let enough time go by that the details of our IVF treatment would be less important.

As the twelve-week mark approached, we celebrated by inviting Lucas and Issa over for dinner to share our happy news. We made a bit of a fuss with the menu and the table setting. We dressed up and waited for them to turn up, giggling and chasing each other around like excited school kids.

It was obvious to them that something was up, but they had the good grace to wait until we raised it. As we sat with our first drink over pre-dinner nibbles, Lucas raised his glass for the customary toast. Liv put up her hand to stop him.

"Actually, we have some news that we want to share first."

All eyes turned to Olivia.

Liv reached out, took my hand in hers and for a moment we locked eyes. Two sets of joy filled excited eyes. Then, just as we had rehearsed, we turned towards them together and announced, "We're having a baby!"

It seemed like it took ages for them to process the news. You could see it didn't add up in their heads. They looked at each other, their mouths hanging open, then looked in turn at each of us before they both erupted with questions.

We giggled and Liv held up her hand, asking for the floor. "Ja," she confirmed. "You heard right, we are having a baby. Let us explain."

It was so good to be finally able to talk about it. They were both excited and happy for us. Lucas was concerned that Oscar didn't know but they could see our reasoning. He was sure Oscar would be thrilled once he found out, except for any possible backlash from Abbie.

A few days later, when we had officially hit the 12-week mark, Olivia joined me on the couch after dinner with a sheepish expression on her face.

I raised my eyebrows, narrowed my eyes and stared at her. "Yeeesss?"

"Umm, you remember the rule we agreed on about not buying anything for the baby until after 12 weeks?"

"Yeeesss?" I was enjoying this, guessing where the conversation was going. "You have a confession to make?"

She opened her mouth, coloured, shrugged. "I may have broken our rule, just a little." She turned those big dark eyes on me, liquid and puppy like.

"You what? I ... I'm shocked, how could you, we agreed." I shook my head in mock disdain and disbelief.

"It's not much, a few things ..."

I grinned at her. "Great, you show me yours and I'll show you mine!"

By the time the conference in Japan came around in July I was almost four months pregnant. Everything was going well except for the fact that I had constant morning sickness. My bump was still fairly easy to hide as I wasn't showing much yet so we hadn't told anyone. We had been spending time planning a big dinner party for our friends for when Olivia was back from the conference.

She had wanted to pull out of the Sapporo conference but I assured her I would be fine. She would be gone for just six days. One day to get there, four days at the conference and post conference meetings and then flying back against time zones to get home. She was very torn and uneasy about it, changing her mind each day, worrying about me.

"It's fine," I said for the thousandth time. "I will go out each day, have a walk in the gardens, get some sunshine, eat my greens, and think happy thoughts. Really, I would be doing the same if you were here."

"I just hate to leave you at this stage. It just doesn't feel right."

"I know that's how you feel, but we both know it's pretty safe now. We are going to be parents for Christmas and you going to Japan for a few days for a conference won't change that. When you get home, we will be booking in for our ultrasound. And, I'll get so big and fat you'll wish you could just leave me stranded on a beach somewhere."

She laughed. "We are going to be parents for Christmas," she beamed back at me. "This Christmas we will be a family of three. I am so looking forward to that. I love you so much." Her face fell as she thought yet again about the decision to go to the conference. "Okay, I will go, but I will miss you so much, more than I normally do when I go away. I wish you could come too."

"We both know that wouldn't be a good idea. I can't have vaccinations, I would probably spew up all the way. Especially with the local food and the pollution, the smells, and I'd be stuck eating rice for a week. Nah, not my idea of fun." A wave of nausea and an involuntary shiver ran through my body at the very thought of it.

Olivia took the taxi to the airport early Saturday morning. She would be home for dinner on Friday night. We held each other for the longest time as we waited in the cool morning air out front of the apartment building for the taxi. "You have the number, you call me if there is even a hint of something that is not right. Call me immediately, day or night."

"Yes, of course sweetheart, we have been over this. I'll be here taking care of our family and I will call you if anything happens. Or ... even looks like it might not be one hundred percent okay. And of course, I'll have Issa and Lucas fussing over me the whole time." I rolled my eyes dramatically. "What does a girl gotta do to get some peace!" I reached out, pulling her close. Cupping her face, I kissed her, savouring the taste and feel of her lips, her tongue. "You just have fun and knock 'em dead with your brilliance."

She put her hand on the small bulge of my stomach and smiled at me through moist lips. "Thank you." She said, a hint of emotion evident in her eyes. "I am so happy I found you in that square in Amsterdam, so happy to have you here with me. I will be thinking of you, of our baby, of our family. I love thinking about our family. I love you so much."

"Hey," I said, holding up both hands in surrender mode. "Don't make the pregnant woman cry!" Then I grinned at her. "You are my life." I said. "Once you saved my life, now we are creating a life together and I couldn't be happier about our future." I nodded confidently, "We are going to make it just fine."

The taxi pulled up then and with one final hug and a kiss she was off to the airport. She turned and waved out the back window of the taxi. I was so happy, so proud of her and so full of love as I waved back, watching the taxi disappear into the distance.

Thirty-two

Olivia called me while waiting in transit in Bangkok. She called me when she arrived Sunday afternoon. She called me as she got ready for bed on Monday night. The conference was going well. She was nervous about presenting her research the next morning. She raved about the wonderful Japanese gardens they had been taken to before dinner that evening.

"Really darling, they were so beautiful, so perfect, so peaceful. We must come back here together. And the food so far has been really delicious."

"You haven't overdosed on wasabi yet have you?"

"Ha ha, no, but I noticed a few people do it. One man spread his sushi with a thick layer of wasabi, I'm sure he believed it was avocado. I watched him take a big bite, chew, chew, then he turned red and started spluttering, grabbing his napkin, diving for the water, didn't help him much. I felt sorry for him but it was pretty funny too. Even he laughed about it later."

"And what are you up to tomorrow apart from presenting the stand out presentation of the whole conference?"

"Ha, maybe not. We have presentations and discussion all morning. After that we go out to somewhere ... along the coast, if I remember, for a bit of sightseeing and lunch. It's really well organised and so interesting but I would rather be at home with you. Are you sure everything is okay?"

"Yes, yes, really, I'm fine. I miss you heaps but you'll be home in a flash."

We talked excitedly about her return and about finally telling all our friends our big news. It was time, I was having increasing difficulty in hiding my growing bulge, it seemed to have popped out all of a sudden.

I woke Tuesday morning to banging on the apartment door. I lifted my sleep mask as my brain struggled through the fog to make sense of the noise. It was still very early though the day was bright and sunny already. I put my dressing gown on and slippers and headed for the door feeling suddenly vulnerable and wondering who it could possibly be at this hour of the morning. It had been ages since Lucas had crashed and he had his own key. I had no idea who else it could be. I peered through the key hole and was puzzled to see Lucas standing there looking somewhat dishevelled.

I opened the door and greeted him sleepily. "Hey Lucas, big night hey, you forgot your key?" I assumed he had been out partying. I headed towards the kitchen, leaving him to close the door and follow me. "You want coffee?"

"I forgot it." He answered somewhat distracted. "Laura ... Laura, I need to talk to you." He turned the tap off, took the jug out of my hand and led me to the couch. I was starting to feel distinctly uncomfortable.

"Come, please, sit down."

I looked at him more closely, realising he was upset. "Hey, what's wrong?" I reached out, putting my hand on his arm.

His lip trembled and his voice came out in an uneven whisper. "It's Olivia," he looked at the ceiling and ran his hand through his hair.

"What is Olivia? What Lucas, what are you saying?"

"There's been an earthquake and a tsunami in Japan. It appears to be close to where she is."

Time seemed to stop as I stared at him for a moment, my mouth open. I was trying to make sense of what he was saying but my brain had frozen. I looked down at my slippers, silly fluffy penguin slippers that Olivia had given me for Christmas. I looked up at him, my face starting to crumple, tears coming into my eyes. "Lucas, that's a weird thing to say, where did you get that story from. I'm sure she'll be alright, I just talked to her ..."

"I am still listed as her next of kin." He spoke quickly as if he wanted to get the story out. "I had a call from the government, from the foreign office an hour ago. She's listed as missing. Oh Laura, I am so sorry."

I looked into his face, desperately searching for a catch, a punch line, anything to tell me what he said was not true. I stood up, filled with a mixture of disbelief and horror, taking in what he had told me. Then I sat down again, reached out and gripped his arm tightly, searching for something to hang on to.

"Lucas, is this true, is this really true?"

"*Ja*, it is true. There have been many people killed both by the earthquake and by the tsunami. The big waves started within minutes, there was no time for warnings. Did she tell you where ... where she would be? It happened at lunchtime today, Tuesday, Japanese time."

I tried to remember, to recall what she had said they were doing. "Umm, I have her hotel address where the conference is in Sapporo but she said ... Umm, I spoke to her yesterday, afternoon. She said ... they were going out. It was ... somewhere, umm, sightseeing along the — oh my God — along the coast, along the coast ... and some lunch. Oh my God Lucas, I don't know, I don't know where they were going, but it was along the coast! Oh fuck! I don't know where she is. I don't know. What else did they say?"

"We need to wait. I ... I'm sure she will be okay, I'm sure she will." His smile and his words were unconvincing.

"Is there anything we can do? She can't be gone, she can't be. We are having a baby, I need her, our baby needs her."

"Oh, I'm so sorry Laura, I'm so sorry. I can't tell you anything more. It is not confirmed, they are searching, rescuing people, they will call here when there is more news. They told me to wait that is all. Everything is chaos there. There is a lot of damage. It will be another day or two until they can get to some areas that were flooded. All we can do is wait." He was shaking his head from side to side. There really was nothing else to say.

As the shock set in and my energy drained I slumped down onto the couch. "Wait? That's it? We just wait? How long do we wait? A day or two?"

"I do not know Laura, I do not know." His eyes slid down to where my hand rested on my bump. "I am so sorry Laura. I will call Issa. We will wait together. I am sure we will hear soon, she will be fine. I will call Oscar too."

I nodded. "Don't call anybody else yet, apart from Issa and Oscar. I don't want a heap of well-meaning people hanging around. And, whatever happens, please let Liv and I tell Oscar about the baby."

We didn't hear soon. The days slipped by as we sat and waited, none of us wanting to leave the flat in case the phone rang. With each day that passed our talk became less optimistic and our hearts heavier. Lucas slept on the couch. Issa reluctantly returned home to Erik each night but came back every morning. We watched a lot of coverage on the TV for the first couple of days, disturbing images and stories of destruction and death. At night I tried to sleep but when I did drift off my dreams were filled with images from the TV. There was destruction, chaos, flotsam and jetsam all over the place and Olivia's voice calling me. In my dreams I desperately searched for her, called her name, then I was looking for our baby. I saw the tiny bundle bobbing in the dirty water. I couldn't get to it. The waves pushed me back. Then I heard Olivia again. Searching, searching. I didn't know who to rescue first. It was like my mind was stuck in an endless loop. I cried out in my sleep, waking myself and lay sobbing uncontrollably.

"Laura, can I come in."

"Yes, yes, sure." I turned the bedside light on.

Lucas came in and lay down on the bed beside me. We rolled into each other and he held me, my head buried in his chest as I continued to sob. The physical pain in my chest was excruciating and I started to worry for our baby.

"What am I going to do Lucas, what am I going to do?" I tilted my head to look into his face. "I don't know if I can do this. We have been so careful, everything has been so well planned. We thought we had covered everything." I caught my breath. "This is not supposed to happen. She's supposed to be on her way home. We were planning a big dinner party, we were going to tell everyone. She didn't want to go to Japan because she wanted to care for me. She was worried about me. Oh my God, oh my God, oh fuck. Oh, so cruel, how can life be so cruel? What's the point? What's the point? It's not right, it's not fucking right."

"No, it's not right, it's not right." Lucas stroked my arm as we cried together.

"Olivia is such a good person. Why can't they take someone else, anyone, but not my Livvy? She's too precious. She has so much to do. She was giving her presentation on Tuesday morning. It was really important, and I don't even know how it went. I have no idea. She didn't get to tell me. And I need her, oh God I need her so much. She's got to come home. She's just got to come home."

I sat up, swung my legs over the side of the bed and looked down at Lucas lying where Olivia should be. He looked so much like her.

"She has to be alive. What am I gonna do if she isn't? How I can live without her? I can't imagine my life without her. I can't breathe without her. I don't want to live, I wanna die, if she is dead I wanna die too, but I can't, I can't." I sniffed, looked down and ran my hands over the growing bulge in front of me. "I have to live, for our baby." I gently rubbed my tummy. "I'm sorry little one. I don't really want to die. If she is dead, I can't even imagine how I will ever get past the pain but I promise you I will." I looked over at Lucas. "I will get through this, I must. I don't know how but I must. Our baby must not be born into a world of grief." Already my emotions were delivering a potent cocktail to our little one. "I can't let that happen. Oh Lucas, what am I going to do?"

Lucas sat up, came around the bed and took my hands. "Come on, sit down, you need to rest. Just get through one day, one hour at a time, Laura. Don't worry about the future, not yet. We cannot be sure what is happening yet." I sat on the bed beside him and he put his arm around my shoulders, drawing me into him. "I will help you all I can and so will Isabella and all our friends, and Oscar when he knows. Just let it happen ... moment by moment and we will take care of you." Tears were gently falling down both our faces. "You are family Laura. Losing Olivia doesn't change that. We will all help you, whatever you need, whatever it takes. It will be as Olivia would want it to be."

Thirty-three

Olivia's colleagues and our friends started calling as the news spread. When Friday arrived and there was still no news Lucas decided to fly to Japan and look for her himself. How I wished I could have gone too. He told Oscar he was going and Oscar immediately volunteered to join him. They met in Narita on Monday, six days after the earthquake. Together they headed over to Hokkaido where a growing number of unidentified bodies were waiting in makeshift morgues to be identified by their loved ones. They spoke to the rescue organisers, describing the tattoo on her forearm, showed them a photo of my matching tattoo. Checks were run, yes, there was a female with words tattooed on her forearm.

On Tuesday morning, they formally identified the body with toe tag number 0173. They were told her body had washed up on the beach.

Lucas rang and gave me the news. I had been hanging onto a glimmer of hope, refusing to give in to despair. When he told me, I let out a cry and sank to the floor. "Noooo, nooo, oh, oh, oh my God, noooo! Olivia! Olivia! No, no!" I lost my voice as huge sobs ripped through my body. Then my thoughts turned to the little life growing inside me. "Our baby, our baby." I sobbed and handed the phone to Issa, standing near me. I rubbed my hand over my baby bump as I begged Issa with my eyes that it not be true.

Issa finished talking with Lucas, put the phone down and turned to me, her face crumpled with emotion. "Oh Laura, oh ..." She slumped down against the couch and pulled me up beside her.

We held each other and sobbed, like little lost children.

I turned to see Smulan watching us from the rug as if she could sense our pain but wasn't sure how to help.

Issa called some of our friends, and they called others. As the day wore on, and then the next and the next, people arrived and left, the fridge overflowed with casseroles, cakes and other bits and pieces that nobody ate. The phone rang often and I let other people answer it. People organised coffee, dished up food and everyone did their best to support me and each other. For myself, I struggled to function. I kept going over and over the facts trying to understand them, to make sense of it all.

I sobbed, I groaned, I screamed into a cushion. After a while I just sat, numb and stared at the parlour palm. I thought of Olivia, of our last phone call, of how nervous she was about giving her talk. We had chatted about how much we were looking forward to her coming home, we had laughed and called each other "Mummy".

I saw her put the phone down, get ready for bed, sleep, wake, shower, breakfast, off to the conference. I Imagined the standing ovation for her presentation, the professional chit chat and congratulations as they all climbed onto the bus to go sightseeing. She would have been so happy. She had so much to come home for, so much to look forward to. She would have chatted with her colleagues on the bus, relishing the professional interest her presentation would bring, enjoying the scenery. Inside, she would feel her mission had been accomplished and she would be anxious to get home. Then what? My mind went blank. Where was she? Had she had lunch? Did she have any warning? What did she think? What did she feel? Was she aware she was going to die? Did she suffer or was she killed instantly? Did she drown or was she fatally injured? How long did death take to claim her? What were her last thoughts? What would she have said if she were able? What would I have said to her?

I asked Issa to tell our friends quietly about our baby, that we were expecting, without explaining anything further or bringing Oscar into it. I didn't want to talk to anybody about it and I didn't want people noticing for themselves. It was more important that they understood the full extent of the tragedy than the possible ramifications of how it came to be. I had confidence in their discretion, there would be no awkward questions.

Everyone was wonderful to me. I was offered a bed at a number of homes, but I politely turned each of them down. I explained that I needed to be at home. Isabella had been staying with me since Lucas left but it was time she went home to Erik. I assured her I would be fine, I just needed to be alone, I needed time to myself. Reluctantly, she returned home of a morning but came back each night and slept in Olivia's place in bed beside me. They seemed to have made a pact that I would not be left alone overnight.

Lucas and Oscar arrived back a few days later, coming straight to home from the airport. They both looked very haggard. They drank a few beers through the afternoon as they told Issa and me all about what they had found. After dinner we sat around the coffee table telling stories about Olivia, crying, laughing. At one point I caught Lucas's eye telling him I was about to raise the subject of our baby.

"Oscar, there's something I need to share with you, now that you are here."

"Something more?" he asked, his face pained.

I nodded sadly. "I'm pregnant," I said simply. "We had been trying for some time. It was done by IVF. Olivia did it. Olivia is the mother ... and you are the father." I ran my hands over my tummy, outlining the baby bump.

Hi eyes opened wide. "What? What are you saying? You are pregnant? How ... how can this be? Why didn't ... why didn't Olivia tell me?" Oscar looked from me to Lucas, to Issa and back to me. Lucas shrugged. Issa looked down and wrung her hands.

I explained everything. He sat and looked at me with increasing sadness, occasionally turning to Lucas or Issa for verification of what I said. He sat, silent for a while as he processed this new twist, then he crumpled forward, overcome by grief.

We all held him as the full weight of realisation washed over him.

When he settled, I continued talking. "I don't want you to think that I need you to take any responsibility for this baby. We always planned to talk to you about what role you might want to play, but ... I ... wanted you to know and we really hoped that you would understand."

"*Ja*. I understand." He nodded slowly. "Our baby. Your baby."

I was so fortunate to have three such beautiful people to care for me at that time. I had moments when I just wanted to kill myself. Maybe if it wasn't for the little life inside me, I would have.

The following morning Jack arrived from Australia. I had called him and Mum after we had received the news from Lucas in Japan. I travelled out to the airport to meet him, buoying myself, determined to show him my best face. It lasted all of three seconds. The moment he reached me I fell to pieces.

"Oh Lozzie, what a bitch, hey?"

"Oh Grub," I sobbed over his shoulder. "I'm so glad you are here. I don't see how I'm going to get through this."

"Like you said to Mum, when Dad died; one day at a time, matey, just one day at a time. You got more than yourself to think about now. You just hang in there."

"I will."

"Mum and Nancy and everyone sends their love. They're all thinking of you."

"Thanks, I'm gonna need that."

I really appreciated him coming. It made a big difference to me to have a family member there at that time. It was a bitter sweet experience though, showing him our little apartment and introducing him to Lucas, Isabella and Oscar. The three boys got along well and that night went out and got completely smashed.

The sun kept coming up and going down despite the chaos around me. It gave me a weird appreciation of just how small a role we actually play in the daily life of our planet. Jack tried to keep me busy, making me take him out sightseeing. It seemed silly, the last thing I wanted to do. At the same time though, it really helped, it gave me a daily distraction while we waited for Livvy's body to come home.

After what seemed a painfully long time, we finally received the news that her body was arriving. It was delivered to the funeral home where it would stay until the funeral service and cremation. I didn't go to see the body. Whatever was there, whatever was left, it wasn't Olivia. I didn't want that image with me for the rest of my life as part of her memory.

The day of the funeral was warm and sunny and there were so many flowers. The room filled to capacity with all of our friends. Olivia's work colleagues were there as were mine, and touchingly, some couples who had become families through the amazing work that Olivia had done. The flowers and cards we received were almost overwhelming.

I looked about me. I was sure Liv would be there somewhere, watching on.

"Not a bad turnout," I whispered to her. "All these people love you, you made a difference in so many lives, you really did, do you see that?"

Despite this, I was glad when the funeral was over. It had been a long-drawn-out process. I was exhausted, and I had so much to think about and organise. Jack took me out for dinner the following night. He was due to fly home the next afternoon.

"Thanks so much for coming."

"Ah Lozzie. You don't need to thank me. It's not much of an effort really, compared to what you're going through."

"Yeah, still ..."

"Are you settled? Are you sure now about what you want to do?"

"Yeah, I need to come home. I don't want to live here without Liv. We need family."

"Ya sure about living in Melbourne?"

"Yeah, that's where I want to be. You guys can come stay or I can visit whenever. I want to be in the city."

"Well, ya know we'll all help as much as we can."

"Thanks Grub, yeah, I know. I also need my own space. It's been pretty crowded lately. I need space and time."

"Do ya think you can get organised in time?"

"I have to. I don't want bubs to be born here. I've got to move quickly now. Lucas and Issa will help."

"They're good people."

"Yeah, I'm going to miss them, I really am. So much to miss." I stopped as my emotions overloaded. "I need to move on. I just want to go now but at the same time, it's so fucking hard to leave."

"Bloody hell. It's a rough spot alright but you realise, you will make it through. You know that don't ya?"

"Fuck, I don't have a choice. I have to make it."

"Well, we'll be doing what we can to get ready for you, alright?"

"Yep, thanks."

I saw him off in the taxi the following morning. I wanted to jump in with him, just go. At the same time, I didn't know how I was ever going to walk out the door of our little home for the last time.

Next it was time for Oscar to leave. He took me out for breakfast before Lucas picked him up to go to the airport.

"What are you planning to do now, Laura?"

"Oh, Oscar, I haven't had time to process everything, but I've worked out a fair bit."

"Okay, what are you thinking?"

"I don't want to raise a child by myself in Sweden. I ... I don't even want to have the baby in Sweden without Olivia. I just want to go home, to Australia, to Melbourne."

He looked pained but stayed silent.

"But at the same time, the thought of leaving our little apartment, I can't deal with the finality of that."

"You understand, I will help you however I can. I will set up an account, send you some money, as soon as I get back to Canada."

"Thank you, Oscar, but it's really not necessary. Olivia had life insurance, with me as the beneficiary, we never imagined we would need it. It's enough to set us up in our own home, and give us a nest egg after all the expenses. We'll be okay."

After seeing Oscar off at the airport Lucas dropped by. I poured us a drink and we sat on the couch.

"How are you?"

"I'm okay. Oscar got away alright?"

"*Ja.*" Lucas was looking down at the drink in his hand. "He told me you have decided to go back to Australia."

I had been dreading telling Lucas and Issa my plans. It was going to be such a wrench for us all. "Yes. Soon. I want to have the baby there. It would be just too sad here. In Melbourne we can have a fresh start. I won't be constantly surrounded by reminders of ... of ... of everything. I will have my fam ... my mother and brother."

"Laura, you are our family. I would like you to stay. Issa and I will help you all we can ..."

I smiled sadly. "Thank you, I know you would but I really need to go."

Lucas moved towards me on the couch awkwardly. He picked up my hand. "Laura, I want you to stay ... I want you to stay as my wife. This child, it is almost my child, my family. Laura, I love you ... I ... I want to take care of you and the baby. We could be happy together, I am sure. I have been wanting to stop travelling ... settle ... find work in Stockholm. We could live here, or find a new place ..."

"Oh God, Lucas," I shook my head sadly. "You are so kind and generous, and you are very precious to me. I really appreciate what you're saying, but ... I'm sorry, I can't do that. I —"

"Just consider it, you don't have to give me an answer now, take some time. It's okay, it's okay Laura."

"No Lucas. I'm sorry. Thank you so much for — my God, for everything, but I don't want to take time to think about this. I want to go home. I can't live here without Liv, I just can't." Tears were running down my face. I looked into his sad, bloodshot eyes and slowly shook my head. "I need to go home. I'm sorry."

He nodded his understanding. There were no winners. We were all losing so much.

"Okay, I understand, I do. It's okay. I am still here for you." He straightened his back and his composure. "You can pack what you want. I will organise for the shipping. Issa and I will look after the apartment. You must do what is best for you and the baby."

Issa dropped by the next day after work. I made coffee and we sat on the couch together. "Lucas tells me you are going back to Australia."

"Yes, I'm sorry Issa, but I just can't stay. I need my home, I need my family. I know you and Lucas are my family too but ..."

She put her hand on my knee. It's okay Laura. I understand. It's awful to think we will lose you and the baby as well but I understand."

"Thank you. Thank you for everything. You've been so good to me, right from the beginning, both you and Lucas. I'm really sorry to be leaving you but I know my priorities ... I have to put myself and the baby first. I couldn't cope here without Livvy, I just couldn't cope."

"I understand. Don't feel bad."

"I'm so glad you have Erik to help you."

"*Ja*. He has been very good. He is very patient."

"You'll be okay?"

"*Ja*. I will be okay. As much as we can be."

I put my arm around her shoulders, drawing her to me. "Yes, one day at a time."

"You will let us know where you are ... about the baby ... everything?"

"Yes, of course. This baby is your family too."

"Thank you, Laura. Thank you. We will help make this happen for you."

I was aware of the limited timeframe I had if I was going to get back to Australia and find my own place in Melbourne before the birth. I could stay with Mum while I looked for a place, but I really wanted to be settled before the baby came.

Thirty-four – Melbourne 2018

Maybe at this point it seems there is too much grief, maybe now, as I reach the end of my story there may seem nothing but sadness. Indeed, this is how it initially appeared to me and I struggled for a long time with that. I could not however let my grief poison the potential of the little life inside me.

I was just over six months pregnant when I said goodbye to Lucas and Isabella at the airport in Stockholm. My things had been shipped already and I had stayed with Isabella for my final week. Lucas and Issa would finish emptying the apartment and take care of any loose ends. Smulan and the parlour palm were settling into their new home with Issa.

When I found out I was having a girl, I thought for a while of calling her Olivia, after her mother. But she is her own person, she needed her own name and I did not need anything further to remind me of my beautiful Livvy. She was the love of my life and we should have raised our daughter and grown old together.

Our daughter, Quinn, was born eight days past her due date. I was glad she hadn't come early as I only moved into our new home three weeks beforehand. She came into the world with little drama and I was relieved as I watched her develop into a happy healthy child. My mother was, of course, ecstatic to have us home. She was a great support in those early years, giving me much needed timeout from parenting, and Jack and Nancy were also great. They eventually had their own kids and Quinn has been like a big sister to them.

Olivia had been spot-on with her predictions, Abbie did not react well to the news that Oscar was a father and gave him an ultimatum. He could choose her or us but not both. Their own childless marriage broke up the following year and Oscar went back to Sweden, taking up a role at the marine science institute at Gothenburg. We kept in touch and he followed all of Quinn's ages and stages. He visited us here, in Melbourne when she was two. She thinks she remembers but perhaps it's really the stories and photos that have been woven into her imagination. He loved her dearly and was so proud of her. He was on his way to visit us again when Quinn was five but he died in a diving incident in the Philippines. That was really hard, going through the grief of losing him without being able to share it with Liv, and not wanting Quinn to notice how upset I was.

I gradually lost touch with Lucas and Isabella. We wrote often for a start then it dwindled down to the annual Christmas cards and a few life updates. It was just too painful for all of us and I hate trying to connect long-distance even though it's much easier these days. We each had to get on with our lives. Lucas made me promise that I would call him if I ever needed him and told me he would visit us one day, but that never happened. The last I heard, he had settled into a long-term relationship with a local girl but never had kids of his own.

Issa and Erik are still together. They had a child of their own, adopted two more and fostered many others. Issa has truly given her all for the troubled children of Stockholm.

I pause, sip my coffee. I am glad my job is nearly done. I had put off writing this down for so long.

I look across the room at the comfy old arm chair. I see our daughter Quinn sitting there as she was just a few days ago. Her dark wavy hair frames her face, she has an air of quiet confidence, slight impatience. Her whole life flashes before my eyes and once more I willingly lose myself in the past. I remember her over at the kitchen table, giggling at age two as she spread blue paint up her arms. Then, laughing again at six as she dressed our Dalmatian in shorts and t-shirt. Later, shaking with shock in my arms as I tried to stem the bleeding while we waited for the ambulance after her bike accident at 14. More recently, calm and contained at 18 as she explained to me after the volunteer trip in Cambodia that she no longer needed mothering. Tears well in my eyes as intense love mingles with guilt and the old well of grief within me.

Outside the window the sky is still red, the frost sits white and crunchy on the grass; the birds announce the arrival of the new day. Inside there is a deep stillness and a slight chill. The clock ticks, the fresh logs crackle in the pot belly, the roof creaks as the warmth of the rising sun hits the freezing iron. I'm sitting at the table with my laptop, savouring the last of my coffee.

Many times, I have been asked why I have never dated, why I have never found myself a new partner. The truth is, after Olivia, there could be no one else. There has not been a single day when I have wanted to be with anyone else. She has remained so close to me. It has been enough for me to raise our daughter who is so much like her. In fact, she has taken after both of her parents with her passion for science. Quinn's field is anthropology, and this gives me great joy as I see both her parents live on in their daughter. They would be so proud.

And, I confess, I dream of death, knowing that my Livvy is waiting for me, my precious, precious love. I interact daily with her, feeling her energy around me. Reaching out, I can almost touch her. Death is an illusion, a veil I long to penetrate, a bridge I yearn to cross. I get up each morning impatient to return to my dreams where I know Liv will be waiting for me. She always has been the patient one. For now, I will continue to carry my duties and wait for the time when we are together again. When we can laugh and love, swim and ski, and watch on together as our greatest achievement, our beautiful daughter, continues to grow and make a difference in the world.

The Secrets We Keep

Acknowledgements

I have had many sources of support and encouragement in my journey to publication. In particular, I would like to thank the online writing community and Indie Publishing groups for their assistance and patience with my questions. I am honoured to be among you. Also, thanks to Carrie, Abra and Helen for your feedback on my manuscript and special thanks to Gabrielle for your early encouragement and wise words.

None of this however, would have been possible without the love, patience and ongoing support of my hubby, Michael, the enthusiasm and assistance of my free-ranging daughter Maia or the dedication and love of my sweet little furbaby, Molly.

And to my readers, thank you. Without you this would be an empty exercise.

The Secrets We Keep

Author Notes

If you liked The Secrets We Keep I would love to hear from you. At the time of publishing, I have two more stories with similar themes in the pipeline so I am keen to get some feedback.

If you liked it, please encourage me by writing a short review on Amazon. I really appreciate any kind words, even one or two sentences go a long way. The number of reviews a book receives greatly improves how well it does. You can also leave a review on Goodreads.

Here are the sites you can reach me on:

My web page: www.drcoghlan.com
Facebook: www.facebook.com/drcoghlan.author
Amazon: www.amazon.com/author/drcoghlan
Goodreads:www.goodreads.com/author/show/18517543.D_R
_Coghlan
BookBub Follow: www.bookbub.com/authors/d-r-coghlan

You can join my mailing list by dropping by my website. If you have any comments, drop me a line at hello@drcoghlan.com. I am always happy to hear from people who've read my work. Your feedback helps me understand what you want, and I try to answer every email I receive.

The Secrets We Keep